CONT

PROLOGUE

A Grand Adventure

Brae was up early. Her father had promised to take her with him on his route today. This would be the first time, and she was too excited to sleep much. She quickly washed and dressed then bounded down the stairs and into the kitchen. In no time, she had a delicious breakfast prepared for both of them. When Elias walked into the kitchen, she was grinning ear to ear. Elias couldn't help the smile that spread across his face.

"Excited to do a little S-23 flying are we?"

Brae's eyes lifted as she nodded. Elias sat down with her at the table and served up their food.

"Where are we going today?" Brae asked as she took her first bite of cooked yulla eggs.

"I've been contracted to survey and geo-map terrain that a wealthy investor is planning to use to expand his agricultural resources," Elias answered in between bites.

That didn't sound very exciting, but Brae didn't care. She could hardly wait to climb into the S-23 side-by-side cockpit and fly. When breakfast was done, Brae began clearing the table.

"Check on the droids and make sure they have their duty instructions for the day, and I'll get the S-23 ready," Elias said.

"Okay, Dad," Brae replied as they finished cleaning up the breakfast dishes.

Brae checked on each of the three droids and verified their duties. She wasn't impressed with the family droids and their abilities, not after hearing about the intelligent and resourceful Rivet droid that was in the stories Elias told.

Before long, Brae and Elias were in the air, flying a few hundred feet off the ground toward their destination. The S-23 was an unusual craft designed for slow speeds and high maneuverability. Its broad wingspan allowed the pilot to navigate terrain at low altitudes for accurate geo-mapping. Much of this kind of flying had been relegated to automated drones, but there were some locations and situations that just couldn't be completed without a skilled geo-mapping pilot like Elias.

Brae loved every minute of the flight and asked to help her father in any way possible. Once the survey work was complete, Elias diverted to a part of the country that was a bit more interesting. There was even a small forest bordering a sizable canyon that would provide some aerial intrigue.

"Can we fly down into the canyon?" Brae asked with anticipation.

Elias smiled then banked to the right, allowing the craft to slip down into the cool canyon air. A few seconds later Brae was pressed up against the glass of the cockpit with a sense of wonder as she watched the jagged edges of the canyon wall fly past. Elias banked left and right in gentle turns to stay centered, being careful to keep a safe distance from the unforgiving rock walls. Brae looked below them and saw a bright blue river punctuated with various rapids and waterfalls. At one section of the canyon, a few of the forest trees spilled down a ravine and populated a section of the canyon floor with a splash of green.

"It looks surreal," Brae assessed as they passed over the area of trees and grass that looked like an oasis amidst the cavern of brown and red rock towers. "Can we stop and explore just a bit? Please?" she pleaded.

Elias slowed the S-23 and made a tight turn back to the lush green area. He gently set the craft down on a plateau of rock just a few paces from the river. Brae giggled with delight as the canopy lifted from its sealed recess.

"Let's not wander too far from the craft," Elias called after her as she clambered over the side of the fuselage and jumped to the ground. "And not too far from me either!" he added.

Brae first ran to the river and dipped a hand into the icy cold water. She lifted a handful to her lips and tasted its sweetness. Droplets spilled down her chin and onto her shirt. She wiped her entire face and the back of her neck with her wet hand, feeling the chilled water breathing new life into her. She stood and slowly turned a full circle, taking in the beauty of this rugged haven.

This will be my secret place forever, Brae thought, letting an uncontainable smile spread across her face. She turned her attention to the grove of trees fifty paces further up the canyon. She looked back at the S-23. Elias was just finishing a quick walk around to inspect the craft.

"Dad," she called out, pointing to the trees.

He looked that way then nodded. Brae started moving in the direction of the trees, being careful about her foot placement since some of the rocks were loose. As she navigated a particularly precarious set of rocks, she vaguely noticed a shadow pass quickly over her. Something triggered a subconscious response—a cloud would not have moved that fast across the sky. She looked up and froze.

"Brae!" she heard her father cry out.

She looked to see him running toward her with a Talon in hand. She bounced from rock to rock, quickly retracing her steps on a path that would take her back to Elias. Before he could reach her, the shadow came at her again. This time it was much larger.

"Get down!" Elias shouted.

Brae dropped to the rocky ground just as an ear-piercing screech permeated the canyon air, echoing and reverberating from wall to wall. She felt a powerful rush of air push down on her from above. Once it was past, she lifted her head just enough to see the winged creature swoop low over the top of her. As it approached Elias, he dove to the ground, rolled on his back and discharged his Talon at the underbelly of the massive creature. It screamed in annoyance but didn't seem to be distracted from its attack. The winged creature landed on top of the S-23 craft, clawing and biting at the ship. Brae stood and ran the rest of the way to Elias. He grabbed her hand and ran toward their ship, finding a large rock nearby to hide behind.

"Why is it attacking the S-23?" Brae asked, as Elias took aim.

"It's mating season, and this thing is defending its territory. It must think the S-23 is a threat. The wing span is about the right size and shape."

Elias fired three shots at the creature, being careful not to hit his ship. This time it was enough to stop the manic attack on his craft before the creature took flight.

"Quickly!" Elias exclaimed.

They ran to the S-23 and clambered into the side-by-side cockpit. There was no time to inspect the damage, but the left engine nacelle looked significantly damaged. As the canopy closed, Elias scanned the sky while trying to ignite the engines, but only the right one took.

"It's circling back behind us!" Brae shouted.

Elias evaluated his instruments and shut down the throttle to the damaged engine.

"We're going to have to make due with one engine," Elias said. "Strap in and hang on, Brae."

With only the right engine functioning, the S-23 was slow to lift off. Elias pushed the throttle up to full speed, leaving a wash of dust and rocks behind on the canyon floor.

"It's coming, Dad!"

The acceleration of the craft was agonizingly slow. Brae let out a scream as the creature opened its jaw of razor-sharp teeth and clamped down on the left wing's control surface. Fortunately, the beast didn't have a solid grip and let loose, but the damage to the craft was more that Elias had to cope with. He banked hard to thwart another attempt, then made for a couple of large rock spires that rose up from the floor of the canyon.

"Hang on, Brae. This is going to get a little wild!"

Elias maneuvered close to the canyon wall then swished in between the two massive spires, their jagged edges perilously close to the craft. Brae heard the creature screech in anger as it tried to keep up with them. For the next two minutes, Elias banked and rolled the S-23 through narrow passages and around canyon wall switch backs with unusual skill. Finally, they outdistanced the creature. Elias pulled back on the stick to lift them out of the canyon and back into the country. He then set a course for home.

"How are you doing, Brae…are you okay?"

Brae turned from looking rearward for the creature and regarded Elias. An ear-to-ear grin covered her face. "That was amazing!" she nearly shouted.

Elias shook his head. "Not amazing," he rebutted.

"How did you learn to fly like that, Dad? I thought we were dead, but you out-maneuvered that thing."

"Remember, I'm a geo-mapping surveyor, Brae," Elias explained. "I have to fly in tight situations all the time, navigating through mountains, valleys, and wooded areas. Although it's slow, the S-23 is built to be extremely maneuverable."

Brae whipped her head back to look out the side of the canopy again.

"Well, that was the best adventure I've ever had, and I can't wait to go again."

That evening when Elias came to tuck Brae into bed, he was unusually somber.

"What's wrong, Dad?" Brae asked.

Elias sat down on the bed next to her, looking deeply into her eyes. "I'm…upset with myself for exposing you to such a dangerous situation this morning."

"I'm okay, dad, really," Brae consoled.

"But you might not have been." He took her hand in his. "I can't lose you, sweetheart. We need to be more careful."

Brae frowned.

"Why do you tell me the stories of Daeson and Raviel if I'm supposed to live a safe and boring life? Besides, you're always telling me I'm going to have a grand adventure one day. I think today was certainly a grand adventure. Please let me come with you again soon!"

Elias looked at Brae and shook his head. "You're too much like your mother, little lady."

Brae smiled. "I wish I could have known her. I'll bet she was something special."

Elias swallowed hard. "Yes, she was," he added quietly.

Sensing that her father might become sad again, she quickly changed the subject. "So can I find out what finally happened to Raviel?" Brae asked. "I know she's not dead...I just know it. You've made me wait far too long."

"Real life doesn't always have happy endings, Brae. Sometimes bad things happen no matter what we want. That's when it's important to trust that Ell Yon is with us and will eventually make all things work out."

Brae thought about that and nodded. "I guess you're right."

"By the way, do you know what kind of creature that was today that was chasing us?" Elias asked.

"Yes, it was a Terridon," Brae answered with a smile.

Elias nodded. "When our people first came to Rayl, there were a lot more of them than there are now. One of them—well, let's start where we left off..."

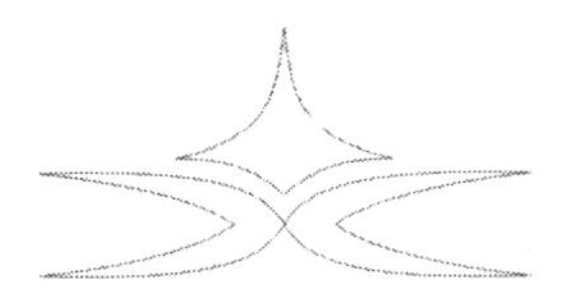

Chapter 1

The Edge of Home

Daeson stood on *Liberty's* observation deck, no other soul with him. The entire wall in front of him was transparent, giving him the sensation that he was alone while drifting in the vastness of space, yet the whole of the galaxy seemed within reach. He held up his hand to the place where his heart had been fractured, that place where his love had perished and his life became gray. The sorrow was always near him, like a shadow that could not be separated from himself, nor would he desire it to be so. The lump in his throat swelled once more as his fingers touched the barrier between him and his love...the barrier of time, space, and death. So permanent...so painful. He allowed himself to be fully submerged in the grief of his loss once more, for in the recesses of his mind he feared that not doing so would cause him to begin to forget.

"Raviel!" he whispered while tears spilled from his eyes. "My love...I miss you."

His hand slowly fell to his side as he ached for a way to reverse time. The day he told Petia about what had happened further intensified his grief, for the tears of the little girl Raviel had rescued clung to his memories.

Two months had passed since the horror of that moment. Two months filled with impossible tasks, sleepless nights, and a hundred dreams of Raviel being sucked out of the slipstream conduit and ripped apart by the shearing fabric of time and space. It was the momentum of life that kept him moving forward—the unrelenting burden of leading the Rayleans on this absurd journey through space. Their needs were overwhelming, and the technological tasks seemed impossible at times. Tig, Trisk, and most of the clan Chieftains helped provide critical leadership, but other leaders among the Rayleans also rose up, often from among the most unlikely. Daeson made sure that new transport pilots and co-pilots were trained as quickly as possible so they always had a skilled pool of pilots available. Master Boytt and the other scitechs became invaluable in procuring the survival of the people in the wasteland of space, for the Protector had led them to the Roth System, a lifeless system of five planets. Here they waited for Sovereign Ell Yon, the Immortal who had led them to this abandoned region of space.

Daeson took a few minutes to recover himself before leaving the observation deck. It was never wise for a commander to reveal such raw emotion to his people. He navigated his way to *Liberty's* largest briefing room, where the twelve clan chieftains, all transport captains, Trisk, Tig, Master Boytt, and a handful of other leaders from the crew of the *Liberty* were waiting. They had modified this large briefing room by removing a bulk head to join two rooms together. Tig and Daeson secretly referred to it as the pit, for there were times when he felt he was being thrown into a pit of vipers.

At the entrance Daeson hesitated. He rallied himself, knowing that in spite of Sovereign Ell Yon's miraculous delivery of his people from the bondage of the Jyptonians, there seemed no end to their petitions and complaints. He was weary of it, yet their concerns were legitimate, especially considering the magnitude of keeping over three hundred thousand people alive in the vastness of space. He looked down at the Protector on his right forearm. Through it Daeson and the Rayleans had seen the impossible happen. But as of late, it was silent...testing. Daeson lifted his chin, pressed the door release, and walked into the pit.

The room was unusually quiet, silent in fact. The officers present snapped to attention. Daeson looked toward Trisk and Tig, giving a slight nod. This was their doing.

"Discipline, regimen, and order are what will keep us focused and alive," Tig had insisted.

"I agree," Trisk had chimed in. "These people may all have been civilians...slaves in fact, but not anymore. We don't have the luxury of treating them as such when resources are limited and the stakes are high. We must implement military protocols...at the very least, for the leadership."

Daeson looked around the gathered men and women. As usual, there was a mix of reactions from the chieftains, some pleasant...some scornful. Chieftain Wescott was Daeson's go-to if he needed a moment of encouragement from an otherwise discouraging crowd.

"This meeting is called to order."

At that, the façade of peace disappeared as the chieftains erupted with questions, complaints, and petitions. Daeson shook his head while Tig and Trisk looked like they were about to unleash on them.

"Nice try," he mouthed to the two of them.

"One at a time," Daeson shouted.

"Admiral Starlore," began Chieftain Cora, "our supplies are dangerously low. We've rationed to the minimums, but even still, I calculate we have no more than one week before my people will begin to starve."

"And besides that," piped up another chieftain, "we're beginning to have mechanical failures with no way to repair them. Two of our six reactor igniters are cracked. We lose one more, and we may never get our engines on line."

One by one Daeson listened to each chieftain's litany of complaints as his executive officer recorded them. When they were finished, Daeson asked each of the transport captains to voice any additional issues that needed attention. Two hours later, everyone had been given the opportunity to speak, and in that span of time, Daeson inwardly despaired. He could fix a handful of the complaints, but in truth, he had no answers for nearly all of them. Yet they expected answers, and not just answers but action. They stared at him expectantly. No amount of talking or promising would satisfy a howling stomach. He knew that dissension was growing quickly with many of the thirty-nine transports.

Daeson looked out at the assembly, frantically searching for the right words to appease them, but none came. All he could do was ask them to persevere a little longer. The Sovereign wouldn't abandon them…would he? As he opened his mouth to speak words he had not yet formed, the Protector awakened and the whisper came. Chills flowed up and down his spine as his eyes filled with the fiery light of the Sovereign.

"Today we set course for our promised homeworld."

Daeson's declaration stunned the occupants of the room.

"It is a world the Sovereign will give us as an inheritance. In three days' time, we will land our transports on Raylean terrain. This will be a world our people will possess forever. Our future generations will celebrate in the victory of this day, for Sovereign Ell Yon has declared it!"

The chieftains and ship captains sat in confounded silence.

"Return to your ships and make ready. We are five slipstream jumps away. We leave in one hour."

At that, Daeson turned about and exited the bay, not waiting for a thousand more questions that would surely follow if he were to remain. He returned to his quarters first to receive further instructions from the Protector without interruption. Thirty minutes later he joined Trisk and Tig on the bridge. Trisk vacated the captain's chair as Daeson entered and sat down.

"Well?" Daeson asked. Trisk stood to his right and Tig to his left.

"They're anxious, afraid, and excited," Tig offered first.

"One question rose above all others," Trisk added. "Is this planet occupied and if so by whom?"

Daeson thumbed the communication panel on the right side of his chair as he glanced from Trisk to Tig. "The Sovereign has never promised easy," Daeson replied.

Trisk pursed his lips. "I see."

"Have they all returned to their ships?"

"Yes," Tig responded.

"Ensign Walla, open a fleet-wide channel."

"Aye, Admiral." With a deft slide of her hand and a tap on a glass instrument panel, the channel-open tone sounded. She nodded.

"This is Admiral Starlore. You have all witnessed firsthand the power of Sovereign Ell Yon and his promise to deliver us from the bondage of the Jyptonians. Now is the time to enter into the promise of our homeworld. Today we journey to our future. Prepare your people and your transports and set course for twenty-four, twelve, fifty-six mark three. Our first slipstream jump will be through the Cordinot gateway. We will be under way in thirty minutes."

Daeson signaled Ensign Walla, and she closed the channel. Tig and Trisk left the bridge to make sure the *Liberty* was ready. Thirty minutes later they returned.

"Are all decks secure?" he asked Trisk.

"Secured and waiting, Admiral."

Daeson then turned to Ensign Kwi.

"Course laid in and set," Kwi offered. "Ready on your command, Admiral."

"Standby. Ensign Walla, have all transports reported in?"

"Yes, sir. The fleet is ready."

Daeson looked at the forward monitor and took a deep breath. Somewhere out in the wilderness of space was their home.

"Ahead three-quarters speed, ensign Kwi."

"Aye sir, ahead three-quarters speed."

Four hours later the *Liberty* led the fleet through the Cordinot slipstream conduit, their first hyperspace jump into the unknown.

Three days later the Raylean fleet of transports exited their fourth slipstream conduit, which positioned them at the fringe of a massive twelve-planet system called Ianis. The Ianis System was completely uninhabitable with multiple gas giants, smaller lifeless planets, and massive asteroid and meteor fields all orbiting two red giant binary stars. The Ianis System and its two gateways rarely saw star ship traffic since there was nothing here to draw the traffic. Colonizing the planets wasn't even in the realm of possibility, and besides this, navigating the system was too treacherous with the millions of meteors and asteroids. In light of this information, Daeson realized that this was a safe haven for his nomadic fleet of Rayleans until they were ready to venture to their final destination, for this region of the galaxy was well known for the many bands of marauders and vicious tribal people groups.

According to the galactic map of slipstream conduits, the next closest habitable planets were in a region of space called the Medarra Cluster, five star systems all within twenty-two light years of each other. One of those systems was the Kayn System, six planets orbiting a yellow dwarf star with three habitable planets. This system had multiple slipstream gateways for it was a significant hub of trade in the Medarra Cluster, if one had the skill and cunning to navigate the intricacies of the often-cutthroat ways of the people there. Two of the planets, Syroc and Jorn, had established single world governments. But the third and smallest planet was a fractured amalgam of various people groups, cities, and governments. It was known simply as Kayn-4 and was a perfect breeding ground for power-hungry tyrants that came and went with the tide of humanity through the years. This planet was the one the Protector had identified, in whispers to Daeson, as their future homeworld.

Daeson suspected that news of their future homeworld might not sit well with the people, so he arranged for Tig and Trisk to embark on an undercover reconnaissance expedition in a shuttle to gather some critical information on the planet before making their final jump.

"Gentlemen, you will navigate to the Kayn System gateway which will take you sixty-three light years from our fleet. Kayn-4, the fourth planet from the system's sun, is your destination. Be careful to avoid any interactions with the other two worlds, Syroc and Jorn. It is my understanding that there is no unified world government on Kayn-4 and ships from other planets in the Medarra Cluster are frequent visitors for the purposes of trade. Therefore, it should be relatively easy for you to enter the atmosphere and set down at a fringe space port close enough to the largest city, Reekojah. Discretion is usually honored at such places where trade profits rely on the exchange of goods with no questions asked. You will offer a few of our tech devices and instruments that should be considered advanced by the people there. Do your best to acquire some critical medical supplies and any smaller necessary equipment for the fleet. I'm giving you four days to discover all you can about the planet's resources, defense systems, and technologies, as well as city and regional governments."

Daeson looked at his two trusted leaders. "Any questions?"

"When do we leave?" Trisk asked.

"As soon as you're ready. The chieftains and their people are already restless. The sooner you return, the better. I'll have the mechtechs prep a shuttle for you immediately."

"Aye, Admiral. We'll be on our way within the hour," Tig replied.

Four days later when Tig and Trisk returned, Daeson called the clan chieftains to the *Liberty*. Just as Daeson had predicted, the announcement concerning their destination was met with disdain.

"Kayn-4 is our destination? This is preposterous!" shouted the chieftain of the Zealon clan. "We've heard the stories of this world and its vicious people. Even if we could somehow land our transports on some uninhabited part of the planet, the people there would conquer us immediately."

"Yes," Daeson replied. "That's why we're not to inhabit some unused parcel of land...we are to occupy the whole planet. Kayn-4 will be our homeworld, and we shall call it Rayl."

"But those people that occupy that world are vicious. Multiple governments rule, and many have advanced weapons and militaries," rebutted Moran of the Simak clan. "I agree with Chieftain Mardan...this is suicide...genocide. We would never survive."

"Yes," shouted another. "I've even heard there are huge, terrifying creatures in the land."

Daeson lifted his hands in the air to calm the chieftains.

"Captains Tig and Trisk have just returned from investigating this planet. I will send a detailed report of their findings to each of you." Daeson turned to Tig and Trisk. "Captains, give your analysis of your findings."

Tig stood first and faced the chieftains.

"Indeed, there are fortified cities, vicious people, advanced technology, and giant creatures...this is all true. But this planet is full of promise and hope. It's a place ripe with resources and land that we can subdue and make our own."

"We are a strong people...a resilient people," Trisk added, looking around the room. "Do not shrink from the victory that awaits us. Have courage!"

"They're right," Daeson added. "There are significant obstacles to overcome, but this means the victory that Sovereign Ell Yon will provide will be great. Have you already forgotten what he accomplished to bring us here?

Do we retreat now...on the very edge of making this planet our homeworld?"

Silence hung in the room as the chieftains considered his words, but Daeson could see by the looks on their faces that they were yet captives on Jypton. He grew angry.

"What you're asking of us is impossible!" declared one chieftain. "How many of our people will die in battle or in the jaws of these monsters?"

"Yes," shouted another. "We have no weapons, no soldiers, and barely enough food and water to keep us alive for a few more days. Such an undertaking is simply preposterous!"

More protests rose up until the pit was full of angry men and women. Galder Wescott from the Baraquet Clan stood and tried to subdue the rising dissension, but the other clan chieftains would not relent. Daeson felt the Protector vibrating in angry resonance. He stood and shouted loud enough to bring a small measure of order back to the meeting.

Asdor, chieftain of the Revitar Clan, stepped forward.

"If you're so confident that Kayn-4 is to be our homeworld, let us first see for ourselves before we risk our lives for it."

His comment was followed by shouts of approval from others. The insult further angered Daeson, but the Protector approved.

"So be it!" Daeson shouted. "Send me one of your best from each clan. We will send them to Kayn-4 in our two shuttles so they can spy out the planet for themselves and report back to you."

Asdor seemed pleased. His nod seemed to abate most of the remaining dissension.

"We're one jump away from the Kayn System. Tell your operatives to report to the *Liberty* briefing room at 0600. We will meet again in ten days when they return." Daeson adjourned the meeting.

The next morning, nine men and three women assembled in the briefing room of the *Liberty*. They all wore expressions of excitement and anticipation. Daeson and Tig briefed the operatives on their destinations, arrival times, mission goals, cover identification, rendezvous points, exit procedures, and emergency extraction protocols. Each of the clan operatives would investigate as much of the surrounding region as possible, evaluating resources, defenses, technologies, city governments, infrastructures, and rural commodities. Each operative was given a Talon and a quantum entanglement communicator or QEC, so they could stay in contact with the *Liberty*. It was decided that one shuttle would navigate close to the largest city, Reekojah, in the eastern hemisphere, and the other would navigate close to the city of Arn in the south. Daeson had Tig handpick two pilots for the shuttles *Venture* and *Excursion*.

Fifteen minutes after the briefing, all twelve operatives had boarded their assigned shuttles and launched. Daeson, Tig, and Trisk made contact each day with the operatives via the QECs to ensure their safety. All in all, the missions seemed to be going well, but Daeson couldn't help but wonder what the final outcome would be. The intensity with which the Protector responded to the protests of the chieftains made him nervous...no...it made him afraid.

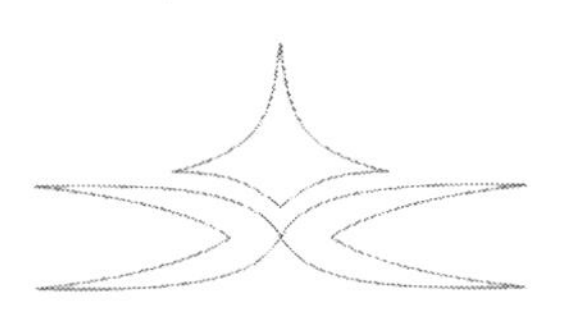

CHAPTER 2

Survival

Spacetime – A conceptual model combining the three dimensions of space with the fourth dimension of time. The spacetime fabric model combines these four dimensions in a relativistic relationship demonstrating their interdependence and variableness one with the other.

Two days later, the last of the food had been rationed, and nearly all the water was gone. Daeson sat in the captain's seat of the *Liberty*, overwhelmed by the looming threat of mutiny. Trisk stood to his right and Tig to his left. They waited expectantly for the return of the operatives, but the pains of hunger and thirst grew severe for the fleet. Even two weeks was too much to ask of them.

What now, Sovereign Ell Yon? How does a future generation inherit Rayl if this one dies tomorrow? Daeson didn't dare voice such thoughts to his people, but he certainly could not deny them.

The fleet was still on the fringe of the Ianis System.

"What are our options?" Daeson asked.

"This is a dead system, and yet we have ships that probably can't make the slipstream jump because of impending mechanical failure," Trisk responded.

"Even if we did jump, the Medarra Cluster is quite hostile. For the safety of our people, the Ianis System is our best bet," Tig added.

Daeson nodded. "We are where we are supposed to be. Although uninhabited, this system is massive. Surely there must be resources here that can help us."

"Resources, perhaps," Trisk said. "But food is another matter in a dead system."

Daeson turned to his sensors officer. "Lieutenant Golan, have you had any success scanning the asteroids for ice?"

"No, sir," Golan replied. "But our scans are only able to reach a fraction of the asteroids in the system."

Daeson turned to his communications officer. "Ensign Walla, have every transport with scanners coordinate with Golan and initiate their own scans. If we need to navigate to a more advantageous position, we'll have the ships separate, safely avoiding all meteors and asteroids. With as many ships as we have, we should be able to cover a lot of space."

"Aye, sir," came the replies.

Daeson then turned to Trisk. "You have the ship, Captain. Tig and I have some flying to do ourselves."

Tig looked over at Daeson as they made their way to the docking bay.

"Are we looking for ice as well or something different?"

"Something different. I was just given a set of coordinates, and I'm hoping it's what I think it is."

Two hours later, Daeson and Tig had arrived at their coordinates.

"Our position is extremely close to the slipstream gateway for the system. There's nothing here," Tig said over the com from the backseat of their Starcraft.

"Yes, it appears that is the case. I guess we wait," Daeson replied.

Thirty minutes passed, and Daeson began to second guess himself.

"Viper One, this is *Liberty*." Trisk's voice was unusually enthusiastic.

"Viper one here. Go ahead, *Liberty*."

"We have good news. Scanners from the *Sojourner* just confirmed a massive section of asteroids that is seventy-two percent ice."

"That's great news, *Liberty*. Work with our scitechs to devise the best way to mine it."

"Copy, Viper One."

Just as the encouraging news report ended, Tig stated with trepidation, "Sensors show something's coming through the gateway."

Daeson armed weapons as a precaution. A moment later the gateway flashed, and eight containers appeared, slowly drifting toward them.

"That's impossible," Tig whispered. "Whatever these are, they have no propulsion system, not even a jump drive engine for the slipstream conduit. It's just not possible!"

Daeson engaged the Starcraft's thrusters to navigate closer.

"It wouldn't be the first time we've seen 'impossible,'" Daeson replied.

Tig laughed. "True, Admiral, true indeed."

Daeson targeted the first container and engaged his grappling field.

"Let's get this one to the fleet and see what's in it, shall we?"

Once the container had been secured in the docking bay, there was great rejoicing when Daeson and Tig opened it to discover perfectly preserved food. Based on the amount in this container, there would be enough food in the eight containers for the entire fleet for a day. And although there were many who would scoff at the meager amount, considering the massive continual needs of the fleet, Daeson didn't trouble himself with these concerns. These containers were proof once again that Ell Yon was with them...he would always be with them. Daeson scanned the food with the Protector, which yielded an impossible zero percent of Deitum Prime contamination.

Six days passed, and each day new containers of food mysteriously appeared.

"You've got to see this, Admiral," his logistics officer said as he escorted Daeson into the docking bay.

"See what, ensign?" Daeson asked.

"At first we thought we could use these containers to expand our living quarters, but then we realized that we would soon be completely overwhelmed by the sheer number of them if this were to keep happening every day."

Daeson looked around the bay and saw only three containers.

"Where are you putting them?" Daeson asked.

"Nowhere. Watch this, sir," the ensign said as he stepped up next to an empty container and struck the side of it with a fusion wrench. Within seconds the entire container cracked into a million pieces, then it fell to the floor in dust. Daeson reached down to scoop up a handful of the debris, but it dissolved away to nothing as it slipped between his fingers.

"Remarkable," Daeson assessed as he looked up at his logistics officer and smiled before standing. "Carry on."

The next day Scitech Master Boytt came to see Daeson in his quarters. His face revealed both excitement and concern. It confused Daeson. Boytt rarely showed emotion, but something was different. Daeson wondered if there was some new technological problem they were facing as space nomads, one without a solution.

"What is it, Master Boytt?"

"I'm not sure how to say this, Daeson." Boytt fumbled for words.

"It can't be anything I'm not prepared to deal with," Daeson said with a smile, trying to lighten the mood.

Boytt looked him in the eye. "I'm not so sure about that."

Daeson's smile faded as he offered Boytt one of the two available chairs. Boytt never teased. Daeson took the other chair and waited. The older gentleman took a deep breath.

"It's been eighty-six days since Raviel—"

Boytt stopped. Daeson's heart nearly stopped too. Hearing her name tore into him like never before. Boytt was right—whatever he was going to say, Daeson wasn't ready for it. He bit his lip.

"With all of the recent use of the Starcraft...," Boytt started again, glancing down at his glass tablet, "the mechtechs were doing some deep level maintenance on it. They discovered encrypted telemetry log files that have been automatically generated between flights of in-range Starcraft. Two days ago, I successfully decrypted the files. They are telemetry logs transmitted by Raviel's Starcraft to your Starcraft at the moment she broke through the conduit wall." Boytt looked up at Daeson.

Daeson leaned forward. "Yes? What does this mean?"

"The log contains all of the flight parameters of her Starcraft...heading, speed, attitude, a hundred other variables, including pilot vital statistics. Your telemetry radio was even able to capture sixty-four milliseconds of data after she left the conduit. After lengthy discussions with the mechtechs, we've come to the conclusion that, barring any quantum bio impact from such an event, she survived the exit from the conduit."

Daeson jumped up from his chair, thrilled and terrorized all in the same instant. He began pacing.

"But you told me—"

"I know, Daeson...I'm so sorry. Based on what we knew then, I didn't think there was any way she could have survived. Then, without some indication of her position and heading, it just wasn't even possible...."

Daeson turned to Boytt, horror gripping his soul. "I killed her...I left her in space to die!" Daeson's eyes filled with tears as he imagined Raviel's slow, cold death in the vastness of space. With no conduit nearby and light years of empty space, she would have been marooned with no hope of rescue. Did she last hours...days...weeks? A new torment tore at his soul, and he knew it would last the rest of his life.

Boytt grabbed Daeson's arm. "No, Daeson...there's every reason to believe that she's not dead...not yet!"

Daeson froze. Boytt's words seemed preposterous. Had he imagined them?

"It's been eighty-six days, Boytt! No one could survive that long!" Daeson nearly shouted.

Boytt shook his head, simultaneously tapping on his glass tablet.

"It's been eighty-six days for us, but not for her. When she exited the slipstream conduit, telemetry data shows she was travelling at near-light speed. According to my calculations, this means that she is, as we speak, experiencing extreme time dilation. For her, only a few hours have passed since the event." Boytt frowned. "But time is of the essence…even with extreme time dilation, she might not have much longer."

Daeson's eyes widened as he considered what Boytt was telling him. The effect of time dilation at near-light speed had always been a known relativity effect, but typically negligible. Before slipstream conduits were discovered, most craft had not been able to attain such speeds to have an impact, since the effect is exponential the closer a traveler gets to the speed of light. Essentially, as a person accelerates and travels at velocities close to the speed of light, time passes slower, relative to the time experienced by another person that did not accelerate to that velocity. At speeds very close to the speed of light, this time dilation can be extreme. Daeson experienced a thousand thoughts and emotions.

"Is this possible? Why would you hesitate to tell me such a thing?" Daeson asked.

"Because I knew what you would attempt to do once I did," Boytt said somberly.

"Save her? Of course I will…she's out there right now!" Daeson could hardly contain himself. He wanted to jump in his Starcraft and begin searching immediately.

"Daeson, all we know for sure is what was happening to her the instant she left the conduit. Even two hours of unknown actions means your chances of finding her are astronomically small. There are a thousand variables that could change everything."

Daeson shook his head. "That doesn't matter…I have to try."

"A one hundredth of one degree shift from the telemetry data would put her millions of miles from the projections I've calculated," Boytt continued. "If you do this, you will probably die trying."

"Calculations? You've already done the calculations?" Daeson's enthusiasm was uncontainable. In just a few moments, despair became hope…loss became gain…death became life. He glanced at Boytt's glass tablet and saw one screen filled with incredibly complex formulas and calculations.

Master Boytt hesitated. He rubbed his forehead. "This has been grievous for me to bear these last two days. I think I shall be responsible for your death, yet I couldn't bear in silence what it would mean to keep this from you. I've gone through the calculations a hundred times. The truth is, your only chance of finding her is if she is unconscious and Rivet is deactivated…fortunately the data seems to indicate both."

"Why is that?" Daeson asked, wondering if he should reveal the truth about Rivet to Boytt.

"Because any flight control or engine input from either Raviel or Rivet would completely alter the outcome of these calculations. They could alter their trajectory or shift the dilation effect. Decelerating a fraction of a percent of the speed of light could change two hours for her to two weeks. You would have to find her at not only a perfect position in space but also at a perfect place in time. You must find her perfectly in four dimensions while she is traveling extremely fast, and you'll have to use the slipstream gateways to leap frog to that intersection in spacetime." Boytt shook his head. "The odds are—"

"I don't care what the odds are," Daeson interrupted. "Because it won't matter. I'm going after Raviel," Daeson affirmed, concluding that Boytt didn't need to know about

Rivet because it wouldn't change the decision to go nor would it change Boytt's calculations.

Boytt's shoulders dropped. "Do you also understand what this means for the fleet? For the people of Rayl?"

Daeson frowned. "Yes," he said quietly. "I have to accelerate my Starcraft to her speed, and I will experience the same time dilation…perhaps twice if we're nowhere near a slipstream conduit. Many months…perhaps years may pass. There's every likelihood that you will all be dead by the time I get back."

"Yes. That conduit spanned 120 light years. Now do you understand why I was hesitant to tell you?"

"Yes, of course I do, but Boytt…how can I not try? You did the right thing by telling me. What must I do to prepare?"

"If you're truly going to attempt this, you need to leave immediately…within the next twenty-four hours. I believe her window of survival is closing rapidly."

Daeson began pacing. The operatives on Kayn-4 were scheduled to return within the next two days. How could he possibly abandon them at this critical time? But how could he abandon Raviel? He had already sacrificed his desire to search for her on behalf of taking care of the needs of the people for over two months. He stopped, looked at Boytt, and asked, "What else?"

"We still have to figure out how to override the jump drive engines to function outside a slipstream conduit. There are a dozen hardware and software safeguards in place to prevent such a thing simply because of the potential disaster it could cause. Additionally, the mechtechs will have to train you how to override Raviel's Starcraft. You won't be able to count on any help from her. Based on the logs, her Starcraft was damaged by the missile, but the damage appears to be mostly to the atmospheric surface controls. As long as you don't try to take the ship into an atmosphere, it should be functional."

"Make the preparations. There are a few conversations I must have in the meantime."

Master Boytt looked long at Daeson, then nodded and left. Daeson went to a view port and stared out toward the place in the galaxy where she was waiting. Deep within him, his soul revived—a feeling he had thought was long dead.

"I'm coming for you, Raviel."

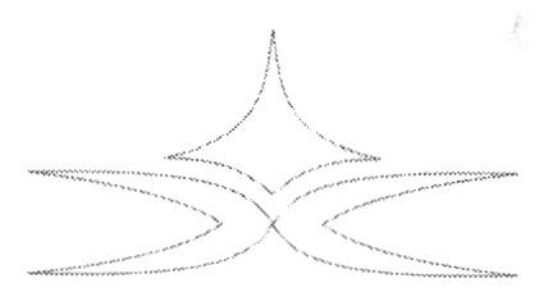

CHAPTER

3

Flight Through Time

Daeson and Tig stood side by side, gazing out the observation deck's viewing window. A dozen Raylean transport ships were visible in the foreground, and behind them was the intricate and vast beauty of the Aurora Galaxy.

"If she's alive, the thought of leaving her out there in the darkness of space is more than I can bear." Daeson turned his eyes from the view of the galaxy to Tig. "I'd rather die."

Tig continued to stare blankly through the viewing window, and Daeson wondered if he'd been listening at all.

"Tig?"

Tig slowly turned his gaze toward Daeson.

"I'm coming with you."

Daeson smiled. Of course he wouldn't allow it, but the loyalty of his friend simply astounded Daeson. He shook his head.

"I can't let you do that, Tig." Daeson put a hand on his shoulder. "Look, my friend, any debt you think you owe me has been repaid a hundred times over." Daeson looked straight into his eyes. "This is something I must do alone. You have a life here."

Tig's eyes didn't soften. Daeson could see his steely resolve was yet untouched by his words.

"You're not coming, Tig. Besides," Daeson broke his gaze from his friend and glanced out across the armada of Raylean ships. "These people are going to need you in the months and years to come. If you want to complete your liege to me, then stay and lead these people."

Tig's eyes narrowed in defiance to Daeson's leveraging words.

"I've talked to Boytt," Tig said. "I know what your odds are. You're going to need help...my help. I'm going with you. Trisk and the other officers are completely capable of carrying on."

Daeson then realized that Tig wasn't just feigning words in some noble gesture...he was serious. It both humbled and angered him. He clenched his jaw. "What about Zee'la? Surely you can't just—"

"Don't you understand?" Tig interrupted. "My oath to you doesn't expire—ever! There's something stronger happening than you or me, Daeson. You're not the only one that hears the whisper of Ell Yon. That oath I made to you was not of my own inspiration, and to deny it now would ruin me. As for Zee'la, that's not really working out."

Tig crossed his arms and glared back at Daeson as if ready for war.

"I am coming with you. This is a rescue mission that I *will* be a part of."

Daeson frowned. "A rescue mission, yes, but it's one with no way home. There's no coming back."

Tig was not dissuaded. Daeson searched for a more compelling argument but none came. The moment hung as his thoughts fumbled for another angle. His gaze dropped then reconnected with Tig's eyes, and Daeson realized Tig was right. Something inside him yielded and rejoiced. The thought of trying this alone was frightening, and having Tig by his side through this venture was a comfort he'd not dared consider until now.

"What about your father?" Daeson asked.

"He understands. He's happy with his people, and he's needed, just as I am needed."

He grabbed Tig's hand and pulled him into an embrace. "You are much more than a brother, Tig. Thank you."

Although time for Raviel was much slower at her velocity, Daeson was eager to put things in order and be on his way since it would take time to travel and find her. Every minute of delay could mean the difference between finding her or not. Daeson met with Trisk, Tig, Chieftain Wescott, and Master Boytt in his quarters before announcing his intentions to the rest of the people.

"Chieftain Wescott, how do you think the rest of the chieftains will take this?" Daeson asked.

Wescott thought for a moment then looked Daeson in the eye. "I can't imagine anyone would condemn you for trying to find her. We all understand the strength of the bonded relationship, but many will undoubtedly feel abandoned, especially when we're on the verge of coming to our own homeworld."

Daeson's gaze dropped to the floor. "Yes, I am concerned about that."

"And besides this, you're taking our only remaining ship with weapons," Trisk added. "It leaves us extremely vulnerable."

These words were hard to hear. Daeson nodded, looking toward Trisk.

"I understand. If there were any way to take a shuttle, I would, but Master Boytt has assured me that the Starcraft engines are the only ones with the ability to accomplish this journey. I've asked him and his scitechs to immediately begin weaponizing every shuttle we have. You'll need to start training pilots and soldiers, Trisk. You know we've been working on plans for building the forcetech and aerotech orders. Accelerate those efforts and start preparing this fleet for the day Ell Yon calls them to Rayl. Whether its tomorrow when the operatives return or six months from now, you must lead them to Kayn-4. It tears at me not to be with the people for this."

Trisk looked a bit overwhelmed but nodded. The four of them talked at length about transfer of leadership, defenses, survival, resource acquisition, trading tactics, and establishment of judicial laws.

"Remember," Daeson said, looking particularly toward Trisk. "I am just a man. It was not I who freed us from the Jyptonians…it was Ell Yon, and he has promised to be with you."

Trisk seemed encouraged by his words.

"And what of the Protector?" Wescott finally asked what the others dared not.

Daeson lifted his arm and gently ran his fingers along the intricate details of the Immortal technology.

"The Protector wasn't given to me…it was given to the Raylean people." Daeson looked up at each of the men. "It stays with you. Unless you have any more questions, I need to speak with Trisk in private."

"I do," Wescott said. "Has the Protector affirmed your decision to do this?"

The others stared at Daeson…waiting. Daeson lowered his head.

"No, but neither has the Protector prohibited it. I've asked Ell Yon a hundred times on behalf of Raviel, but—," he paused and looked up into the eyes of his friends. "But he has chosen to remain silent."

"The heart of a man chooses his path, but the Sovereign will establish his steps," Wescott said as he placed a hand on Daeson's shoulder. "I believe that the oracle that gave us those words is offering encouragement for a good man during the times when Ell Yon chooses to remain silent. He will be with you."

Daeson found great comfort in his words. Wescott then turned and exited the room. Boytt and Tig followed as Daeson turned to look at Trisk.

"You've been faithful to Ell Yon, Trisk. You are capable, and you are called to this." He looked down at the Protector. "Your ability to lead these people will depend on how well and how willing you are to hear the voice of Ell Yon."

Trisk swallowed hard. "You know I'm not a fearful man, but this...this frightens me."

"And it should. It scares me every time I hear him," Daeson replied. "The power of the Protector and your ability to use it is directly related to your body's level of Deitum Prime assimilation. I must scan you before yielding the Protector to you. Are you willing?"

Trisk straightened. "I am willing."

Daeson lifted his hand toward Trisk, bringing his thumb and forefinger together. He then spread them apart, and a bright horizontal amber beam of light emanated outward toward Trisk. Daeson moved his hand so the scanning beam passed from Trisk's head to his feet. When it was done, Daeson looked at the percent of Deitum Prime then closed his hand, and the display disappeared. He looked at Trisk, hesitating.

"To say that any amount of Deitum Prime assimilation is acceptable would be a gross misstatement, however, you've done well, Trisk. Be ruthless in abstaining from Dracus's genetic poison and lead the people in this endeavor as well."

Trisk looked relieved, nodding. Daeson grabbed the Protector with his left hand and hesitated, knowing the chasm of loneliness he would feel once disconnected from Ell Yon. He remembered the words of an ancient oracle, proclaiming that one day the voice of Ell Yon would be ever-present in the minds of those who would follow him. Without the Protector, Daeson couldn't imagine how such a thing were possible, and he wondered if he would ever see that day. All he knew right now was that the Immortal's voice through the Protector was life itself to him. Without it, he wondered if Ell Yon was done with him. He lifted the vambrace upward, and the Protector yielded its grasp on his arm and on his mind. He immediately felt as if he were floating in the emptiness of the dark. He caught Trisk's gaze as he held the Protector above his outstretched arm. He *was* afraid. Daeson slowly pressed the Protector onto Trisk's arm. Trisk's eyes opened wide, and Daeson thought for a moment that he could see the milky glow of a trillion stars in his eyes. Trisk winced, then fell to his knees, clutching the Protector with his left hand.

"It's too much!" He yelled.

"Breathe," Daeson said calmly. "Focus on one singular thought and let it calm you. Ell Yon is your protector...not your destroyer."

Trisk took a breath and slowly relaxed. Daeson fully understood the experience, feeling as if at any moment the waves of a tsunami would carry him away. Moment by moment, Trisk was able to absorb the impact of the Protector until he could stand and face Daeson. Daeson smiled sadly. He recognized the glow of Ell Yon in Trisk's countenance and mourned for himself.

"Guard your heart, Trisk. Even the Protector can be used for selfish gain. On that day, great will be Sovereign Ell Yon's indignation over such a thing."

Trisk looked at Daeson. "I understand."

The next morning, Daeson met with the fleet leadership and chieftains before making his announcement to the rest of the fleet. Trisk had gained the respect of all of the clan chieftains, perhaps even more so than Daeson himself. When Daeson explained his intentions and the plans they had made to carry on, surprisingly little was said. For some, there even seemed a hint of satisfaction and relief. Daeson couldn't deny the sting that he felt as a result. He hoped Trisk would fare better as their leader than he had.

After the fleet-wide announcement, Daeson and Tig spent most of the morning going through the details and training required with Master Boytt, his scitechs and the Starcraft mechtechs. They were given the tools and software required to modify Raviel's Starcraft.

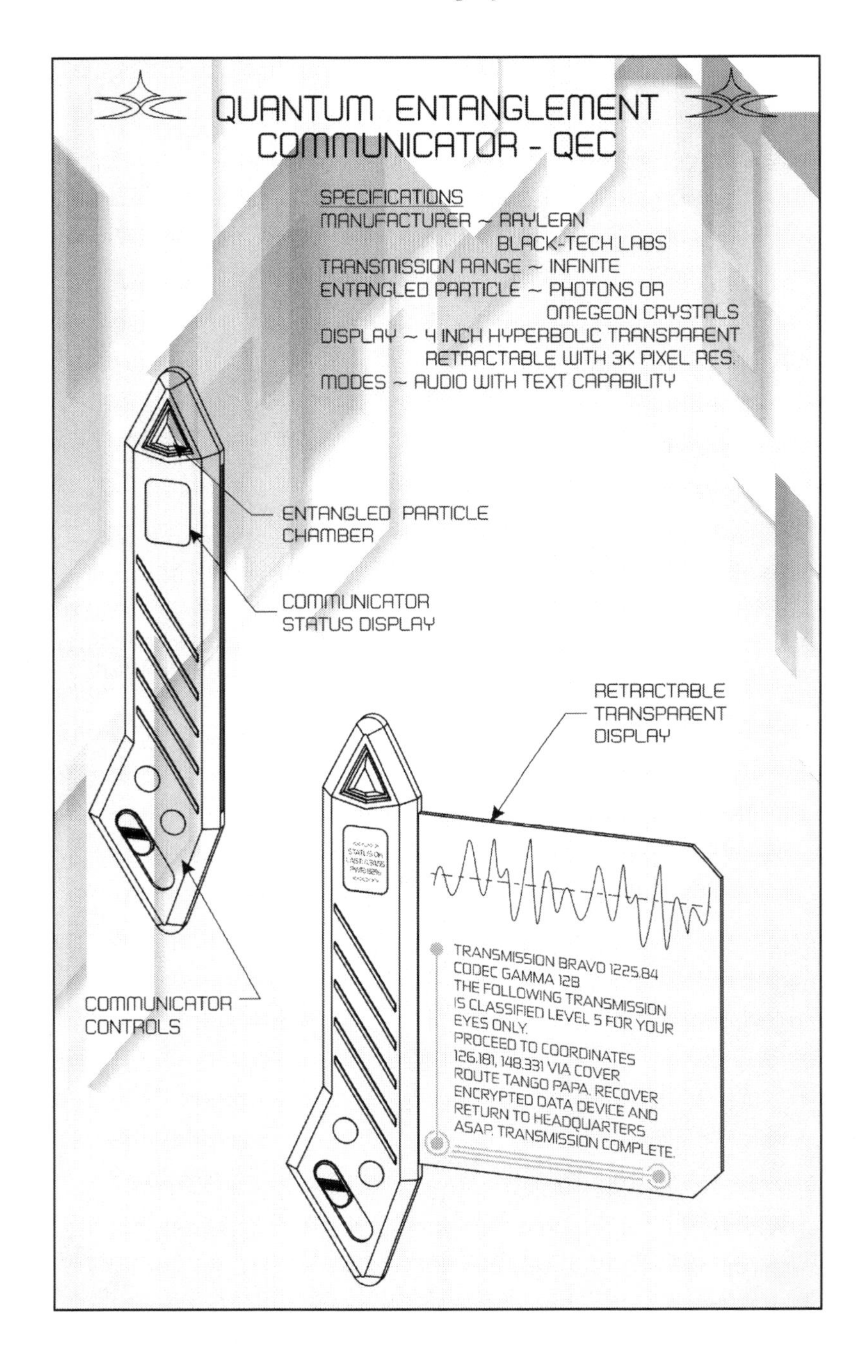
QUANTUM ENTANGLEMENT
COMMUNICATOR - QEC
SPECIFICATIONS
MANUFACTURER ~ RAYLEAN
BLACK-TECH LABS
TRANSMISSION RANGE ~ INFINITE
ENTANGLED PARTICLE ~ PHOTONS OR
OMEGEON CRYSTALS
DISPLAY ~ 4 INCH HYPERBOLIC TRANSPARENT
RETRACTABLE WITH 3K PIXEL RES.
MODES ~ AUDIO WITH TEXT CAPABILITY
ENTANGLED PARTICLE
CHAMBER
COMMUNICATOR
STATUS DISPLAY
RETRACTABLE
TRANSPARENT
DISPLAY
COMMUNICATOR
CONTROLS
TRANSMISSION BRAVO 1225.84
CODEC GAMMA 12B
THE FOLLOWING TRANSMISSION
IS CLASSIFIED LEVEL 5 FOR YOUR
EYES ONLY.
PROCEED TO COORDINATES
126.181, 148.331 VIA COVER
ROUTE TANGO PAPA. RECOVER
ENCRYPTED DATA DEVICE AND
RETURN TO HEADQUARTERS
ASAP. TRANSMISSION COMPLETE.

Boytt and the mechtechs were quite concerned with the planned modifications to Raviel`s Starcraft however, since they didn't know how the Malakian's upgrades to that craft would be affected. They had to hope for the best.

By noon, Daeson and Tig were ready. A small cadre of friends had gathered to send them off. After a final check of the Starcraft by the scitechs and the mechtechs, Boytt handed Daeson a QEC communicator.

"The most significant calculations will allow a forty-five-minute launch window. If you can't arrive at your departure coordinates and launch within that window, you'll have to abort. When you get to the designated launch point, I'll send you additional parameters so that you will have the most current and accurate calculated numbers," Boytt said with an edge of concern in his voice. "Once you receive the new launch parameters, you will have sixty seconds to set your final orientation and engage your jump drive engine. That will initiate a thirty-second, automated jump drive powerup sequence that you cannot stop, so be sure you're ready when you engage the drive."

"Will our long-range sensors work at near-light speed?" Daeson asked.

"Yes, and we've boosted the range of the subspace scanner, but you still need to be within three light years to get any signal at all."

Boytt looked sternly at Daeson. "Everything has to be absolutely perfect for this to work."

"I understand," Daeson said.

"I don't think you do, Daeson. If you overshoot her by just two weeks, she'll be—," Boytt stopped short of saying it. "I really wish you would reconsider."

"It's okay, Boytt. I know the risk. Regardless of what happens, I am indebted to you. I promise to take care of your future family."

Boytt smiled, but the sadness in his eyes remained. Trisk stepped up beside Boytt.

"Raviel's your bonded, but she's also my cousin. Find her, Daeson. Find her and bring her back to her people."

Daeson nodded. There was one more goodbye to make. He stepped around Boytt and Trisk and walked to the little girl who had known so much pain already. He knelt down to face Petia eye to eye. She tried to smile, but tears formed instead. She threw her arms around Daeson's neck and held on tightly. Daeson gently hugged her.

"It will be okay, Petia. Nynna and Jarden love you so much and will take good care of you," Daeson said softly into her ear.

Daeson felt her shoulders shaking. She finally released her hug and faced him, wiping tears from her eyes. "I know you'll find Raviel...and Rivet too. When you do, tell them I love them."

Daeson's eyes hurt as his own tears threatened to fall. "I will, Petia."

Petia then leaned into Daeson and kissed him on his cheek. "I love you too," she said quietly, then turned to bury her face into Nynna's leg.

Daeson could hardly speak. "I love you, little miss," he finally said, then turned toward his Starcraft. He joined Tig in strapping into a ship that was about to take them to the far reaches of space...to a place in time and space where Raviel was trapped.

The canopy whirred as it closed down on them from above.

"You said that Boytt told you the odds of our success?" Daeson asked Tig over the com.

"Yes, he did," Tig replied.

"And you still want to come?"

Silence, then the com mic clicked. "He also told me that my presence on this mission doubles your chances of finding her."

Daeson smiled. "Doubling nothing still leaves you with nothing, my friend. I wouldn't blame you if you bowed out."

"Rear cockpit checklist complete," Tig responded.

"Copy," Daeson replied. He saluted the men and women in the docking bay, then waited for everyone to exit. Once clear, he fired up the Starcraft engines.

"*Liberty*, Viper One requests docking bay doors open."

"Roger, Viper One. Docking bay doors opening now. May Ell Yon be with you!"

Eight hours later, Daeson and Tig were about to enter the final three conduits that would take them to the Omega Nebula, then to Jypton, then to their launch point.

"Omega slipstream conduit in two minutes," Tig said over the com.

"This is it, Tig. We'll transition through the Omega and the Jypton conduits quickly. Hopefully we won't encounter any serious resistance in the Nyson System from Jyptonian Planetary Aero Forces. I doubt they've recovered from the decimation they experienced during our escape, but we'll need to be careful just the same. There we navigate to the Oriot conduit which Boytt calculates will put us on a close intercept course for Raviel's Starcraft, based on her telemetry logs. If all goes well, we should have plenty of time to make our launch window."

"Copy," Tig replied.

"Once there, we'll have to be quick about it all, but our launch parameters must be perfect. So I need you to triple check the numbers we get from Boytt before we engage our jump drive engine."

Tig double-clicked his mic to acknowledge.

After a few hours of flight, they realized that their navigation near the Omega Nebula and through the Nyson System had taken longer than expected, but Daeson calculated that they would still have time to make their launch window. They began positioning their Starcraft for its near-light-speed launch outside of a conduit. It was something the scitechs couldn't test because of the risk of time dilation for the testing pilots. Daeson set up their initial flight parameters then radioed Boytt via the QEC.

"Daeson, I've calculated new launch parameters for you, but you need to know what's happening here first."

Daeson could hear multiple voices in the background. He checked their time for the approaching launch window.

"Go ahead," Daeson replied.

"The operatives have returned, and Trisk is meeting with the clan chieftains as we speak. It's not good," Boytt added.

Boytt continued transmitting so Daeson could hear the proceedings of the meeting.

"I am Tearan of the Revitar Clan. Kayn-4 is indeed a planet rich in resources as Captain Trisk and Captain Tig have reported, but this is well documented and known throughout the region, so I will tell you what you don't know...what isn't in the planetary survey reports. Six of us spent most of our time in the city of Reekojah. These are vicious and ruthless people...nearly barbaric. Slavery is commonplace, and there are arenas where games to the death are fought. And although their technology is limited, they understand the value of it and are aggressively acquiring that which will increase their power in the land. Frankly it's a frightful place."

There was a pause as Daeson heard a clamor rising from the chieftains. Then the operative's voice came back loudly.

"We would be better off back on Jypton."

Daeson clenched his jaw, but before he could speak the Simak Clan operative stood and gave his report, which was even more discouraging than the first. Daeson's heart sank as he listened to each operative give similar accounts, testifying to the overwhelming odds they would have to overcome to make this planet their homeworld. At one point, a young woman gave a terrifying account of their encounter with a creature as they made their way to one of the cities.

"It was the most horrifying creature I've ever seen!"

"Worse than a Kolazo beast?" asked one chieftain.

"Ten times worse and ten times larger...with wings!" she replied. "This thing could swallow a man whole."

Daeson heard the clan chieftains and their deputies gasp in horror.

"Daeson, we are out of time," Tig interrupted. "We have to launch now. The window Boytt gave us ends in two minutes."

Daeson was grieved to the heart. How could he leave them now? But how could he also leave Raviel to die in the cold of space alone? Trisk could recover the people, he told himself.

"Okay, Tig. Begin the sequence."

"How can anyone survive such a place?" Daeson heard another voice from the QEC exclaim.

"Why did Starlore bring us here and then abandon us?"

Daeson tried to concentrate on his launch checklist, but the QEC kept filling his headset with more dissenting questions and comments directed not only at Daeson but at Ell Yon as well.

"Boytt...let me talk to Trisk," Daeson said as he checked his timepiece.

"Daeson, the reports from the operatives have enraged the clan chieftains." Trisk's voice was strained.

Daeson considered aborting once again, but then realized his presence wouldn't change a thing. These were Sovereign Ell Yon's people, not his.

"Has the Protector spoken?" Daeson asked.

"Yes, Daeson, with great severity."

Trisk hesitated. "Sovereign Ell Yon is going to destroy them all!"

Daeson could imagine the fierceness of Ell Yon's words as the Protector permeated Trisk's mind with such a frightful message.

"Plead with him, Trisk!" Daeson exclaimed. "Ask him to remember the pride of the Jyptonians and how they will gloat at the destruction of the Rayleans. Fall on your knees and plead for their lives!"

"I will, Daeson!" Trisk replied.

"Now, Daeson!" Tig interjected.

"Our time is up, Trisk. Ell Yon be with you!"

"And with you!" Trisk replied, then Daeson shut the QEC off.

"New parameters received and set," Tig said through the com. "These parameters are good for sixty seconds."

Tig started a countdown on the Starcraft's nav computer. Daeson did his best to double-check the parameters with the ship's attitude, heading, and all engine parameters, but the final words of Trisk continued to echo in his mind.

"You okay?" Tig asked.

"I don't know...are we doing the right thing, Tig?" Daeson asked.

There was a long pause.

"Do you really think you could have convinced them more than Trisk?" he finally asked. "Raviel's out there...it's now or never if we are going to save her."

Daeson took a deep breath, encouraged by Tig. "Let's go!"

He flipped up the cover that protected the jump drive engine launch switch. A red warning popped up on his display, stating that the Starcraft must be within range of a slipstream conduit to activate the jump drive engine. The countdown clock was now at twenty seconds and decreasing. At ten seconds, Daeson took a deep breath. A moment of fright threatened to break his resolve as he thought about the chances of the jump drive engine tearing the Starcraft apart within the first few milliseconds. That Tig was willing to take this risk with him made the burden and the fear all the worse. At five seconds he placed his finger over the launch switch.

"All systems normal," Daeson heard Tig's calm voice through the com. Four...three...two...one.

Daeson flipped the switch to "LAUNCH." He felt a tremor in the structure of the Starcraft, unlike anything he had ever felt before as the automated power-up sequence initiated. A new thirty-second countdown timer displayed on his front glass panel.

"How we doing, Tig?"

"Reactor coils energized. Quantum ignitors charged. Inertial dampeners at full power, and E-shield at 100 percent...all systems—"

Tig's voice broke off. The timer read nineteen seconds.

"Status, Tig...are we good?"

"We've got a problem," Tig's voice was strained.

Daeson felt the entire Starcraft shudder. He saw his heading shift by 0.13 degrees. He tried to adjust.

Fourteen...thirteen...

"The jump drive engine temperature is out of tolerance. We've got to abort."

Daeson struggled to reset the Starcraft to the parameters Boytt had sent them.

Ten...nine...eight...

"There is no aborting! Help me get—"

The Starcraft lurched to the starboard side. Daeson felt his legs and arms fill with adrenaline as he desperately fought to regain parameters. He felt the crushing avalanche of disaster coming at them.

Four...three...

He made a desperate final effort to align the Starcraft's bearing using two nose vectoring thrusters, but the controls seemed to resist.

Two...one....

All at once, the space around them split open and swallowed them.

"We're in trouble, Tig! Our heading is off by 2.6 degrees. We need to shut the jump drive engine down."

"Working on it, but the shutdown sequence Boytt gave us isn't working," Tig replied.

At this speed, Daeson knew they were traversing many light years of space every second. He also realized that they were traversing many years of time relative to the rest of the galaxy. They had to get control of the jump drive quickly, or they would never have a chance of finding Raviel.

"You keep working on shutting it down. I'm going to plot this new course and make sure we don't obliterate ourselves in some giant star."

Daeson and Tig worked frantically to gain control and recover to normal space and time. Daeson finished plotting their projected course—his heart sank.

"Tig, unless you can get this jump drive shut down in the next sixty seconds, we're as good as dead."

Daeson displayed their plotted course on the left glass panel.

"Is that what I think it is?" Tig asked.

"Yes…and it's too big to miss. We're heading straight for the Omega Nebula. We'll be pulverized the instant we enter."

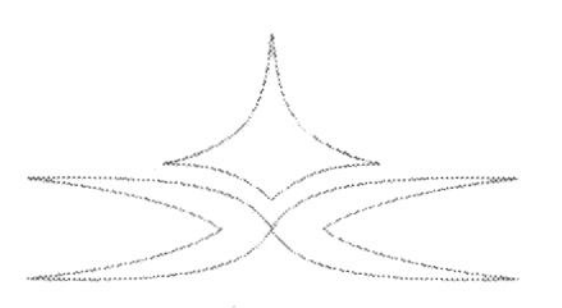

CHAPTER 4

The Other Side

Daeson and Tig were hurtling through time and space at near-light-speed velocity, the Omega Nebula staring them right in the face. Daeson redirected his efforts to help Tig get the jump drive shut down.

"I think the over-temp is causing the problem, but I don't know how to normalize the reactor cores."

"Let's try pre-emptively opening the exhaust ports," Daeson offered. "Maybe that will decrease the temperature of the entire drive."

"It's worth a try," Tig replied. "I'm out of ideas."

"Opening exhaust ports…now!" Daeson said as he touched the control panel.

Daeson heard the exhaust ports latch into the open position near the aft of the Starcraft.

"That's helping, but it's not enough."

Daeson glanced at their position. The Omega Nebula was screaming toward them. They only had seconds left.

"Try the shutdown sequence now," Daeson ordered.

Five long seconds passed.

"No luck," Tig responded.

The nebula was on them, and Daeson mourned. He had killed Raviel, and now he had killed Tig. He felt like such a fool.

"I'm sorry, Tig."

He heard Tig's mic click, but it was too late. They hit the boundary wall of the nebula. The first time Daeson had seen it, he and Raviel were nearly hypnotized by its majestic beauty and power. Then they had barely escaped death by its Omegeon particle radiation. Now it would finally have its way with him.

Brilliant white-hot light filled the cockpit as both men shielded their eyes. *Was this death?* Daeson wondered.

He blinked, and for one split second, his vision cleared just long enough to see an image. Then the world went black again. A billion faint stars became visible as his eyes adjusted to normal space. Daeson felt it first...the Starcraft shuddered.

"Tig...you did it!" Daeson shouted. "The jump drive is offline!"

"That wasn't me," Tig replied. "The jump drive temp is back to normal, so the shutdown sequence must have initiated." He paused. "Why aren't we dead?"

Daeson glanced at their course and position. They had exited on the far side of the Omega Nebula.

"The E-shield must have protected us from the plasma discharges and debris," Daeson replied. It was a fairly absurd explanation, but it was the best he could offer.

Both men remained silent for a minute...reflecting on what had just happened. Although grateful they hadn't been obliterated to dust, the thought that their mission was a disaster was too much for Daeson to absorb.

Daeson heard Tig's mic activate. "Did you...see something?"

Daeson hesitated...not sure how to answer. "Yes...but I'm not sure what. It lasted less than a second. Could you make anything of it?"

"Not really," Tig said. "Just that there was something there."

Just then the subspace scanner alarmed to indicate a contact. Daeson's heart skipped a beat, then he chastised himself for even hoping. According to Boytt's calculations, they were way off course and more than likely way off time. They had probably overshot Raviel by trillions of miles and perhaps hundreds of years. It was impossible to say without running calculations. Daeson narrowed the subspace scanner beam in an attempt to get an ID on the contact.

"We've resumed normal space time," Tig said. "According to the Starcraft's computer, 186 years have passed in normal galaxy time while we were traveling."

It was a frightening number.

"We're off course and off time, Tig…I think—"

The scanner alerted again, this time with an ID. It was the signature of another Starcraft.

"Impossible!" Daeson whispered.

"Are you seeing this?" Tig asked.

"Yes…it's impossible. If that's Raviel, she shouldn't be here."

Daeson couldn't suppress the hope that swelled within him, but then a thought of horror drifted into his mind. What if they were fifty years too late? Perhaps all they would find was a derelict Starcraft and the frozen remains of his love. The image haunted him.

"Perhaps she or Rivet altered their course," Tig said.

Tig's words triggered a sequence of thoughts…Rivet… Lieutenant Ki…inexplicable jump drive malfunctions…the Omega Nebula! Did Ell Yon and the Malakians have a hand in this sequence of events? Perhaps Ell Yon was not yet done with him, even if he was centuries out of time. Daeson dared let hope live in his heart once more.

"I'm laying in a course for the contact. We should be there in twenty minutes," Tig said.

As soon as the course was laid in, Daeson brought both thrusters up to full speed. As they closed in, he tried to make radio contact multiple times but was met only with static.

His heart began to race. Dreadful thoughts filled his mind as he considered the odds. Tig was silent. Tig would know that any idle talk or even an attempt at encouragement would be trite at a time like this.

"I'm getting telemetry data, Daeson…it's Raviel!"

Daeson's chest hurt as his heart pounded.

"Evidently the Starcraft at least has battery power. That means…"

"That means she could still be alive!" Daeson exclaimed. "What are her vitals…does the telemetry give us that?"

"There's so much data, it's hard to tell. I don't know," Tig responded.

Daeson closed in quickly, positioning the Starcrafts nose to nose. He looked through the canopies and, for the first time in over two months, set his eyes on the beautiful, still face of Raviel.

"Canopy coming open!" he said over the com to make sure Tig's helmet and suit were in place.

"Copy. Clear to open," Tig replied.

Daeson released his harness and clambered through the growing space between canopy and craft. He pushed toward Raviel's Starcraft and grabbed onto the side, now just inches away from her, reaching for the external lever to open the canopy.

"Daeson!" Tig shouted. "We need to verify the integrity of her suit before you open.

"Copy…can you tell from the telemetry data?" he asked.

Long, agonizing seconds ticked by.

"No," Tig's response finally came.

Daeson swung himself across the top of the canopy multiple times, trying to discern the condition of Raviel's suit and helmet. He felt a tug at his waist and looked down to see Tig attaching a tether.

"We have enough to deal with without creating another emergency," he said, tapping Daeson's shoulder to indicate he was secure.

"Copy," Daeson said. "As near as I can tell, her suit hasn't been compromised."

Tig swung himself to the opposite side of the cockpit as Daeson reached for the canopy lever. He hesitated then pulled. The air inside escaped and instantly crystallized...a good sign. Daeson reached for her, aching to hold her closer. Tig grabbed Raviel's arm and tapped on her suit's forearm status display.

"She's alive, Daeson. Her vitals are off, but she's alive!"

A lump formed in Daeson's throat as he fought back a wave of emotion. He closed his eyes.

"Thank you, Ell Yon," he said quietly.

"Daeson, look at Rivet," Tig said.

When Daeson opened his eyes, he looked to the second cockpit. The android sat perfectly still, his right hand on the stick, his left on the throttles, with a cable attached from his power pack to Raviel's life support panel.

"Looks like it was trying to control the Starcraft after Raviel lost consciousness," Tig assessed. "It drained its power pack to keep her alive."

Daeson didn't even know how to process what he was seeing. Rivet was obviously shut down, but what about Lt. Ki? She had promised to keep Raviel safe and had clearly been true to her word.

Thank you, Lieutenant. I hope you're okay, Daeson thought. He consoled himself, knowing that if anyone could help her, it would be the Malakians.

Daeson and Tig quickly set to work recovering Raviel's Starcraft. They transferred Raviel to the second seat in their Starcraft and ensured she was stable with oxygen, heat, and power being supplied to her suit. They secured Rivet then began working on modifying the Starcraft. After two and a half hours of often frustrating work, they were ready.

"What's the plan, Daeson?" Tig asked. "The closest slipstream gateway is fifty light years away, but it's on the other side of the Omega Nebula, and I don't think we should push the test button on that one again. The Gordenot gateway is eighty-six light years, but in the wrong direction. Based on how our Starcraft responded, there's no guarantee that either of our ships will work as planned."

"True enough," Daeson radioed. He looked at his friend as they hovered over the cockpits of the two Starcrafts. "Raviel's vital signs are getting weaker by the minute. If we journey back the way we came, it would take us over ten hours, and going further away isn't an option. I don't think she'll make it if we do."

"Agreed," Tig replied. "Then let's set a course directly for Kayn-4. We're going to experience time dilation anyway, and although this will make it worse, it will also make our journey minutes instead of hours."

"That's brilliant, Tig."

Daeson was so used to thinking in terms of traveling through gateways that Tig's solution hadn't even entered his mind.

"Kayn-4 is over one hundred eighty light years away. If this doesn't go perfectly, we could end up trillions of miles apart and many years as well, but we don't really have a choice, do we?"

"No," Tig answered. "No, we don't."

"We'll set coordinates for the Ianis System, our last known position of the fleet. Then we'll make one slipstream jump to the Kayn System, where they should now be. Since we don't know if our modifications to Raviel's Starcraft are going to work, you launch first in her Starcraft, then I'll follow. No matter what happens or where we end up, we both navigate back to our people on the planet. If for some reason we end up in an unpredictable situation, don't forget to encrypt your Starcraft start code."

"Agreed," Tig said. He held up his hand, and Daeson took it.

"Thanks, Tig. I..."

Tig nodded. "See you on the other side," he said with a smile.

Tig took the Starcraft with Rivet, and Daeson strapped in with Raviel. They took their time setting up the new coordinates for the Ianis System and triple-checked their Starcraft systems and jump drive engine parameters.

"Viper 2," Daeson radioed. "It is absolutely critical that our jump drives are engaged for exactly the same amount of time, or we will miss each other in time and space. A tenth of a second too long and we'll miss each other by days, not to mention millions of miles."

"Copy, Viper 1," Tig acknowledged. "I've set my auto shutdown to disengage the jump drive at 116.722 seconds."

"Roger and copy," Daeson replied.

"All systems go for Viper 2," Tig radioed.

"All systems go for Viper 1," Daeson replied. "I'll be right behind you."

Tig looked over at Daeson and saluted. "Initiating jump drive...now!"

Daeson mentally counted down the thirty seconds for Tig's automated power-up sequence to complete. Then for one fraction of a second, Tig's Starcraft stretched forward and disappeared in a brilliant flash of light. Daeson reached for the jump drive launch switch, suddenly feeling immensely alone in fifty light years of nothingness. He hoped with all his might that his jump drive would initiate. He lifted the protective cover and flipped the switch to LAUNCH. Daeson felt a tremor shimmy across the fuselage of the Starcraft once again as the jump drive powered up.

Here we go again, Daeson thought. The heading of the Starcraft shifted 0.14 degrees. This time he was ready, making micro adjustments, and the craft responded.

Five...four...three...

Daeson made one final push of the stick to bring the heading deviation to 0.00013 degrees.

Two...one...

The stars became streaks as Daeson and Raviel exploded into the world of relativity, traveling aboard a Starcraft that was stretching time and bending space. Daeson was elated to see that all of the jump drive engine parameters were within normal operating ranges. Now if the auto shutdown sequence functioned properly, they would be home free. The eighty-six seconds of near-light speed seemed to stretch on forever. It was hard for Daeson to believe that years were passing by in normal galaxy time as the seconds were for him. What would they find on their new planet, Rayl? Daeson imagined a homeworld filled with Rayleans who loved and served the Immortal Sovereign Ell Yon…a world set apart as an example to the rest of the galaxy…a world leading the way in defeating the evil plots of Lord Dracus and establishing true freedom for all worlds. Daeson's anticipation mounted as their non-conduit jump drive journey came to an end. They would arrive 271 years after they had left. What would the future be like when they arrived?

At 116.722 seconds after launch, the Starcraft's automated shutdown procedure initiated. Daeson had arrived within range of the Ianis System as planned. A short fifteen-minute flight should bring him to the Kayn System gateway. When Daeson and Raviel returned to normal space, Tig was nowhere to be found. All attempts at radio contact failed, and Daeson was becoming anxious about Raviel's condition. She hadn't revived on her own, and there was nothing he could do for her while they were in space. He risked waiting thirty minutes, then set a course for the Kayn System slipstream conduit gateway, the place he had left the Raylean fleet over 270 years earlier. As soon as he entered the section of the Ianis System where the gateway was located, he quickly realized that something was drastically wrong.

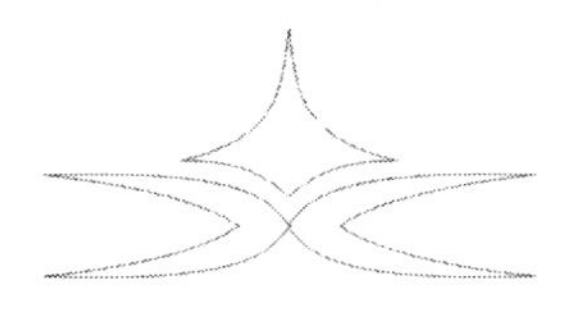

5

Vagrants

Time Dilation – A relativity phenomenon where two persons or objects moving relative to each other experience different rates of time flow. The relative time flow for a person or object that accelerates to near-light speed will be slower than for the person or object that does not experience acceleration. The effect is irreversible.

What Daeson expected to see in the Ianis System was space devoid of any life, with empty and dead worlds orbiting two red giant binary stars. But his scans indicated something entirely different. Just above the plane of the largest asteroid field in the system, his scans showed a massive array of ships and debris. This made no sense. Could these be the remnants of his Raylean Fleet? They would have needed all of their transports to get the people to Kayn-4, their new homeworld of Rayl. Very little should have been left behind. He scanned for life forms. A few seconds later the number that appeared on his right glass panel shattered everything he had hoped for—462,382. He tried to imagine what could have possibly gone wrong. The Rayleans were still here after 271 years!

Daeson shook himself out of a stupor, realizing that regardless of the fate of the Rayleans, Raviel needed help immediately. He checked her vitals and nearly panicked when he saw how weak they were. He pushed his thrusters to full speed and made for the fleet. As he closed in, his idyllic vision for his people collapsed further. This was no fleet he was approaching, but a massive amalgam of derelict metal containers, joined in no apparent logical fashion. He had never seen anything like it. As he approached, he tried to identify anything familiar then barely recognized the form of his ship, *Liberty*. Four small vessels approached him with great speed, each of them a different type of craft. Two looked like they had some sort of modified weapon retrofitted to the fuselage. One vessel he barely recognized as an original transport shuttle. They all had carbon scoring and damaged surfaces. Daeson was impressed with the courage these pilots must have had to even attempt to fly them.

"Unidentified spacecraft approaching the colony, stop immediately or you will be destroyed!" Daeson's radio shrieked.

Colony? He wondered.

His alert system flashed a red warning, indicating that they had targeted his Starcraft with weapons armed. He raised his E-shield and realized that until he could discern the state of these people, he would have to proceed very carefully.

"This is Starcraft Victor 56. My intentions are not hostile. I have an injured pilot on board who needs immediate attention. Please escort me to the nearest medtech facility."

"Negative, Victor 56. We have no facility that can serve you. Return to the gateway at once!"

By now the four vessels were on him. Two positioned themselves directly in his flight path, forcing him to come to a complete stop. The other two took cover positions on his port and starboard. He could easily outmaneuver and outgun them, but that would end his chances of getting help for Raviel.

"Comply, Victor 56, or we will fire on you," came the stern warning.

"The injured pilot is Raylean and needs immediate attention, or she will die," Daeson radioed.

There was no response. Daeson waited. Two minutes later...

"Victor 56, drop your shield."

Daeson had no way to gauge the mindset of this vagrant people. To have survived under these conditions for this long in this dead system, they had to have adopted a cunning and ruthless perspective, especially in regard to outsiders. Was this a trick to destroy him? He tried to suppress the anger he felt as his finger hovered over the ARM selection on his front panel. He took a breath then disengaged his shield.

"Shield disengaged. Requesting escort to the nearest medtech facility now!"

The two vessels to his front remained still.

"Victor 56, do not deviate from course, or you will be destroyed...acknowledge!"

Daeson calmed himself, recognizing that his previous tone was not helping.

"Starcraft Victor 56 acknowledge."

A few minutes later Daeson was shutting down the engines of his Starcraft in one of the bays of a transport that was interconnected with three other ships. Once the bay was pressurized, Daeson flipped the switch to open the canopy as the bay walk-through doors slid open. Six armed personnel quickly positioned themselves about the cockpit. Daeson stood in his seat and leaned over to reach Raviel.

"Remain seated!" shouted one of the men.

Daeson ignored the command and reached for Raviel's helmet. He released the latch then carefully removed the helmet. A commotion erupted on all sides as he reached to touch her cheek, but before he could reach her, two burly men whipped him out of the cockpit and onto a raised platform, pinning him flat beneath a set of knees.

"Don't move!"

"Please, help her. Her vitals are—"

"Quiet!" shouted the voice again.

Daeson yearned to be with Raviel, but he was instead bound and rushed out of the docking bay. A few minutes later, he was pushed into a holding cell without any hope of knowing the state of Raviel. Daeson paced back and forth in his cell for over an hour, fretting over Raviel's condition and wondering if Tig were a hundred years further into the future…or even alive. Tig had warned him, and now his friend was gone…probably forever. None of this was turning out how he had hoped.

Finally, the door slid open to reveal a woman with a sergeant insignia on a ragtag uniform and a burly guard beside her. Her tough-looking demeanor complemented her handsome Raylean beauty. Olive skin, dark hair, and eyes with an edge of fierceness.

"Come with me. I'm taking you to your interrogation."

"What of my copilot? Will she be okay?" Daeson asked.

The sergeant scrutinized Daeson with narrow pale-blue eyes.

"She's being treated by our medtechs. That's all I know…come!"

Daeson could hardly contain himself.

"Please…I must see her."

"That's not possible," the sergeant replied. "You're an outsider who has come to our colony. You must be thoroughly interrogated first."

Daeson didn't know how much authority this sergeant had, but he had to see Raviel.

"She and I are both full-blooded Raylean. Do a genetic scan and you'll see for yourself."

"That's irrelevant," came the sergeant's terse reply. "The admiral trusts no one that comes from outside our colony." She motioned for the guard to take him.

"I must see her…we're bonded," Daeson finally said.

At that, the sergeant held up a hand to stop the guard. She eyed Daeson closely.

"Scan him," she ordered.

The guard withdrew a sub-dermal scanner. He didn't wait for Daeson to offer his hand but instead punctured his neck for a sample. A few seconds later the guard turned the scanner display toward the sergeant. She smirked.

"Bring him," she ordered.

The guard grabbed Daeson's arm, pushing him out of his cell and down the corridor to follow the sergeant. After a few minutes of traversing corridors and hatches, Daeson was escorted into a spacious medtech bay that was a strange mix of antiquated and futuristic equipment. Raviel was lying on one of the central medical beds with a host of medtechs and assistants surrounding her. A chief master sergeant and another guard also stood ready.

Daeson tried to make his way to Raviel's side, but the guard restrained him.

"Why is he here?" demanded the chief, his eyes red with anger. His chiseled jaw, stocky build, and large square hands told Daeson this was not a man to be trifled with. The female sergeant that had brought him to the room looked uneasy.

"It's okay, Chief Bern," said the master medtech working on Raviel. "I need to talk to him...come," he encouraged, looking briefly at Daeson, then back to Raviel.

Daeson pulled loose from the guard's grip and hurried to Raviel's side. One of the medtech assistants stepped out of the way to make room. There she was...lying perfectly still. Her face was pale but her beauty undaunted by impending death. Daeson tenderly placed his hand against her cheek. For months he had ached to see her again...to touch her...and here she was before him now.

"Raviel!" he whispered.

The medtechs and assistants seemed to understand that she wasn't just a fellow pilot to Daeson. They allowed the moment to happen.

"They are bonded," Daeson heard the sergeant whisper to the chief as she showed him Daeson's genetic scan results. The information did nothing to soften the chief's demeanor.

Daeson could hardly take his eyes from Raviel. "Will she make it?" he asked, looking up briefly into the face of the master medtech.

He pursed his lips. "I don't know. Nothing we've tried seems to help her, and she continues to fade. I've never seen anything like this. We can't identify her malady. What happened to her?" he asked.

Daeson fixed his eyes back on Raviel, remembering every single detail leading up to the moment he lost her.

"She suffered an accident inside a slipstream conduit and was lost to a tear in the barrier's wall. She's been unconscious for hours."

This news stunned every occupant in the medtech bay, prompting quiet conversations among them.

"That may explain some of our readings," the master medtech said, looking across to catch the eye of another medtech who nodded in return.

"It seems to me that this is something our scitechs could help with," the other medtech offered as she reviewed Raviel's vitals on a glass tablet once more.

"Send for Master Olin," the master medtech said to the chief. Chief Bern scowled then nodded to the sergeant.

Raviel suddenly arched her back and began convulsing. The medtechs pushed Daeson out of the way as Raviel's body contorted, her stomach heaving its contents. The medtechs rolled her to one side to clear her airway of fluids. Daeson could hardly keep himself from her as the medtechs worked quickly. The master medtech administered a shot, and a few seconds later Raviel's convulsions subsided. Slowly she fell back to the bed, limp. Daeson tried to get back to her, but the chief grabbed his arm.

"Stay clear!" he ordered, yanking Daeson back. The other guard stepped in and gruffly pushed Daeson to the wall.

Daeson glared at the chief over the man's shoulder.

"I'm not an enemy. Please, I just want to be near her," Daeson pleaded.

Chief Bern stepped closer to Daeson as the guard stepped aside.

"And if you were an enemy, you'd say something different?" rebutted the Chief. He leaned in and came within inches of Daeson's face. "Everyone's a ravager until proven otherwise. Ravagers like you have killed many of our people. Once we determine your guilt...you will be executed."

"He and the other must come from the same ravager band," the guard said as the chief backed away.

"Other?" Daeson asked. "There's another like me here?"

The chief's eyes narrowed. "That's how we know you're up to something. He arrived five days ago in the same type of craft you were flying."

Daeson breathed a sigh of relief. "Don't you see? He witnessed her accident." Daeson motioned toward Raviel. "He would be helpful here."

"Not on your life!" Chief Bern snapped.

The master medtech heard the exchange and came to stand next to the chief.

"I don't know how long she has left," he said. "If the other pilot can add some details to what happened, it might help."

"Why are we trying to save these ravagers anyway?" the chief barked.

The master medtech crossed his arms and glared eye to eye with the chief. "Because that is our creed as medtechs. Once we heal them, you can do what you want with them, but for now I need more information. Bring the other here while I ask this man some more questions."

Anger flushed the chief's face, and he looked like he was about to tear into the medtech. He growled some unintelligible words then turned to his guard.

"Bring the other man here," Chief Bern ordered his guard. When the guard hesitated, the chief nearly came unglued and shouted at him. The guard quickly exited the medtech bay as the master medtech nodded for Daeson to follow him back to Raviel. He asked a dozen questions about the incident and more about her medical history. A few minutes later, Tig entered the medtech bay.

"Tig!" Daeson exclaimed. He went to his friend and embraced him. "Thank Ell Yon...I thought I'd lost you for good."

Tig returned Daeson's embrace.

"Don't tell them who you really are...I'll explain later," he whispered into Daeson's ear.

Daeson stepped back. A week here must have revealed some critical information. He nodded.

"How is she?" Tig asked as they stepped to Raviel's side. As Daeson gently lifted her hand, the deep ache in his heart soothed just a little.

"Not good, Tig," Daeson replied. "They're trying to stabilize her, but she continues to grow weaker."

Tig's face looked pained. "I'm sorry."

The sergeant appeared in the doorway of the medtech bay. "Master Scitech Olin said he didn't have the time to spare for outsiders," she announced. "So instead, I brought the lad."

Daeson looked their way, his heart sinking to despair. The lad looked to be about sixteen years old. He was handsome, with an air of quirkiness and disheveled hair piled on top of a slender head. Deep, penetrating eyes let Daeson know there was something unusual about him. He was either looking clear into your soul or not looking at all...Daeson couldn't quite tell. What Daeson *could* tell was that the chances of getting help here among the Rayleans appeared dismal. He thought perhaps he should have risked taking her to Jypton where their medical knowledge and treatments were second to none...at least that was true 270 years ago. Surely it would have been better than leaving her fate in the hands of a teenage boy!

"He's good with this sort of thing," the sergeant added. Daeson thought the comment a bit odd coming from a forcetech sergeant.

The master medtech eyed the boy.

"Yes...so I've heard. Come here, Avidan," he said. "We would like you to examine her."

The boy looked confused. He glanced over at his escorting sergeant, and she nodded.

"Why?" the lad asked.

"Because we believe this patient has experienced some sort of quantum event that is affecting her biological stability," the master medtech explained.

The boy's brows furrowed slightly, as if he didn't believe him. He stepped up next to Raviel, directly across from Daeson.

"How is this possible?" the boy asked, reaching for the glass tablet with Raviel's statistics.

Daeson explained what had happened once again, but with more detail on how Raviel was ripped out of the slipstream conduit as a result of the missile explosion. As he recited the story, Avidan's eyes lifted to meet Daeson's. When Daeson was through, the boy just stared at him. There was a knowing in the mind of the boy that not another person in that room seemed to grasp. His eyes quickly scanned Daeson's and Tig's uniforms. He then broke from his gaze and turned to examine Raviel.

"I need blood and tissue samples," he stated to the medtechs. "Quickly!"

A few minutes later the boy had his samples. As he exited the medtech bay, he turned back.

"Do not under any circumstance give her any more sedatives. If she awakens...keep her awake regardless of what happens."

The next hour was agonizing for Daeson as he watched Raviel slip further and further away from him. Tig tried to encourage him, but the chief limited their interaction. Daeson was on the verge of attempting something drastic, being convinced that the limited knowledge and resources of the Raylean colony would not be able to save her. When Chief Master Sergeant Bern stepped out of the medtech bay to respond to an urgent call, the other sergeant took his place as watchguard over Daeson and Tig. She dismissed the third guard and then turned to Daeson, her penetrating pale blue eyes capturing his attention.

"Avidan isn't an ordinary boy...he's a prodigy," the sergeant said. "And he isn't just gifted in scitech. He has a mind for astrotech and phystech as well, which is why I brought him here. If anyone can understand what's happening to her, it will be him."

Daeson looked over at the sergeant. Her dark hair was pulled back, revealing sharp facial features. She looked tough, especially carrying a plasma tactical rifle. Since she was the only guard in the bay, Daeson knew he and Tig could overpower her quickly and devise a plan to escape from the colony with Raviel then on to Jypton. It would be a long shot, but watching Raviel die...again...was not an option. Tig stepped up next to the sergeant and crossed his arms, seemingly knowing what Daeson was considering.

"I think we need to trust somebody, Daeson," Tig said with a quick glance toward the sergeant.

Daeson took a breath and nodded. Her words had been kind, something Daeson acknowledged at that moment. "Thank you," he said. "His parents must be proud to have their son earn such respect within the tech orders at such a young age."

The young woman's face saddened. "Four years ago, his parents were killed or enslaved by ravagers...we're not sure which. I found him, and no one else would take him in, so I've rather adopted him as a younger brother."

Ah...that makes sense, Daeson thought. She seemed soft toward the lad, uncharacteristic for a sergeant in forcetech, especially while on duty. This story was sure to be the first of many tales of woe that Daeson didn't really want to hear. Was this all his fault?

When the boy returned, he had an equipment case and two glass tablets. He opened the case then went to Raviel, scanning her with an instrument that Daeson had never seen before. His eyes looked wild as he tapped out numbers and formulas on a tablet. The sergeant allowed Daeson to step closer to Raviel.

"What have you found?" he asked.

The boy ignored him as he continued to analyze new data. Daeson was about to lose his mind. Finally, Avidan looked up at the master medtech.

"You're right. She is indeed experiencing the consequences of a quantum event. This isn't a diagnosable medical condition. It's a quantum phasal anomaly affecting every cell in her body. And it's not happening just at the cellular level, but at the atomic level."

Avidan then looked directly at Daeson. "It's as if her cells are somehow quantumly stuck at near-light velocity."

Daeson reached for Raviel's hand again.

"Look at this," the boy said, showing a recorded moving image of Raviel's cells on one of his glass tablets. Thousands of cells were displayed, all vibrating at an incredibly high frequency. "Watch as some of the cells seem to fade away then return."

"What does this mean?" Daeson asked.

"The slipstream conduit protects travelers from the effects of relativity time dilation," the lad explained. "We still don't understand how this Immortal technology works, but the conduits have the ability to shift the spacetime impact on us so we can travel great distances at speeds greater than light without experiencing time distortion. When she prematurely exited the conduit, her cells lost that protection and are, for lack of a better way of saying it, confused as to *when* she belongs. Every atom in the galaxy is affected by the reality of quantum mechanics. When those mechanics are disrupted or circumnavigated, such as through conduit technology, we run the risk of a quantum phase anomaly."

Avidan looked down at Raviel.

"Unless we can discover a way to stabilize her, she will either die or dissolve to a future time, possibly existing in a never-ending unresolved quantum state of molecular phasal confusion."

Daeson shook his head, not even sure he understood what the boy was saying.

"How do we stabilize her?" he asked desperately.

Avidan continued to stare at Raviel.

With eyes closed, her lips barely moved in a whisper. "Daeson."

Daeson's heart nearly stopped. He leaned close. "I'm here, my love."

Suddenly her eyes opened in stark fear. "Daeson!" she screamed. "It hurts...make it stop!"

When she abruptly sat up, Daeson grabbed her. "Hang on, Raviel...hang on!"

Her arms wrapped around his shoulders so tightly he was shocked by her strength. Pain-filled moans crushed his heart as he hung on, trying to soothe her. Then as quickly as she revived, she fell still and silent. Daeson held her a moment longer then gently laid her back to the bed.

When he looked up, his moist eyes filled with angst. He looked about the room. "Please...please help her!"

The medtechs, assistants, and forcetech personnel alike stared back in stunned silence.

"I must think on this," the boy named Avidan mused as he turned away and left the room.

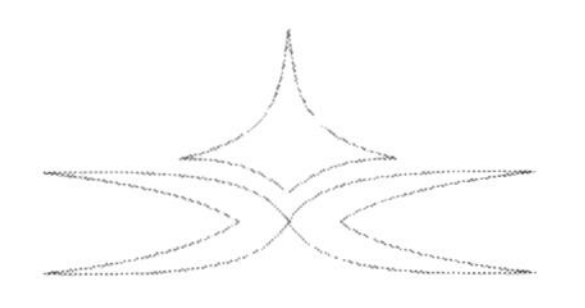

5

A Rebel Plan

Once Raviel seemed somewhat stable and the medtechs had exhausted their use of Daeson, the chief, who had returned to the medtech bay, insisted that the sergeant take Daeson and Tig back to their holding cells, where they were given a meager meal. Although separating from Raviel was painful, he was anxious to talk with Tig and find out what his friend had discovered since his arrival.

Just before the cell door closed, Tig turned. "Sergeant," he called.

She looked over her shoulder.

"Thank you."

She turned to face him. "If her condition changes, I'll bring you word," she said, her countenance softening for just a moment. Then she donned the rigid face of a veteran soldier and closed the door.

Daeson and Tig did a quick scan of their cell to see if they could detect any monitoring devices. Once they were reasonably sure there were none, he turned to Tig and spoke in low tones just to be safe.

"What happened, Tig? How did you arrive five days before I did?"

"I don't know. Our jump drives must have shutdown at slightly different times," he said, looking toward Daeson. "This place...our fleet...Daeson, something went drastically wrong. Did the Protector say they were supposed to be here for 270 years?"

Daeson shook his head. "Just before we jumped, Trisk said that Ell Yon was going to destroy the people. Obviously that didn't happen, but something else must have. This was not Ell Yon's plan for them, at least not at the beginning."

Daeson sat down and ran his hands through his hair. "I shouldn't have left them. This is my fault."

Tig came to Daeson and put a foot up on the bench near him. "It's not your fault, Daeson. It's their fault. Besides, Raviel would be dead if you hadn't decided to come."

Daeson nodded, looking up at Tig. "What have you learned these past five days?"

"Not as much as I wanted to," Tig replied. "They won't tell me much. The only information I have I've gotten from the young woman that delivers my meals." Tig hesitated. "These people are desperate. They're often attacked by marauders, which they call ravagers. Most of their records were destroyed because of it. Evidently, long ago bands of ravagers began stealing critical tech and components when the fleet had no way of defending themselves—computer systems, memory cores, plasma generators, jump drives, and even their proto-ion engines. More recently, the Reekojans from Kayn-4 have started taking prisoners to serve as slaves in their fortified city. The man in charge of the colony is Admiral Bostra. He's not liked but respected because of his tenacity to protect and defend the colony in spite of the great odds against them." Tig lowered his head. "It's a wonder they're still alive. Of course, stories have been passed down from generation to generation. The one most relevant to us is the one regarding a great leader that abandoned them in space centuries ago."

Daeson felt as if a knife had pierced his heart. Tig looked at him, his eyes reflecting the grief Daeson was already feeling.

"That's why I don't think it wise that we reveal who we are or from when we come," Tig continued. "During my interrogation, I devised a story about a small group of

Raylean slaves that had escaped to Jypton long ago. A few of us had been trained as mechtechs in the Jyptonian Aerotech order and devised a plan to escape and find our original colony. My genetic scan being part Jyptonian and part Raylean helped in the ruse, but they also suspect us to be spies for a larger ravager band."

Tig frowned. "They're extremely suspicious, and I don't blame them…they have to be to survive."

"Makes sense. You were wise to hide our identities, and your story will be easy to corroborate since it's so close to the truth."

"What's our plan?" Tig asked.

"Eventually we need an audience with the admiral," Daeson said. "But for now, we have to find a way to help Raviel. What's the status of Rivet?"

"The last I saw of him, there was still no response," Tig said, shaking his head. "Whatever happened to Raviel must have also affected him in some way. Maybe his power cells are just drained. I have no idea what they've done with him. I would imagine they are analyzing his technology as we speak."

Daeson was concerned for Lt. Ki. If Raviel was affected, was she too? The fact that Rivet was plugged into Raviel's life-support was evidence that Lt. Ki had at least been conscious for some of their journey.

"What about the Starcrafts?" Daeson asked.

Tig shook his ahead again. "*Liberty* still seems to be the center of command and technology, and the docking bay is large enough to hold both of them, but your guess is as good as mine."

Daeson and Tig talked at length about their options as Tig continued to fill in details about what he'd learned. Although the Rayleans did have a rudimentary forcetech order and although their procedures and training were paltry, Daeson surmised it would be quite difficult to thwart them. Two hours later their conversation turned back to Raviel. Daeson was becoming desperate for news regarding her condition.

"I don't think she could travel well, Daeson." Tig said. "That lad seems pretty intelligent. Do you think he might be able help her?"

Daeson stood up and walked to the cell door then turned around. "I don't know. It looks to me like they're barely keeping their own life support systems operating, yet some of their technology is extremely advanced." He looked at Tig. "If he doesn't come up with something soon, we may have to figure out a way to get her to Jypton."

Tig nodded his agreement. Daeson wanted to discuss their options further, but he felt his body collapsing from the fatigue of his last twenty-four-hour ordeal. He laid down to rest for a few minutes and fell asleep instantly. Three hours later he was abruptly awakened by the opening of their cell door. There stood the female sergeant from the medical bay and the genius boy. The cell guard was standing behind them. Daeson sat up and wiped away the sleep from his eyes as the sergeant and the boy entered the room. She then turned to the guard.

"Wait out there," she ordered.

"But the chief—" the guard began.

"Chief Bern isn't here, and I'm taking full responsibility for the boy and their security," she said sternly.

The guard looked past them to Daeson and Tig, then nodded and closed the door. The sergeant turned around and eyed them carefully, her plasma rifle at the ready. A moment later she relaxed her grip and lowered the weapon to her side, the rifle's harness strap across her shoulder carrying the weight.

"I'm Sergeant Antos. I saw the mark on the young woman's shoulder, and although the medtechs can't get a clean genetic scan on her, I believe she is Raylean as you say." She looked at Tig, lifting her chin his way. "You...I've heard the story of your arrival and how you could have easily destroyed the ships that were firing on you, but instead you surrendered. That's not the way of a ravager." She looked back at Daeson. "I'm here because Avidan seems to believe you too...well, most of your story. He presented a way to heal the young woman to the master medtech, and he in turn presented it to Admiral Bostra but was denied because of the risk and resources required. For some reason, Avidan wants to talk to you before giving up on her." The sergeant turned to the lad. "What did you want to ask them?"

Avidan looked at Daeson with stern eyes...questioning eyes.

"From when do you come?"

Daeson's eyes lifted. He glanced toward Tig then back to the lad. He considered trying to carry the ruse Tig had started, but something told him this boy already knew more and wouldn't easily be tricked.

"When Raviel, the young woman you are trying to help, was thrown through the tear in the conduit wall, she lost consciousness and was traveling at near-light speed. As a result, she experienced extreme time dilation because of the velocity of her Starcraft."

Daeson looked directly into Avidan's eyes for a reaction. There was none.

"In order for us to rescue her," Daeson continued, "we had to bypass our jump drive safety protocols and initiate near-light speed travel outside of a conduit on an intercept course to bring her back."

Avidan was deep in thought. "But you didn't bring her back, did you?" he asked. The lad's eyes narrowed. "You brought her forward...through time."

Daeson took a deep breath. "Yes."

"How long ago are you from?" Avidan asked.

Daeson looked over at Sergeant Antos. She was mesmerized by what was being said.

"Two hundred seventy-one years."

"What?" Sergeant Antos exclaimed. "This can't be!"

Daeson shrugged his shoulders.

"Actually, they're fortunate it was only that far," Avidan added. "And the odds of you finding her in space and in time are pretty astronomical. It's the hardest part of your story to believe."

Daeson chuckled. "You are a smart one," he added. "Our course and our own time dilation were altered somehow. We passed through the Omega Nebula and something... happened."

The lad looked intently at Daeson, not even blinking. "Are you him?" Avidan asked straightforwardly.

The question nearly knocked Daeson off of his feet. He stared blankly at the lad, not sure how or if he should answer. The sergeant looked confused.

"Most of our early files and records have been stolen, lost, or destroyed due to the ravagers," Avidan said in response to Daeson's silence. "Some stories of our ancestors were kept alive, but as is true of most tellings, after a few generations they hardly represent the truth anymore. Nearly all of them are either embellished or forgotten. In my family there is one story that my mother swore was true...one that was passed down with a promise to maintain the truth...one that we kept to ourselves because of unbelief."

Avidan's face softened, and his eyes filled with yearning. "Are you him?"

"What's your family name, son?" Daeson asked.

"Yuten, but my mother was Ketura Boytt," Avidan replied.

"Of course it is," Daeson said with a smile. "I am he."

The lad's eyes filled with wonder and hope. In him was a realization that the destiny of their people was about to change, and he was the only one in the colony that knew it.

"Who?" Sergeant Antos asked. "What story? Who are you?"

Avidan turned to her. "Kyrah, we have to do everything in our power to help them—no matter what," Avidan affirmed.

"What are you talking about? What is going on?" she asked.

"There's too much to explain right now. We don't have time...*she* doesn't have time," Avidan urged. "Just promise me you'll help them."

Sergeant Antos glanced at Daeson and then at Tig before pulling Avidan a few steps away, a gentle hand resting on his shoulder just as an older sister would do.

"Avidan, I've never seen you like this," she said quietly.

"Then you know that what I'm asking of you is serious." Avidan turned and looked briefly at Daeson and Tig. "This isn't just about saving the woman...it's about saving the whole colony."

"That's a little dramatic, don't you think?"

"Have you ever known me to be dramatic?" he asked.

"No...no I haven't. But you're asking me to commit treason, Avidan," the sergeant clarified. "You're asking me to go against everything I was trained to be."

"I understand, but I'm not asking you to go against what you know to be true...what your gut is telling you." Avidan looked down at the floor. "When we are attacked by ravagers, we can hardly defend ourselves." He looked back up into her eyes. "When they kidnap our people and haul them off to be slaves, we do nothing. I believe that helping these men and this woman, right here, right now, is the beginning of changing all of that. That's not treason, Kyrah...that's helping our people. Promise me you'll help." When she hesitated, Avidan grabbed her arms. "Promise me!"

"Okay...okay. I promise."

Avidan turned to Daeson and stepped toward him. The sergeant slowly followed. "I don't think Raviel has more than a few hours before she slips away forever."

Daeson swallowed hard. "I can't lose her a second time. You said you have a way to heal her...what do we need to do?" Daeson asked.

Avidan looked back at Sergeant Antos. "We're going to have to break some rules," he said with a sheepish grin then began pacing, talking quickly as he went.

"I believe the only way we are going to be able to stabilize her and stop the cellular phase quantum anomaly is to finish the journey she began." He stopped and looked briefly at Daeson. "I'm assuming that your journey here was direct and not through any gateways?"

"Yes…yes that's right."

"That's fortunate. Had you travelled through any entrance gateway or exit gateway other than the one she missed, I believe she would already be gone."

"Why?" Daeson asked.

"I theorize that the Immortals built the slipstream conduits so that as matter enters a gateway, it is quantumly tuned and in phase with that gateway. The exit gateway of that same slipstream conduit releases that matter's phase, tuning it back to normal spacetime. The atoms in Raviel's body were never released by that exit gateway."

"So if we take her back through a slipstream gateway, her matter will realign with this spacetime?" the sergeant asked.

"Not just any gateway," Avidan stated, encouraged by the sergeant's engagement with them. "The exact gateway she missed."

"But that gateway is the Omega Nebula gateway…three jumps away," Tig interjected. "You said she wouldn't survive traveling through a different conduit. Why don't we just engage our Starcraft jump drives and fly her there directly? We would experience another time dilation event, but it would be worth it if it saves her life."

Avidan became solemn. He looked at Daeson. "That is an option, but there's serious risk no matter what you do. She might not even survive entering one gateway. I'm nearly finished building a quantum phase containment field generator. It should stabilize her cells enough to make the journey, but there's no guarantee."

The lad looked at Daeson apologetically. Daeson rubbed a hand down his face as he considered the options.

"How large is the containment field generator…will it fit into the cockpit of a Starcraft?" Daeson asked.

"No," Avidan replied. "Raviel needs to be in a shuttle. That would give us enough space for the generator and some medtech equipment to keep her stable."

Avidan looked sadly at Daeson. "Honestly, Admiral Starlore, I don't think she'll make it out of the medtech bay without that field containment generator."

Sergeant Antos raised her eyes at the way Avidan addressed Daeson.

"Okay," Daeson nodded. "A shuttle it is. And let's keep that name a secret for now, okay?"

Avidan flashed a quick smile. He turned to the sergeant with fresh excitement in his eyes. "I need to finish the quantum field containment generator, and you need to help them steal a shuttle."

Her right eyebrow lifted.

"If I had known that's what you were going to ask, I would have never brought you here," she said with a frown.

"I know—I'm sorry." Avidan tilted his head. "You promised."

"Do you understand that whether your plan works or not, life for you and me here on this colony is over?" she asked.

"It is for everyone," Avidan countered. "The new ruler of Reekojah is ruthless, and we won't survive another week under his attacks anyway."

Sergeant Antos was clearly wrestling with her loyalties and sense of duty. She scrutinized both Daeson and Tig with a look that said, *this better be worth it!* "This won't be easy...we're going to need help. I know another forcetech we can trust, and he owes me a few favors."

Tig stepped forward and offered a forearm handshake to the sergeant. Such a gesture among Rayleans was binding, a sign of trust. Daeson realized Tig was asking her to give them her word of honor.

"I'm Tig."

Sergeant Antos hesitated, knowing exactly what this would mean. She glanced toward Avidan then reached for Tig's arm.

"I'm Kyrah. Let's do this."

CHAPTER 7

An Ally and a Friend

Having Kyrah as an ally changed everything. She knew schedules, access codes, security strengths and weaknesses, and she was armed. Daeson couldn't help but wonder just how far she would go for them. She was a loyal Raylean with a strong conscience. Her devotion to Avidan might have limits.

It was decided that Kyrah and Avidan would leave so the lad could complete his work on the quantum field containment generator. Kyrah would return later in the evening to retrieve Daeson and Tig under the guise of taking them for further medical evaluations and interrogation. When she arrived, their guard was more than willing to end his duty at the cell door early. In the night hours of the colony, very little activity took place in the corridors, making it easier for Kyrah to escort them to the *Liberty* docking bay where only one forcetech guard was on duty. When she attempted to send him on a bogus errand, the guard became suspicious, and they were forced to overpower him, securing him in a nearby cargo bay. Kyrah was more than a little anxious about what had happened…she had now fully crossed the line.

Daeson and Tig did a quick inspection of their Starcrafts before moving to the shuttle. Both vessels had access panels open and instruments connected, especially Daeson's, but they still seemed to be in flyable condition.

Once they accessed a shuttle, Daeson and Tig began preparing the craft for launch while Kyrah returned to help Avidan transport the quantum field containment generator to the medtech bay. This was where Kyra's contact proved extremely helpful. The remaining and most challenging part of the mission was getting Raviel out of the medtech facility and to the shuttle. The master medtech accosted them on their way out, but then turned a blind eye to what was happening once he discovered what they were up to. He even found an opportunity to distract Chief Bern when he nearly discovered the plan. After two hours and more than a couple of near-discoveries, Daeson, Tig, Kyrah, Avidan, and their patient Raviel were on board the shuttle for departure. Just before they closed the doors to the shuttle, the docking bay walk-in door opened and Daeson's heart sank. Had they been discovered? Was a contingent of forcetech guards about to end their mission?

The master medtech appeared in the docking bay walk-in door, then ran to the shuttle and jumped in through the doorway. "I'm coming with you," he stated. "She might need medical attention if you're successful."

Daeson, Tig, Kyrah, and Avidan were shocked.

"You did force me, correct?" he asked with a sly smile.

Kyrah smiled back. "Kidnapped you right from the medtech bay. One false move, and I'll shoot you," she said with a wink. "Let's move…they'll be coming soon!" she instructed Tig. He fired up the engines on the shuttle from the co-pilot seat on the right side of the cockpit in advance of Daeson's arrival in the cockpit.

The master medtech immediately began scanning Raviel. "I'm Gilzan, by the way," he added with a quick glance toward Daeson.

"How is she doing?" Daeson asked Gilzan as Kyrah and Avidan worked to secure both Raviel and the quantum field containment generator.

Gilzan looked concerned. "She's barely hanging on," he replied. "Whatever you're planning, you need to do it fast."

When Daeson squeezed Raviel's cool hand, it felt almost as if her skin was pulling away from him.

Avidan finished securing the controls for his device to the side of Raviel's gurney. "I'm powering up the quantum field containment generator," he announced. "No one can touch her anymore."

Daeson leaned over and kissed Raviel's cheek, then went to the cockpit and strapped in to the pilot seat. He could hear Avidan's generator powering up and saw an immediate draw on the ship's power grid.

"I think we forgot one small detail," Tig said as he flipped a few switches while checking their fuel status.

"The bay door," Daeson said.

"I've got that covered," Avidan said, tapping rapidly on his glass tablet. A few seconds later he looked up. "If Kyrah's codes are good, that should do it." He tapped one last time on the tablet, and the docking bay alarm sounded. Ten seconds later the bay door began to open. Daeson powered up the engines and maneuvered the shuttle toward the bay door.

"Is everyone secure back there?" Tig asked, looking over his shoulder. "This could get rough."

Kyrah, Avidan, and Gilzan sat down and tightened their straps.

"Shuttle Bravo One Three, you are not authorized to depart. Return to bay immediately," the radio shrieked.

"They'll try to override the bay door," Daeson stated.

"That shouldn't be a problem," Avidan responded calmly. "I've encrypted the access code."

Daeson ignored the continued threats being broadcast over the radio, fully expecting to be fired upon once they exited the bay doors. As soon as the door was open wide enough, he pushed the throttles to one-quarter speed. Once clear of the docking bay, he pushed the throttles up and began zooming in and out of the massive colony structures in an attempt to avoid detection, but two small weaponized craft were in pursuit and closing in on him.

"There's not much chance this shuttle can outrun them," Tig said.

"Shuttle Bravo One Three, return to the docking bay or you will be fired upon!"

"Looks like we'll have to make a run for one of the asteroid fields and then to the gateway," Daeson said.

Tig looked at him with concern in his eyes.

"Did I hear you say you're taking us through an asteroid field?" Kyrah exclaimed.

Tig diverted reserve power to the shuttle's E-shield then looked over his shoulder.

"Don't worry, Sergeant, he's rather fond of asteroids. Flies through them all the time."

Daeson couldn't help the grin on his face.

"Just a reminder," Tig said quietly. "This is no Starcraft."

"You're not kidding," Daeson replied as he tried to adapt to the sluggish controls. "Let's just hope they don't have the guts to stay with us."

Daeson flipped the shuttle upside down, pulled back on the stick, and executed a barrel roll around one of the smaller colony modules. Then he dodged between two attaching corridors. The two small craft in pursuit had a difficult time staying with them in spite of their maneuverability advantage. Daeson heard Avidan and Gilzan groan behind him.

When Daeson felt like he had enough distance, he pointed the nose of the shuttle toward the nearest asteroid belt and pushed the throttles to full. It would be close. Once the pursuing craft were clear of the colony, they fired two warning shots.

Daeson pushed the mic button on his radio. "Pursuing craft, this is Shuttle Bravo One Three. We are on a medical rescue mission and will return in eight hours. Our patient is Raylean and our crew is Raylean. Please stand down."

"Do you really think that is going to get them to back off?" Tig asked.

"No, but it might buy us the thirty seconds I need to get us there," Daeson said, nodding toward a few hundred thousand asteroids that were in a distant orbit around the binary stars.

"Shuttle Bravo One Three, return to colony or be destroyed," came the reply from the pursuit craft.

Daeson searched for his entrance and found it.

"These sensors are weak, but it looks like they're locked on this time," Tig warned.

Daeson made his move just as a plasma burst slammed into one of the larger asteroids in front of them. Seconds later Daeson had slowed the shuttle to maneuvering speed and carefully worked his way to one of the larger asteroids.

"Any pursuit?" Daeson asked.

"Negative," Tig replied.

After a few minutes, Daeson maneuvered clear of the asteroid belt and made for the gateway. Ten minutes later they were energizing the shuttle's jump drive engine. Avidan unstrapped and went to check on Raviel and the containment generator.

"You should stay strapped in," Tig warned.

"Can't," Avidan stated. "I need to make some critical adjustments before we enter the gateway, or it could kill her. If I'm right, I'll need at least a minute in close proximity to the conduit entrance to tune the containment field to the gateway before we enter."

Avidan was feverously tapping commands and making adjustments as he referenced his glass tablet. Daeson had to bring the shuttle to a dead stop to keep from entering the gateway.

"We've got company," Tig said. "Those two pursuit craft are closing in fast!"

Daeson's left hand gripped the shuttle throttles tightly. Tig's hand hovered over the slipstream jump drive switch. The seconds ticked by as Daeson and Tig watched the distance between the pursuing Raylean craft and the shuttle drop quickly. Daeson looked over at Tig.

"We're okay," Tig said. "We're not going 'til she's ready."

The Raylean craft were now within weapons range.

"Any time now, Avidan." Daeson urged. At a dead stop, they were an easy kill.

"Almost," he said.

Daeson's heart was pounding. The shuttle's E-shield might not be able to withstand even one shot from the craft. It completely depended on the power level of the pursuing crafts' weapons.

WHAM!

The shuttle shook violently from a plasma burst, and Avidan slammed up against the side of the shuttle wall.

"E-shield at five percent," Tig spoke with a false calm.

The next one would kill them.

Avidan recovered and entered one last number.

"Now!" he shouted.

Daeson slammed the throttles to full speed as Tig engaged the jump drive engine. A second later they were gone.

"Aaahh!"

Daeson heard Raviel's terrifying scream. He unstrapped and jumped to the back, reaching out for her.

"No!" Avidan shouted, grabbing Daeson's arm just as he was about to penetrate the quantum phase containment field. "If you compromise the field, you and she will both die!"

Kyrah unstrapped and pulled Daeson back. He felt his soul tearing apart as Raviel arched her back in agonizing pain. Gilzan released his seat harness and began monitoring her vitals with a bio scanner while Avidan adjusted the containment generator. Raviel screamed again.

"Can't we do something?" Daeson pleaded. He could hardly watch, wanting desperately to hold her. Then Daeson saw something that turned his blood cold. Raviel fell unconscious, momentarily fading to a wisp of her bodily form. A second later she was back, her eyelids and hair covered in a thin white frost. She began shivering uncontrollably.

"What was that?" Daeson asked. "What just happened to her?"

"I'm not sure what's happening, but her body temperature just dropped two degrees in a split second," Gilzan stated, his eyes filled with concern.

Avidan looked up from the controls. "The atoms of her body are on the verge of completely losing phase with this spacetime," he explained. "I was able to stabilize her but just barely."

"Is it the conduit?" Daeson asked.

"The gateway may have triggered it, but this will happen no matter where she is unless we get her to the Omega Nebula exit gateway soon."

"If we don't make it, what will happen to her?" Kyrah asked the question Daeson couldn't bear to verbalize. "Where will she go?"

"The question isn't *where* but *when*," Avidan replied. "Traveling through time is always a one-way ticket…forward. If the matter in her body is able to synchronize in phase with a certain time in the future, she would resolve then. If not, I don't know."

Daeson was gripping the edge of Raviel's gurney, remaining so close to her yet unable to comfort her with his touch.

"I'm here, Raviel. Fight this…stay with me!"

"Coming up on the conduit exit," Tig said from the front cockpit.

"As soon as we're out, full speed to the next gateway," Daeson ordered.

"Aye, Admiral," Tig replied.

"We have two more conduits to go through," Daeson said quietly. "Will she make it?"

Avidan looked up at Daeson. He didn't answer. Daeson heard the jump drive disengage as he watched Raviel's face intently. She seemed to endure the exit through the gateway much better than the entrance. The next two slipstream conduit entrance gateways were equally as horrible as the first. On the last one, Raviel's eyes opened, and she screamed out for Daeson. Gilzan and Kyrah both had to restrain him from reaching for her. When she fell unconscious a third time, she faded almost to nothing. Avidan worked incessantly until Raviel finally resolved. When she reappeared, her body temperature had dipped dangerously low once again before slowly recovering. She looked like she had been locked in a freezer for hours.

The next gateway was the entrance to the Omega Nebula slipstream conduit. Daeson hadn't envisioned the torture the thought of this entrance would be to him. He would have rather taken her pain a thousand times over than to see her endure it once more. Tig piloted the shuttle to the threshold of the gateway and waited. With tears in his eyes, Daeson leaned as close as he dared to his love...his bonded soul mate.

"Raviel, this is the last one. You're tough...stay with me one more time."

Avidan finished his adjustments then looked up at Gilzan. "I'm not getting any valid bio scans," he said quietly. "It's now or never." Then Avidan looked at Daeson and nodded.

Daeson bit his lip and clenched his fists. "Take us in, Tig."

Five seconds later it began. This time Raviel winced with great anguish but did not scream. As she began to fade, she opened her eyes and turned to Daeson. With her eyes, she beckoned to him, expressing the love that held his heart and soul together. *I love you!*

There was no sound, just the gentle movement of her lips, and then she was gone.

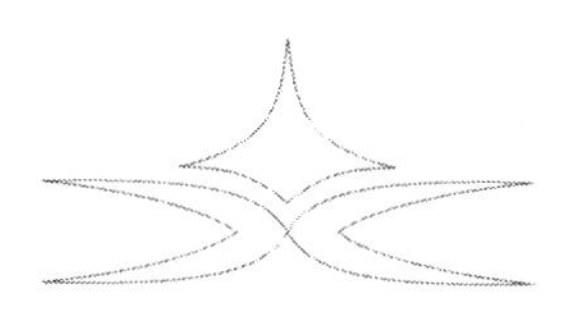

CHAPTER 8

Raviel!

"No!" Daeson screamed. "Come back to me, Raviel!" But she was not there.

Daeson fell to his knees in agony and wept bitterly. He was unaware of anything except his own utter grief. He had lost her twice, and it was too much. The seconds wrapped around Daeson like a ribbon of thorny grief and held him hostage to his absolute misery.

"I need more power for the generator," Avidan shouted to Tig.

"You already have everything except life support," Tig replied.

"Give it to me!" Avidan screamed.

Daeson looked up to see the lad's fingers flying across the glass instrument panel. Then, for just one fraction of a second, a faded image of Raviel appeared. Daeson's heart revived. He came close to where she should have been. "Come back to me, Rav…come back!"

The shuttle was becoming cold, but Daeson didn't notice. Then another flash of her body, and this time it lasted for a few seconds. "You still have her," Daeson exclaimed.

Avidan didn't break his concentration as he flitted from his glass screen to the control panel in a flurry. "I have to stabilize her in this spacetime before we hit the exit," he uttered, his voice strained.

"How long to the exit, Tig?" Daeson shouted.

"Forty-three seconds."

The next few seconds became a battle with quantum mechanics that only Avidan could wage. He fought like a valiant warrior desperate to rescue his people. Raviel appeared three more times, each appearance longer than the previous, but each time she was noticeably paler.

"Ten...nine...eight..." Tig counted.

Raviel faded away. Time was out.

Please Ell Yon...only you have power over this unknown terror, save Raviel! Daeson implored from the depths of his heart.

"Five...four..."

The gurney was empty.

"Three...two...

Raviel's frosty-white body resolved as solidly as at any time since entering the slipstream.

"One!"

The jump drive disengaged, and Raviel clutched the sides of the gurney in panicked silence as she fought for air. She was a frightful sight—frozen skin, eyelashes and hair, with portions of her clothing shredded and torn as if some dimensional monster had raked her from head to foot. Daeson, Kyrah, Gilzan, and Avidan were momentarily paralyzed. Nothing was left to do—she was there!

"Drop the containment field!" Daeson ordered.

Avidan tapped the control, and the generator fell silent. Still unable to take a breath, Raviel looked at Daeson with fear in her eyes. He grabbed her off of the gurney and pulled her close. She was freezing cold. Gilzan wrapped a thick blanket around them both.

"Breathe, Raviel...breathe!"

All at once her lungs filled with air, and she clung to Daeson, burying her face in his chest. Tears spilled from Daeson's eyes as he held tightly to the one who owned him. He let the warmth of his body melt away the frosty edges of the deadly cold she had experienced. She was shivering uncontrollably.

"Tig, get the heat and oxygen back online," Kyrah shouted to the cockpit.

"Copy that," came his reply.

Daeson adjusted the blanket to cover all of Raviel's head except for her face.

"D-D-Daeson," Raviel's shivering voice was barely audible. "You ca...ca...came for me."

"I'm here," he whispered. "I'm here."

Daeson held her tightly for a long while as she sank into his embrace. Slowly she warmed, and her shivering subsided. He felt his soul healing from months of agony.

Gilzan began scanning Raviel while Avidan finished shutting down the field generator. Kyrah made her way to the front cockpit where Tig was.

"How's she doing?" Tig asked.

"She's here and she's conscious. Gilzan says her body temperature is starting to return to normal. I guess that's a win," Kyrah replied. She reached for the nav system and entered the coordinates for the return gateway.

"Looks like you know your way around a shuttle too," Tig said.

"In the colony, you learn quickly to master many things," she acknowledged without looking at him. "You never know who might be taken from you."

Tig piloted the craft toward the coordinates she had laid in.

"What you sacrificed for us...there's no way we can thank you," he said. "I know because my father was a sentry on Jypton, and he had to make the same choice one day. I'm alive and here today because of his courage. Raviel owes her life to you."

Kyrah seemed deep in thought as she stared at nothing. She then turned her penetrating pale blue eyes on Tig. "I don't think he's coming back to his seat for a while," she said with a quick glance back toward Daeson and Raviel. "And we've got a few-hours' journey back. Mind filling me in on what I just threw my life away for?"

Tig nodded. "You deserve that."

He began to regale Kyrah with their long and bizarre story as Daeson and Gilzan ministered to Raviel.

"She needs fluids and nourishment," Gilzan said.

"I don't think I can keep anything down," Raviel replied.

"You must try, Rav," Daeson encouraged, offering her a container of water.

She drank a little to start and then much more. Once she started eating, she was shocked by how ravenously hungry she was. With each passing hour, Daeson could see life returning to her...and to himself, but in a different way. When she had consumed her fill of food and water, she leaned back, closed her eyes, and took a deep cleansing breath.

"Feeling better?" Daeson asked.

"Yes...much."

She opened her eyes, and for the first time since being fully restored, she looked at each of the crew members. Daeson could see the confusion in her eyes. There was much to explain.

She first set eyes on Gilzan. "I don't know you, sir, but I'm certain I owe you my deepest gratitude."

Gilzan smiled. "I am Master Medtech Gilzan at your service. But I am not the one you need to thank." Gilzan looked toward Avidan who was sitting quietly in his seat reviewing a plethora of data on his glass tablet, collected during the ordeal.

"This is Avidan," Daeson said. "He's the one who figured out what needed to be done to save you."

Avidan looked up and offered a weak smile.

"Thank you, Avidan." Raviel leaned forward but kept the blanket wrapped tightly around herself. "I can only hope that one day I'll be able to repay you for saving my life. I am truly grateful."

Avidan blushed slightly then resumed his preoccupation with his tablet.

"And that is Sergeant Kyrah Antos," Daeson said, pointing to the cockpit. "She's the one who made the shuttle heist from the colony possible."

Kyrah turned and gave a quick two finger salute.

"Thank you, Sergeant," Raviel offered. "I don't know why you would all risk so much to save me, but I will endeavor to make your sacrifice count."

Raviel turned to Daeson. "I'm extremely confused. We have a colony...on Rayl?" she asked. "How could this have happened so quickly? How long was I unconscious?"

Daeson took her hand in his.

"There's a lot I need to explain, Rav. And much of this isn't going to be easy to hear," Daeson warned.

Over the next two hours, Daeson explained what had happened after the slipstream conduit accident. Gilzan and Avidan also listened intently as he told of the plight of the fleet before they left and of the two-hundred-seventy-one-year leap through time. At that, Raviel's face turned to stone as she absorbed the impact of her new reality. Everything she had known was gone, including the people she had come to love.

"Petia," she whispered, shock filling her eyes as she looked to Daeson.

He simply put an arm around her and held her close. The rest of the crew became silent while Raviel mourned a life lost.

"What of Rivet?" Raviel asked. "Is sh...he okay?"

Daeson shook his head. "His power cell was depleted to keep your life support systems online as long as possible. I don't know what his fate will be."

Avidan leaned forward. "The android...you're speaking of the android you brought with you?" he asked.

"Yes...is he okay?" Raviel asked.

"I've heard they tried to restrain him and power him up, but there's been no response. Master Scitech Olin is quite amazed at his technology. Where did he come from?"

"That's a story for later," Daeson responded.

"And what of this time…what has happened to our people?" Raviel asked, looking from face to face.

Kyrah exited the cockpit and took up a seat directly across from Raviel.

"Like you, I'm finding all of this a little hard to believe, but the truth is that we are a derelict colony, orbiting the Ianis System. We're barely surviving day to day. Many of our people have lost faith in Ell Yon, despite miraculous provisions of food and supplies that appear each day through the gateway."

Kyrah glanced toward Avidan.

"And Avidan believes that your arrival in our time is the beginning of something new," Kyrah concluded. Then she looked at Daeson. "Is it? Because as soon as we get back to the colony, everything is going to come crashing down, and I just need to know if this is some crazy expedition without a meaning or if we sacrificed our lives for something worthwhile."

Daeson turned to face her. "I can't tell you what's going to happen tomorrow or the next day, but I can tell you that Sovereign Ell Yon has not abandoned his people nor forgotten his promise of giving us a homeworld. And neither will he abandon us now."

Kyrah pursed her lips and nodded. "Okay."

"Ianis exit gateway in thirty seconds," Tig announced. "Here we go."

"Do either of you know the status of our Starcrafts?" Daeson asked.

"They haven't been able to power them up yet, if that's what you mean," Kyrah answered.

"We encrypted our start codes," Daeson explained. "But are they impaired in any way?"

"Hard to say," Avidan added. "The scitechs and the mechtechs are pretty enamored with one of them. The tech is way beyond ours, and they're trying to decide how to analyze it. I don't think they've done anything irreversible yet. Is it Immortal tech?" he asked, looking at Daeson.

"Exiting…now!" Tig interrupted.

As soon as the shuttle exited the gateway, four Raylean pursuit craft greeted them with weapons armed and locked.

"Shuttle Bravo One Three, make your course for *Liberty* docking bay and do not deviate, or you will be fired upon. Acknowledge."

Daeson looked at Raviel. "Are you okay?"

Raviel nodded. He kissed the back of her hand then went to the cockpit and sat down.

"This is Shuttle Bravo One Three. Instructions received. We will comply," Tig said as Daeson finished strapping in.

Daeson flew the shuttle as gently as he could, eventually setting it down in the docking bay. As soon as the bay was pressurized, thirty forcetech personnel led by the chief master sergeant quickly surrounded the shuttle. Before he opened the shuttle door, Daeson turned around in his seat to face his heroic team.

"I don't know what the next ten minutes or ten days will hold, but you are some of the most courageous people I have ever served with. No matter what happens, today you served Ell Yon well. We are one under the Sovereign!"

In that moment, Kyrah, Avidan, Gilzan, Raviel, and Tig resounded with a valiant echo, "We are one under the Sovereign!"

Ten seconds later that courage seemed to shatter as they were forced face-first onto the docking bay floor with charged plasma rifles pointed at the backs of their heads. Kyrah was yanked upward into an uncomfortable position on her knees with her head pulled back. Chief Bern stood in front of her, glaring down with a countenance of fierce indignation. He slowly shook his head. "One of our own! Antos, what have you done? Do you know what the penalty is for treason?"

When Kyrah didn't answer, Chief Bern leaned down. "Do you?" he shouted.

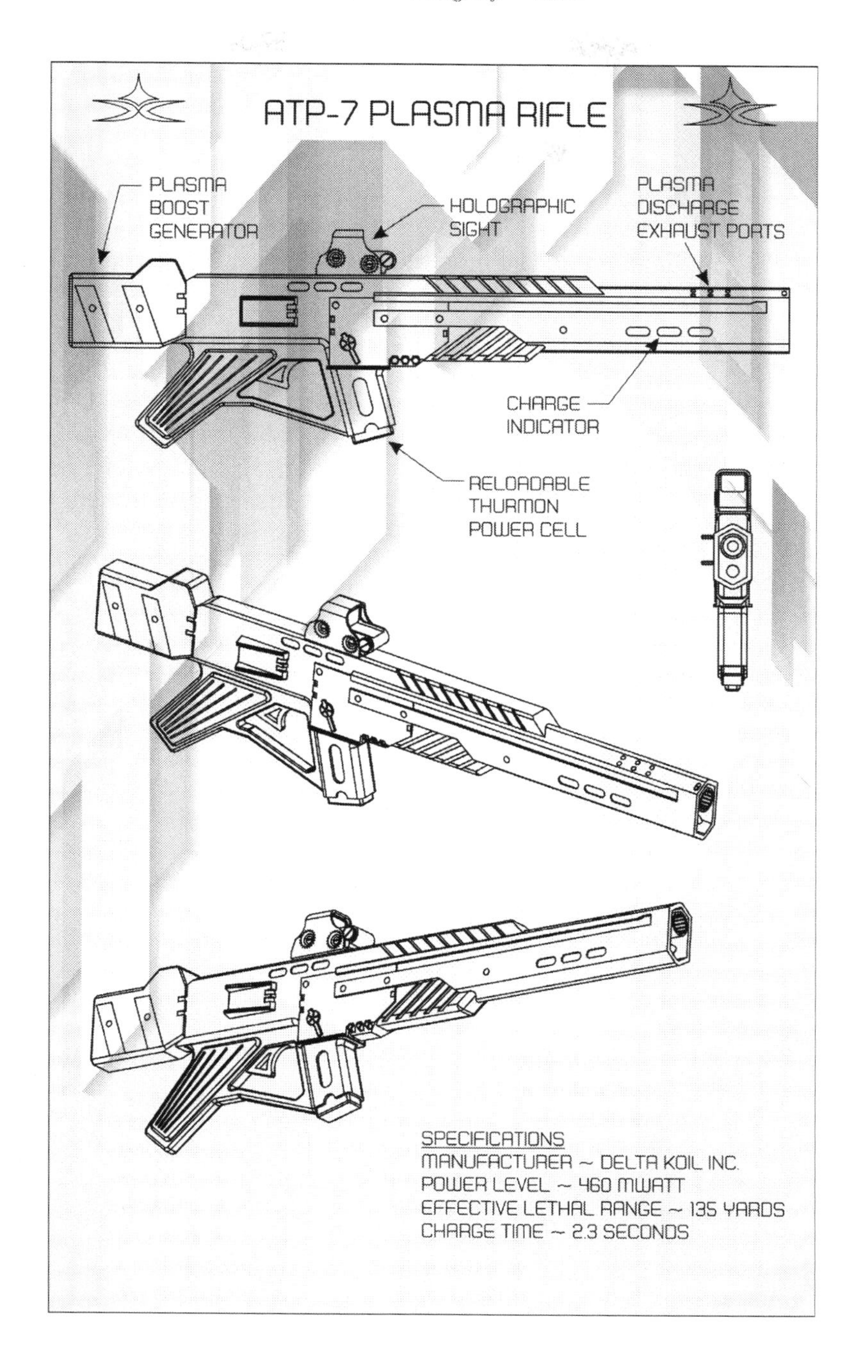
ATP-7 PLASMA RIFLE
PLASMA BOOST GENERATOR
HOLOGRAPHIC SIGHT
PLASMA DISCHARGE EXHAUST PORTS
CHARGE INDICATOR
RELOADABLE THURMON POWER CELL
SPECIFICATIONS
MANUFACTURER ~ DELTA KOIL INC.
POWER LEVEL ~ 460 MWATT
EFFECTIVE LETHAL RANGE ~ 135 YARDS
CHARGE TIME ~ 2.3 SECONDS

"Sir, yes sir. Death by firing squad."

"No!" Avidan shouted. "Kyrah…no!"

One of the guards kicked the boy in his side, and the pain caused Avidan to curl up and groan.

"The master medtech and the boy had nothing to do with it," Kyrah stated. "I forced them to help us."

The chief smirked. "You disgust me. I thought you were a better soldier than to be lured into joining with a band of thieves and ravagers. Take them to their cells!" Chief Bern ordered.

A few minutes later, Daeson, Tig, and Raviel were thrust into one cell, while Kyrah, Avidan, and Gilzan were placed into another.

Daeson went to Raviel. "How are you feeling?" he asked.

Raviel rubbed her wrists where tightened fetters had been. "I'm fatigued, but I'm feeling all right," she said, taking a deep breath. "It was the most bizarre feeling I've ever experienced, but I am feeling better with every minute that passes. I don't ever want to go through that again."

Daeson pulled her to him in an embrace, thankful once more that they were together. The three friends talked at length about their options and obligations to a people that now considered them enemies.

"I must see the admiral," Daeson decided.

"If the chief has his way, we'll all be executed tomorrow," Tig replied.

"Then let's hope the chief doesn't have his way," Daeson responded.

"Do you think they'll actually execute her?" Creases on Tig's forehead let Daeson know that he was very concerned about Kyrah.

"Please, no," Raviel said. "I couldn't bear the thought of her dying because she came to help rescue me."

"She didn't desert, she didn't steal anything, and she didn't cause any damage to the colony," Daeson stated. "Her only crime was to help rescue a fellow Raylean. Once they reason it through, there will be no justification for execution."

"I hope you're right," Tig said. "She's gutsy. If we make it through this, she could be a great asset."

"Very true," Daeson replied. "And we're going to need all the help we can get!"

Daeson looked at Raviel. She looked bone-tired. Something was different about her. He hoped it was just the extreme fatigue.

"Come...you must lay down and sleep."

As she sat down on one of the beds, she gripped Daeson's arm. The intensity in her eyes alarmed him.

"What is it?" he asked as he sat down next to her.

"Thank you for coming for me...for rescuing me."

Daeson pulled her close under his arm. "That's what we do, Rav...we rescue each other every day."

She held tightly onto his waist for a while until she was ready to lie down. Daeson covered her with a blanket and watched her closely as she drifted off to sleep. He and Tig quickly followed suit since the last few days had been grueling for them as well.

Raviel closed her eyes, but she was afraid to fall asleep. A new terror was fighting for control of her mind. In a strange way, it felt as though she had been sleeping forever, yet her body was heavy with fatigue, as if every cell had been utterly drained of its energy. The pain of transitioning in and out of different spacetimes was indescribable, like she was being disassembled and reassembled over and over.

She took a deep breath and fought for control of her fear. *Sovereign Ell Yon, even here I know I am within your reach...grant me peace and strength...please!*

Slowly, the agony of the twenty-four hours released its grip on her, and she drifted off to sleep. The next time she opened her eyes, Daeson was offering her a plate of food for breakfast.

"How long did I sleep?" she asked.

"It's been over twelve hours," Daeson answered. "How are you feeling?"

Raviel stretched and actually felt somewhat normal, like she had two feet on solid ground again. "Much better," she said with smile.

Though the breakfast was rather meager and the water somewhat stale, Raviel devoured it enthusiastically. She then went to Tig and gave him a hug. Tig awkwardly received it with flushed cheeks. She stepped back and looked up at him.

"I don't even know how to thank you, Tig," Raviel said. "I am in awe of you. You are one of the most spectacular men I've ever known. Thank you!"

Tig grimaced a smile and was clearly at a complete loss as to how to respond. Raviel squeezed his arm and turned to Daeson.

"So, what's the plan now?"

Evidently Daeson's request to have an audience with the admiral had fallen on deaf ears. That afternoon a contingent of forcetech guards appeared at their cell door. They were fettered and escorted out of the cell and down the corridors of the *Liberty* to a destination and fate of which they knew not.

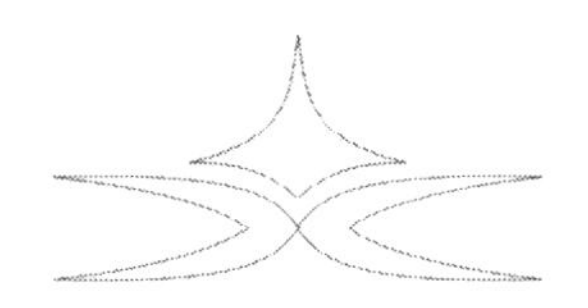

CHAPTER 9

Fireball

Daeson, Raviel, and Tig could hear the unified chants of thousands echoing throughout the corridors of the ship like some eerie call to sacrifice. As they were led through one of the ship's hatches and a connecting corridor to another ship, Daeson could feel the slight shudder of the walkway beneath his feet coinciding with the syncopated shouts of the people. The hatch opened, and they were greeted with a scene that felt as if they had walked into a technological dystopian world of near barbarism. A huge cargo ship was permanently moored next to the *Liberty* and had been converted into an arena for some purpose they had yet to discover. The three of them gawked in stupefied wonder at the sight. Their guards brutishly shoved them forward into a holding area off the end of the main arena. Circular in shape and spanning over one hundred feet in diameter, the arena was made up of twelve sections encompassed on all sides by seating for over two thousand spectators. Daeson immediately recognized the clan symbols annotated above each section. Multiple cameras were positioned strategically around the perimeter of the arena to broadcast the games throughout the entire colony. A hovering drone was also used for this purpose. A smaller separate section in the seating area was elevated to allow a privileged set of spectators a superb view of whatever spectacle was to take place. Here on a grand seat sat a man who clearly possessed all authority over the colony—Admiral Bostra. On his right sat another man of importance, and to his left stood the arena announcer.

Raviel looked over at Daeson, her eyes filled with pain. "What has happened to our people?"

Daeson was too angry to answer. He'd had glimpses of their collapsed civility, but this scene exemplified just how far they had fallen.

The crowd hushed as Bostra lifted his hand. Daeson's heart skipped a beat. Though in the distance, he could just make out the distinct form of the Protector encircling Bostra's right forearm.

"Daeson!" Tig said quietly.

"I see it," he replied. *At least the Protector remains.*

When all were silent, Bostra dropped his arm, and the announcer stepped forward. "Welcome to Fireball!" he began, his amplified voice filling the space of the arena. The crowd roared its approval. After a few seconds, the announcer hushed them by waving his arms. "This evening we have special entertainment for you. Three imposters claiming to be Raylean have come to us." Jeers and shouts of disdain rose up. "Already they have attempted to incite discord among our people and even stolen one of our shuttles while coercing one of our very own to join them in their thievery."

More shouts of disapproval followed as Kyrah was brought out from a different doorway. Chief Master Sergeant Bern shoved her toward Daeson, Raviel, and Tig.

"You schemed with them...now you can die with them," he sneered.

She looked the worst of them all. A cut above her left eye and a swollen right cheek was evidence of the abuse she had endured. Her despairing countenance was hard to look at. She offered a confident nod, but Daeson could perceive the beginnings of a broken spirit.

"Kyrah!" Tig breathed quietly.

She offered a faint smile then looked away to the arena.

Daeson looked around to see if Avidan and Gilzan would be added to the sacrificial games.

"What of Avidan and Gilzan?" Daeson asked. "Are they all right?"

"Thankfully Avidan is too valuable, and Gilzan is too beloved," Kyrah answered without turning his direction. "Bostra wouldn't dare jeopardize the entertainment of the games by engaging them here, but I don't know what will become of them."

Daeson could read the concern on her face.

The arena announcer's booming voice regained the crowd's attention. "These four are worthy of judgment, but perhaps a test is in order to help determine their fate. In this arena, we value the courage and skill of contestants. And so, this evening we will test them so that you can determine for yourselves what manner of consequence they deserve...if they survive."

A thunderous roar of cheers and applause ensued. Admiral Bostra glared down at the accused in smug silence, as one with complete control over their destinies. The announcer motioned to the opposite of the arena, and a man appeared. He wore a form-fitted uniform that was as clean and advanced as anything Daeson had seen since arriving, yet still revealing evidence of savagery. There were some similarities to the Talon training uniform he used to wear back at the academy on Jypton. The man that wore it was a specimen of superior athletic form. Tall...strong...agile.

"I give you Seerok!"

The man was a tower of supreme strength and confidence. Whatever this Fireball contest was, Daeson could see why this man was its champion. The crowd's cheers amplified even further at the sight of him. Behind him two more men and a woman followed...all fit for battle and just as daunting as Seerok.

"And I give you Joran, Morat, and Kamla!" Bostra added, bringing the crowd to their feet.

Kyrah tilted her head toward her fellow prisoners. "Admiral Bostra doesn't intend for us to survive," she said. "These are the most ruthless fighters of all."

"Bring the imposters and the traitor," the announcer continued. "Let us see if any of them can survive the Fireball contest against our best!"

"What debauchery has come to our people?" Daeson said quietly. "Where have they acquired such a vile form of entertainment?"

"This was adopted from our tormentors...the Reekojans on Kayn-4," Kyrah offered. "Not as vicious as them, but it's brutal just the same," she said with a scowl. "Contestants often don't survive—welcome to the colony."

As the four of them were pushed toward the center of the arena, the crowd cheered and jeered, relishing in the anticipation of the games. At a distance of thirty feet from the game champions, they were halted. A small cadre of arena attendants came to them and presented each with a case that held weapons with which they were to defend themselves. Within each case was a studded right-hand glove and a modified Talon-looking baton weapon. Kyrah stepped forward, first lifting the glove out of the case.

"This is an arc glove," she said, slipping her hand inside it. Once the glove was in place, she tightened the strap around her wrist. An array of electrodes ran from the palm of the glove up and down each finger and thumb. The wrist of the glove bulged around its circumference, which Daeson thought must surely house a power supply for whatever the device was to perform. Kyrah then closed her hand into a fist.

"Open your hand quickly and..." she opened her fingers swiftly, and the action immediately created a melon-sized arcing sphere of plasma energy. She looked their way.

"It creates a contained plasma sphere called a fireball that will last thirty seconds once it leaves the glove. With some skill, it can be thrown at your opponent. Watch out for ricochets and don't let one hit you. If it does, pray it hits a leg or an arm because it will fry your brain and stop your heart if it hits anything else."

Daeson, Raviel, and Tig stared at the beautifully terrifying sphere of constrained energy. Kyrah slowly closed her hand, and as she did the sphere decreased in size.

"Smaller spheres are easier to throw but lack the punch to take your opponent down," Kyrah said as she finished closing her hand to a fist, at which point the energy sphere disappeared completely.

They each donned their gloves.

Kyrah then reached for the other weapon. It was eighteen inches in length with Talon-type nozzles at each end. Kyrah pressed a button, and both ends extended a Talon blade with that all-familiar stasis field buzz encasing the fluidic metal molecular structure.

Daeson grabbed his and did the same. He looked at Tig and Raviel with a steely gleam in his eye. "I think I like this."

Tig and Raviel each grabbed their own weapon, knowing they wouldn't have time for much instruction.

"This a modified double-bladed Talon called a Talon-X," Kyrah said.

"Does it have a discharge weapon like a standard Talon?" Raviel asked.

"No, but it does have this," Kyrah said, pressing a button near the center of the baton with her thumb. A two-foot diameter energy shield appeared on the side away from her arm. It only lasted a moment then disappeared.

"It only lasts a few seconds then needs a couple of minutes to recharge, so use it sparingly. You'll need to time it perfectly with any of the energy spheres that come your way," she explained.

The arena attendants closed their cases and filed off of the arena combat circle. The four opponents were taunting the four accused ones and spurring the crowd to new heights of gleeful anticipation for the violence.

"Don't lose heart," Daeson said, hoping to encourage his team. "We are perhaps the four best trained in the entire colony."

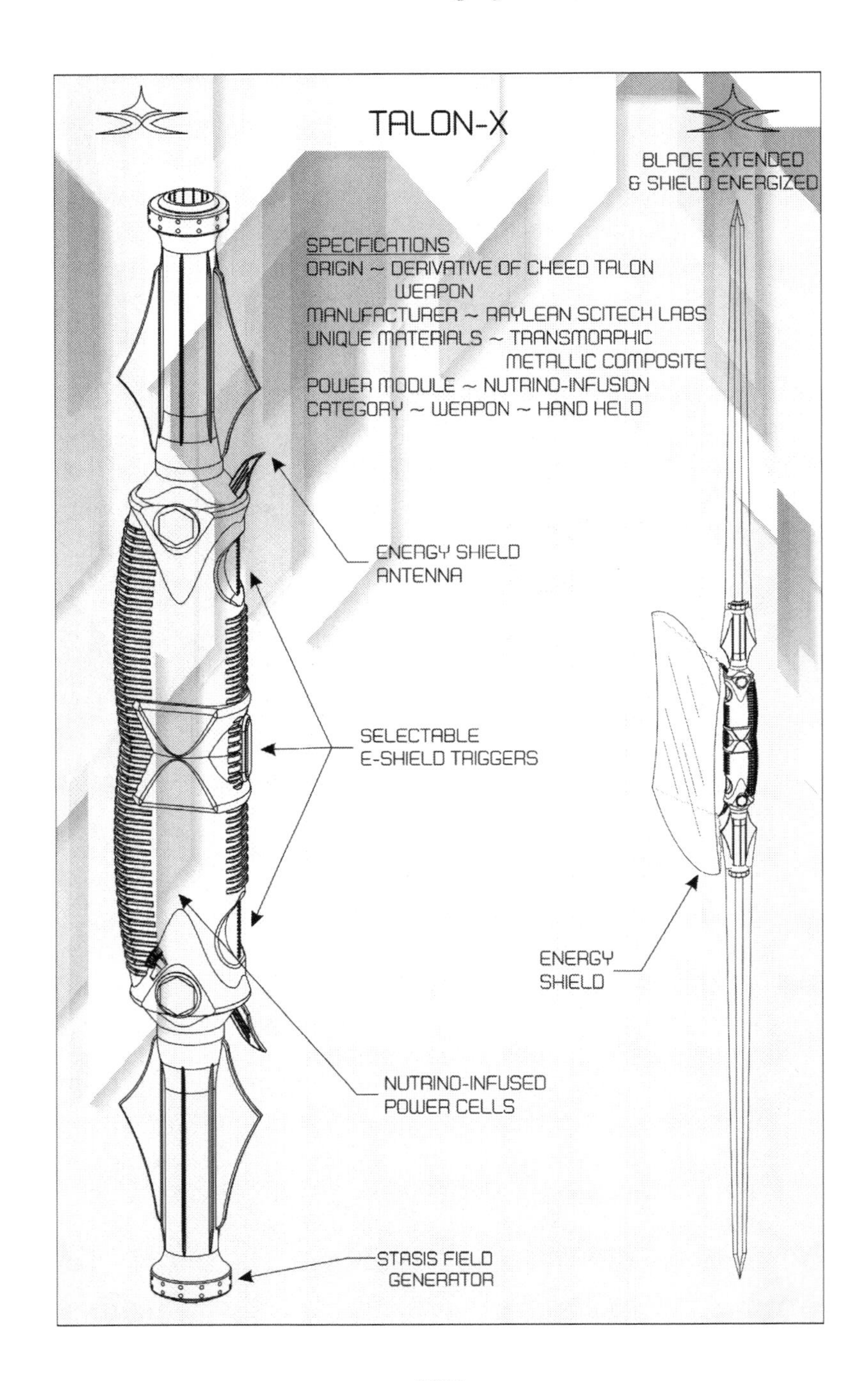

TALON-X
BLADE EXTENDED
& SHIELD ENERGIZED
SPECIFICATIONS
ORIGIN ~ DERIVATIVE OF CHEED TALON
WEAPON
MANUFACTURER ~ RAYLEAN SCITECH LABS
UNIQUE MATERIALS ~ TRANSMORPHIC
METALLIC COMPOSITE
POWER MODULE ~ NUTRINO-INFUSION
CATEGORY ~ WEAPON ~ HAND HELD
ENERGY SHIELD
ANTENNA
SELECTABLE
E-SHIELD TRIGGERS
ENERGY
SHIELD
NUTRINO-INFUSED
POWER CELLS
STASIS FIELD
GENERATOR

"Trained...really?" Kyrah looked skeptical. "Have you ever used an arc glove or a double-bladed Talon?"

"No," Tig replied as he swung his Talon-X from side to side, trying to get the feel for it. "But Raviel was trained as a spy who infiltrated the Jyptonian Aero Forces for years." Tig paused in his weapons practice and looked her squarely in the eye. "Daeson and I were pilots in the Jyptonian academy. We've all had extensive hand-to-hand combat training with the Talon. You're not alone here, Kyrah."

A rare smile slowly spread across Kyrah's face. "I knew I liked you guys from the beginning. Let's rumble."

Daeson looked at Raviel, concerned that she was not yet at full strength after recovering from the quantum anomaly event. She caught his eye. "I'm ready," she said with confidence, but Daeson noted the absence of the fiery spark in her eyes that he usually saw there.

With hope renewed, the four friends turned to face their combatants, but that hope was short lived as the one named Seerok touched a button on the vambrace of his arm. Beside him, panels in the floor recessed away and a huge robotic canine creature leapt up and onto the arena floor.

"Behold...Demon!" shouted Seerok with his Talon-X lifted high above his head.

Once again, the crowd jumped to their feet in riotous applause and cheering. On all four of its legs, the robotic creature stood as tall as Seerok's waist. Red eyes, long vicious fangs, and a deep synthetic growl sent chills up and down Daeson's spine.

Kyrah frowned. "This is new. I've never seen that frightful thing before," she acknowledged.

Their hope now shattered, the odds had completely turned against them.

"We fight as teams of two and as a team of four...Never alone," Daeson stated. "In scenarios like this, the team that loses their first combatant loses it all, so no one falls...no one. With that electronic beast, they outnumber us, so we must quickly even the numbers."

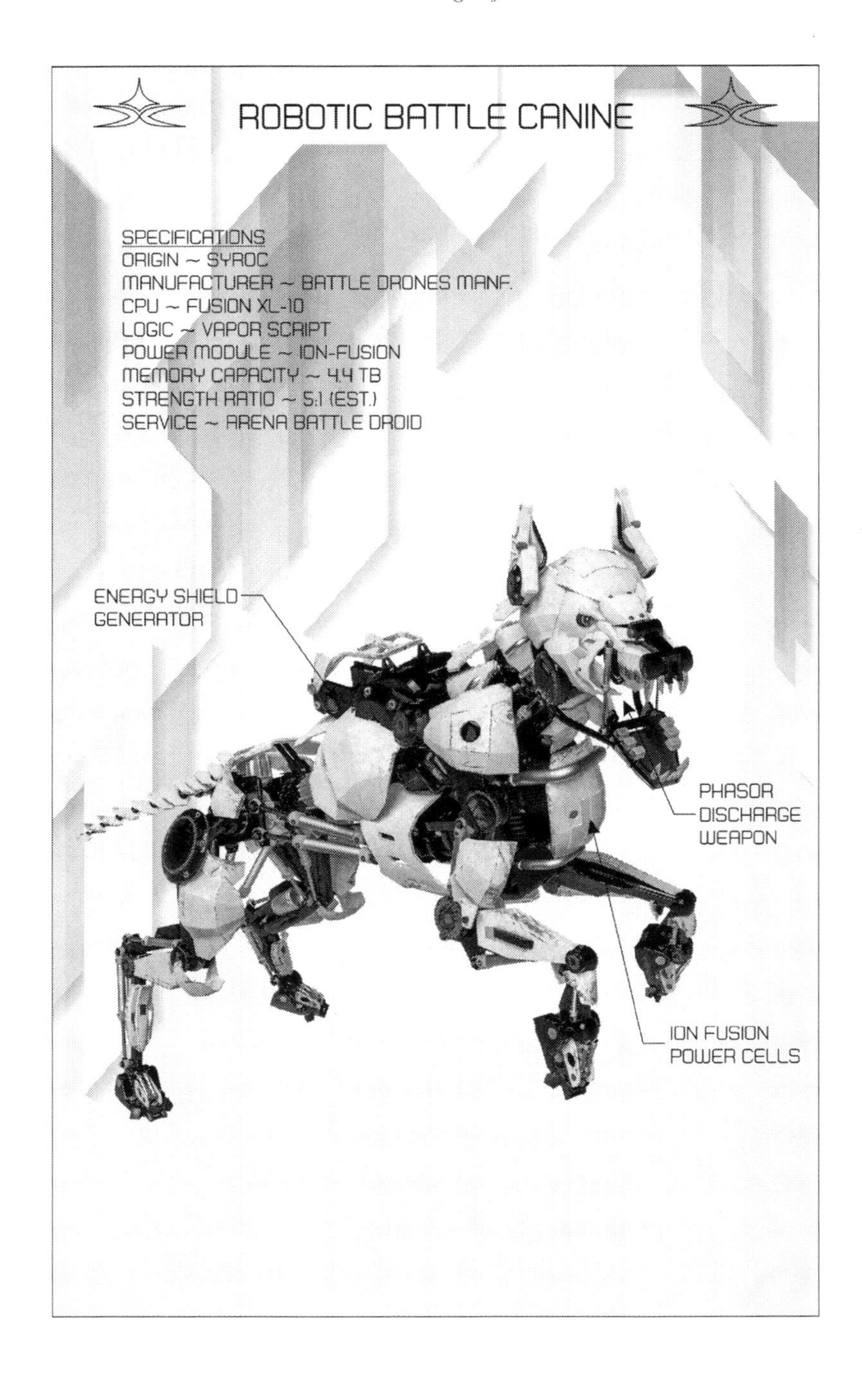
ROBOTIC BATTLE CANINE
SPECIFICATIONS
ORIGIN ~ SYROC
MANUFACTURER ~ BATTLE DRONES MANF.
CPU ~ FUSION XL-10
LOGIC ~ VAPOR SCRIPT
POWER MODULE ~ ION-FUSION
MEMORY CAPACITY ~ 4.4 TB
STRENGTH RATIO ~ 5:1 (EST.)
SERVICE ~ ARENA BATTLE DROID
ENERGY SHIELD GENERATOR
PHASOR DISCHARGE WEAPON
ION FUSION POWER CELLS

"Ell Yon is here," Daeson said, scanning the arena. "He is here, and he is with us."

"Let the contest of Fireball begin!" the announcer shouted.

The arena filled with the sound of an oscillating siren. Then between each of the twelve sections of seating, large semi-circular beams with energy shield generators rose up from the floors and, pivoting near the edges of the arena, rotated inward such that when they were locked in place, they formed a half-spherical barrier between the crowd and the arena. All at once, the eight semi-circular beams energized, and a transparent energy field began to encase the arena beginning from the floor and moving upward. Once complete, the energy field would isolate the combatants from the spectators, although it would do nothing to insulate the combatants from the cheers and chants of the crowd.

The energy field was now as high as their heads and rising. It was then that a glimmering flash of metal caught Daeson's eye. Faster than a man could move, a metal machine shimmied up one of the beams and leapt over the top of the rising energy field. With perfect agility, an android fell twenty feet to the metallic floor with a thud, landing on his two feet and one fisted hand to spread and balance the impact to his frame. The crowd instantly hushed, waiting for some explanation from the announcer as to this novel addition to their entertainment—there was none. Bostra leaned forward in his seat. Slowly, the android rose and stood before Daeson, Raviel, Tig, and Kyrah. Its robotic countenance was hollow and empty as it focused its eyes on the four.

"Rivet!" Raviel exclaimed, taking one step toward him.

The android looked at her, silence his only answer. She stopped, confused.

"Rivet," Daeson said to gain the android's attention. "Is Lieutenant Ki with you?"

The android looked at Daeson as if he were thinking about the question.

"I do not know Lt. Ki. My original programming has been restored. It is my core directive to protect and serve my liege. My liege is Daeson Starlore. Please confirm your identity."

The energy field finished encapsulating the arena as the crowd began to murmur.

"No!" Raviel said quietly, shaking her head.

"I am Daeson Starlore."

Rivet's eyes glowed momentarily as he scanned Daeson's face.

"Scan complete. You are in danger. I suggest we prepare for battle. I've scanned and analyzed the robotic creature's abilities. It has a discharge weapon and a miniature E-shield generator. Its power cells are larger than mine, but it is not as intelligent. I do not have the ability to destroy it but can distract it long enough for you to fight your own battles. Is this acceptable?" Rivet asked, waiting for a response from Daeson.

"I'm not sure who this tin bucket is, but if he's for real, I'd say the odds are now even," Kyrah evaluated as she activated her arc glove.

"Can we trust him?" Raviel asked.

"How can we not?" Daeson replied as they each prepared themselves for battle. "Yes, this is acceptable. Contend with the robot."

"Yes, my liege," Rivet said while immediately turning toward their opponents.

Seerok commanded the robotic canine to attack, and Rivet didn't hesitate. He sprinted toward the attacking electronic beast—they would meet first while the humans followed. The canine opened its mouth wide and released an explosive blast of white-hot plasma at Rivet's center mass. Rivet ducked, narrowly escaping the scorching energy as it passed. Daeson and Kyrah had to twist to avoid being hit as well. With fifteen feet remaining, the canine lunged at Rivet. Rivet didn't break stride as he jumped, tucked into a ball, and spun forward over the top of the canine. He slammed a fist into the top of the canine's head with one hand while opening from his tuck position and grabbing the tail of the creature with his other hand. This had the effect of transferring their closing momentum from a linear direction to a circular direction. Rivet used this to swing the electronic beast by its tail one hundred eighty degrees in a circle right back at its charging human combatants. The flailing creature shrieked in anger as it careened past its master and into the energized arena wall behind him. The impact sent a shower of sparks in every direction, except toward the crowd, which erupted in thunderous applause at the opening action. The beast fell to a heap on the floor, but it was only momentarily dazed. It rose up and shook itself, its glowing red eyes refocusing on Rivet.

Daeson and Raviel paired off and took on Seerok and Kamla, while Tig and Kyrah faced the ones called Morat and Joran. The fight was on.

Daeson attempted to throw his first fireball, but it went grossly wide, and Seerok taunted him for it. A few seconds later the arena was filled with ferocious robotic battles and flying energy plasma balls. Slowly the individual fights moved closer and closer until they were within striking range of the double-bladed Talons. Daeson tried to keep an eye out for Raviel, but Seerok was more than he could handle, especially since these weapons were unique. At one point, Seerok charged Daeson but at the last second threw a fireball at Raviel, who was fifteen feet to Daeson's right.

"Raviel, nine o'clock!" Daeson shouted.

Raviel had just enough time to turn and block the fireball with her shield, but it left her exposed to her opponent. With only ten feet of separation, Kamla threw a quick underhanded fireball that Raviel couldn't avoid. The fireball careened into her left shoulder and sent her flying. When she hit the floor, she lost her grip on her Talon-X, and it slid a few feet from her, the blades now retracted. Daeson disengaged and ran to cover her. Both Seerok and Kamla allowed the reprieve so they could soak up the applause and taunt their opponents for the crowd's pleasure.

Raviel was grimacing in pain with her eyes tightly shut. Daeson lifted her to a sitting position.

"Rav…are you okay?" he asked, but she wasn't able to speak yet.

Daeson took a quick glance toward Tig and Kyrah. They were holding their own against the other two combatants, but just barely. Without weapons, Rivet was taking a beating from the vicious robotic canine. Somehow, they had to gain the advantage quickly, or they would all meet their end.

"Raviel…can you get up?" Daeson asked. "I need you to get up!" he urged.

Seerok and Kamla were coming. Raviel was finally able to catch a breath, the grimace on her face dissipating as her body recovered from the shock to her nervous system. She opened her eyes, and Daeson saw it…the fiery spark that had inspired him to rise from ignorant Jyptonian pawn to leader of a nation. She grabbed his forearm.

"It's time our people understand why we're here," she said with a steely-eyed gaze.

Daeson stood and lifted her to her feet. She recovered her double-bladed Talon and glared at Kamla. Daeson and Raviel stood side by side, poised and ready. The fight resumed. Daeson heard a scream behind him from Tig and Kyrah's fight but couldn't break from his own to find out where it came from. Raviel advanced on Kamla with renewed energy, fueled by a heart of resolve. The warriors had to be always mindful of fireballs rebounding off the arena energy shield walls, as well as a deflection from a combatant's Talon shield. Daeson noticed that when a fireball rebounded, its speed doubled but then quickly disappeared.

Seerok unleashed two spheres and charged. Daeson ducked to miss the first then dove to the right, barely avoiding the second. He calculated the first rebound of both spheres from the energy field and deduced he was safe for at least four seconds. But he was not safe from Seerok. The man was now nearly upon him, and Daeson was still rising from the ground. He deflected a newly thrown fireball then lunged at Seerok. The man's blade flew near to Daeson's face, but Daeson parried with his own and countered. Now he was within Talon-X range. Seerok tried to back away, but Daeson stayed with him as their Talons collided in brilliant bursts of vibrant electrolyzed stasis field explosions. Seerok's countenance displayed great alarm as he realized that Daeson's skill in close combat was far superior.

Daeson saw Seerok forming a new fireball, so he formed his own. Seerok tried to strike first with his fireball, but Daeson was ready. He met the fireball head on with his own, and the resulting collision was blinding. Daeson took the moment of confusion to strike Seerok's glove with one blade of his Talon-X, which effectively demolished the device. With blinding speed, Daeson formed another fireball, tossed it a few inches in front of him, activated his Talon-X shield and punched the fireball right at Seerok's chest. The fireball accelerated toward him with such velocity that Seerok had no time to react. It exploded into his chest and sent the man flying twenty feet through the air and into the arena energy shield. He crumpled to the floor with a thud. Daeson formed another fireball and covered Seerok with it and his Talon-X in a fraction of a second. Once he saw that the man was incapacitated and unconscious, he turned to help Raviel, but there was no need. She had just successfully landed a fireball on Kamla's right leg and advanced on her with the speed of a cat. Kamla's painful retreat ended when Raviel executed a quick cut with one blade then deftly rotated the Talon to execute another cut with the other blade, which landed on the center section of Kamla's Talon-X. The weapon exploded in her hand in a display of blue and orange sparks. Kamla shielded her face, falling to one knee.

"I yield!" she screamed.

"Discard your arc glove," Raviel commanded.

The woman unstrapped it and threw it across the arena. Daeson and Raviel then sprinted to Tig and Kyrah's aid. The two remaining combatants fought for a few seconds but then quickly yielded and disarmed.

"Daeson...Rivet!" Raviel yelled.

Daeson turned to see the robotic canine on top of Rivet, its jaws in the process of clamping down on the android's neck. Rivet's hands were gripping the canine's upper and lower jaws in an attempt to stop it, but he was slowly losing the fight. Daeson could hear the creature's plasma discharge weapon building power. One shot at such close range would end Rivet.

Daeson threw a fireball then sprinted toward the creature. The fireball hit its mark, but the canine's E-shield dissipated the energy so that the effect was minimal. Its fangs were now closing on Rivet's neck. Just as Daeson approached striking distance, Rivet tucked his legs up under the canine and heaved the three-hundred-pound robot into the air. Daeson swung his Talon-X downward with all his might onto the mid-section of the creature. The stasis field of his Talon-X collided with the E-shield of the canine in a brilliant flash of explosive energy. When the air cleared, the robotic canine lay in two sections, one on each side of Rivet. Rivet regained his feet, a little worse for wear.

"Well executed, my liege," Rivet acknowledged.

The fight was over. Bostra and his crowd sat in stunned silence as the announcer gawked with mouth open, not knowing what to say. Daeson glared up at Admiral Bostra as he threw his expired Talon to the ground. Slowly turning so that all of the crowd could see him, he let the moment hang.

"What has become of you?" Daeson shouted to the assembly. "Is this the plan of Sovereign Ell Yon for his people...to become barbarians? It's an abominable thing what you have done...what you have become!" Daeson walked toward Raviel, Tig, and Kyrah. "We are your fellow Rayleans...the people of the Immortal Sovereign Ell Yon, yet you force us to fight one another for your entertainment?"

Daeson went to Kamla and offered his hand. She hesitated, then took it, rising to her feet.

"Have you forgotten to whom you belong?" Daeson continued. "Have you forgotten the power of our Sovereign? Have you forgotten why he led us out of Jypton to this place? We must fight together, not against one another!"

"Silence!" Bostra shouted as he stood to his feet. "You do not lecture us, criminal! Guards!"

The arena energy field dropped, and six guards quickly surrounded the five comrades. As they were escorted from the arena, Bostra glared down at them, his countenance full of disdain. Daeson caught the eye of the man sitting to Bostra's right. The look in his eyes was distinct from that of the admiral's.

The prisoners were taken out of the arena and back to one of the holding cells. At the door, Rivet attempted to follow Daeson in, but a guard moved to stop him.

"The android comes with us," the guard announced. Rivet quickly turned on the man, as though he was going to take him out. The other guards charged, aiming their plasma rifles at Rivet.

"No, the android comes with us," Daeson countered.

Kyrah stepped forward. "Come on, Pars," she said, stepping between the guards and Rivet. "Haven't you seen enough? There's more going on here than you realize. Open your eyes."

The guard hesitated, then stepped back and signaled for the others to drop their weapons.

"I want to see Admiral Bostra," Daeson demanded.

The guard stared at him before stepping back and closing the door.

It took them all a few minutes to absorb what had just happened.

"You all fought well," Daeson complimented. "Rivet, do a self-diagnostics check."

"I already have, my liege," Rivet replied. "My power cells are at thirty-two percent, and I am in need of minor repairs on three sensors and two mobility actuators."

Raviel came close to Rivet, carefully evaluating him. "I need to look at your circuitry," she stated.

Rivet looked to Daeson.

"Allow it," Daeson ordered. "You are to take orders from any of these people as though their orders are my own."

"Acknowledged," Rivet replied. "As long as those orders do not interfere with my core directive."

Raviel raised an eyebrow as she circled to the back of the android and opened its access panel. The door slid smoothly and quietly away, revealing Rivet's ingenious electronic design. A minute later she closed the panel and looked at Daeson.

"The alien device that was connected to the mobility analytics processor is missing," Raviel confirmed with a frown. "She's not here."

"She?" Tig asked. "What are you talking about?"

Rivet's head tilted slightly. "Raviel Starlore, I have just discovered a message in my memory banks that I am programmed to deliver to you. Would like me to relay the message now?"

Daeson and Raviel looked at each other.

"Yes," Raviel said. "Relay the message."

Rivet stared straight ahead as if thinking about what he was to say.

"Raviel, I am sorry that I was not able to spare you from this unfortunate event. It will have severe and lasting consequences for us both. There are circumstances that even a Malakian cannot control, especially when Dracus is involved. I have done everything within my power to prolong your survival. It is my hope that Sovereign Ell Yon will direct Daeson to you before it is too late. When he finds you, love, serve, and protect each other well. I've reinitialized this android's original programming but have modified it to continue my directive as your protector. You'll find it quite resourceful in the challenges that lie ahead, and there will be many. Sovereign Ell Yon will always be with you!"

Rivet paused then looked her way. "That is all, my lady," Rivet said. "May I shut down to preserve my power cells?" he asked Daeson.

"Yes…and Rivet—"

"Yes, my liege?"

"You did well today. You saved us."

Rivet nodded then sat down and became perfectly still. Daeson put an arm around Raviel as she rested her head on his shoulder.

"I hope she's all right," Raviel said.

"Me too," Daeson replied.

Tig and Kyrah stared blankly.

"Rivet was never really just an android," Daeson began. "He was a mimic bot controlled by one of Ell Yon's own Malakian warriors. The Sovereign was with us in more ways than we realized."

"Well, that certainly explains a lot," Tig said with a smile.

After some rest, the four prisoners considered their best recourse for revealing the truth about who they were and what their mission was. Kyrah was key in helping them understand the current leadership and colony culture, as well as outside threats, as they evaluated their options.

"Admiral Bostra is the least of your worries now," Kyrah said.

"Why's that?" Tig asked.

"Because some of those clan chieftains were affected by what he said," Kyrah answered, nodding toward Daeson. "But more than that, the ravagers from Kayn-4 have become brutal. I believe they want to destroy us."

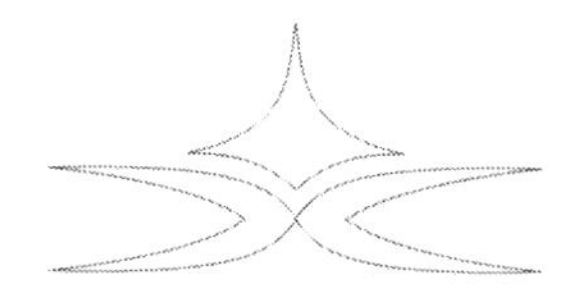

CHAPTER 10

Conquered

"In the day of Navi's return, I will return my favor to Rayl and will bring my people to a new world."
~Darnullay, Oracle of Ell Yon.

The next day, the door to their detention cell slipped away to reveal two security guards and a man of obvious authority, the same man who had been sitting next to Admiral Bostra in the arena. Like many Daeson had seen in the colony, this man was a veteran of battle with many scars to prove it. Though slender in build, he looked as strong as steel.

"I am Vice Admiral Orlic. Your presence and actions while aboard this ship have caused great concern. Regardless of your genetic scans, we consider you a threat to the safety and security of this colony."

Daeson walked toward Orlic, but the guards prevented his approach.

"Vice Admiral Orlic, we've been searching for the colony for...many years. I assure you that we are not ravagers. I request an audience with Admiral Bostra."

Orlic's eyes narrowed. "The Admiral is extremely skeptical of your story, and your words in the arena greatly insulted him." He paused, his countenance softening. "But I must admit, there are some who heard your words and took them to heart. That's why I'm here...but it wouldn't be appropriate for the admiral to come to a detention cell."

"Then please...take us to him. We're servants of Sovereign Ell Yon, and I have a message for him. One that will have an impact on the entire colony."

Orlic hesitated, eyeing Daeson closely.

"I'll be back."

A few minutes later, Orlic and the security guards returned, this time accompanied by Chief Bern.

"Very well, come with me. I'll take you to the Admiral." Orlic looked Daeson in the eye.

"This probably won't go the way you hope, but considering your performance in the arena, you've earned the right. Be warned—you may end up worse off than before."

Daeson nodded. "I understand. That's a risk we're willing to take."

"Sergeant Antos and the android stay here," Orlic ordered.

Tig glanced her way.

"You okay?" he asked.

Kyrah nodded. "Vice Admiral Orlic, is Avidan all right?" she asked.

Chief Bern started to move her direction, but Orlic held up his hand, looking over Daeson's shoulder at her.

"He's confined to quarters and under guard, but he's fine." Orlic then turned and exited the cell. "Bring them!" he ordered.

Vice Admiral Orlic, Chief Master Sergeant Bern, and their security team escorted Daeson, Raviel, and Tig to the bridge of the *Liberty*. Daeson hardly recognized his ship. There was clearly some sort of tribal hierarchy of order among the troops, but it was nothing he had ever seen before. The tattered uniforms of the ranking members were festooned with various displays of conquest, perhaps of the member they had previously defeated to attain their current status. When the door of the bridge slid away, the murky command center left no question as to who was in charge. The eyes of the entire bridge crew fell on the prisoners and then to their leader. Admiral Bostra sat casually skulking in the captain's seat, his left arm perched atop the back of his chair. He wore patched dark leather armor, knee-high black boots, and a tattered scarlet half cape. His right hand rested on the hilt of an extended Talon, its tip embedded into a crack on the floor near his right foot. The weapon's stasis field was off. Daeson felt as if he were looking at a sea pirate from some ancient legend of a water world he had once heard about. He glanced toward Raviel, then Tig. They were as stunned by the spectacle as he was. Daeson's gaze fell to the jeweled vambrace on Bostra's arm. The Protector looked out of place in this world of nomadic vagabonds. Though silent and still, its technological magnificence was obvious. Daeson wondered if the man had any idea as to the power of the Protector. Admiral Bostra sneered.

"Aah...so you *are* just a band of ravagers like so many before you." He looked down fondly at the Protector. "You have come for the jewel of the galaxy. Not many know its value, but I see by the look in your eyes that is not the case with you."

Bostra looked at his vice admiral. "You see, Orlic, it's wise to be cautious."

"We're not ravagers," Daeson replied. "We are Rayleans, like you. Our...predecessors were separated—"

"Silence!" Bostra shouted, his casual demeanor dissolving in an instant.

Their escorts charged their plasma rifles and stepped closer to Daeson, ready to execute the bidding of their commander at a word.

Bostra gripped his Talon and stood. Slowly he walked toward them. "I have heard of your lies, and I don't care what genetic scans say about you. My people have survived centuries in space because we don't trust anyone we don't know." Bostra leaned over to within a few inches of Daeson. "And we don't know you!"

Bostra shortened his Talon to knife-length, pushing it up against Daeson's neck. Orlic stepped forward.

"Your wisdom is our survival, Admiral. But even if they are ravagers, the genetic scans have been verified, and we have laws against executing our own—laws that must be followed."

Bostra sneered. "I suppose you're right, Orlic." The admiral dropped his Talon away from Daeson's neck and turned away. "But our laws don't prohibit administering the test of Yashar. The Protector will tell us if he's lying."

Bostra lifted his hand before Daeson and spread his fingers. A brilliant amber scanning beam formed between his index finger and his thumb. He began to scan Daeson, but when the scan was midway down his body, the *Liberty* ratcheted from an explosion on its port side.

"Admiral, we're under attack!" the sensor officer exclaimed. "Multiple fighters and breaching ships have exited the gateway and are closing in fast."

Vice Admiral Orlic went to the scanning station and pushed the officer aside.

"It's the Reekojans again," he said, turning to face Bostra.

"No!" Bostra exclaimed. "It's only been two weeks. They know we can't sustain these raids this close together!"

Bostra began barking orders to his bridge crew as another round of plasma fire hit the ship. Over the course of the next few minutes, chaos reigned as the colony deployed what was left of its paltry defense forces and tried to survive the ferocious onslaught of the Reekojan marine forces. Damage and casualty reports began flooding in over the communication channels. Daeson, Raviel, and Tig could hardly contain themselves as they watched the remnants of their once noble fleet crumble around them. Hull and hatch breaches were being reported from all ships, including the *Liberty*. A few moments later, the doors to the bridge opened, and after a fierce but brief plasma firefight, twelve Reekojan marines commandeered the bridge. One of the Raylean security guards was killed, and Chief Bern took a shot to his left shoulder, leaving him crumpled against a support. The rest of the bridge officers quickly surrendered. Once the Reekojan marines had secured the bridge, a fierce-looking leader entered. Beside him stood a brutish warrior, his second in command. Both scoffed at the sight of Admiral Bostra and his crew.

"Prefect Verdok...I don't understand," Bostra began. "We've paid you all we can, and just two weeks ago at that. Why have you attacked us?"

Verdok pointed to the ops station. His second in command leveled his plasma rifle at the officer there and blasted him. The officer fell backward onto the counsel...dead. The ruthless commander grabbed the man's body by the neck and threw him to the floor then began scanning the ship's systems. Daeson heard Raviel gasp at the shameless act.

"We've played this game with your petty people long enough," Verdok scowled. "You Rayleans are space locusts consuming resources that belong to us. My predecessor, Prefect Taran, tolerated your presence in our region of space because he seemed to think there was some value in your technical prowess, but I do not."

Verdok scowled at the cowering *Liberty* bridge officers.

"We will take from this hodgepodge of space junk anything that is of worth and make slaves of your youth. The rest of you will die."

He scanned the room for any defiant faces. "I am Prefect Verdok of Reekojah, and I have spoken!"

Every Reekojan marine snapped to attention. "Reekojah!" they shouted in unison while lifting Talons in the air.

Verdok lifted his chin with self-righteous satisfaction. The *Liberty* jolted from more cannon fire without while sounds of Talon-induced death and chaos rang from within. Daeson glanced at the bridge displays and cringed at the sight of the merciless destruction of an already tattered Raylean fleet. *Why didn't Admiral Bostra call upon the Protector?*

Verdok's second in command pulled away from monitoring the controls at the ops station.

"Prefect, this is one of the few ships worth salvaging. We can transfer anything of value here before destroying the rest of the colony and then transport it to Reekojah."

"Can you fly it without the crew, Commander Kasix?" Verdok asked.

"I need him and her," Verdok's second in command pointed to the Raylean officers at the navigation station and the communication station. "That is all."

Verdok smiled as he turned to exit the bridge.

"Good. Kill the rest of them!" he ordered as he left the bridge to join the ships already departing to return to Reekojah with prisoners.

A dozen Reekojan marines leveled talons at the remaining bridge crew, waiting only for Verdok's second in command to give the order.

"Daeson!" came the whispered plea from Raviel. Without the Protector, Daeson was just as vulnerable as any other man on the bridge.

"Commander Kasix, if you execute them now," Daeson said, stepping forward, "you will lose the most valuable possession in the quadrant...perhaps in the entire galaxy."

Every head turned to look at the forgotten prisoners.

"Silence, you traitor!" Admiral Bostra shouted.

Kasix held up his hand to stay his executioners. He tilted his head and walked toward Daeson, Raviel, and Tig. Deathly silence hung in the air as the brutish commander pondered the odd trio. He looked back at Admiral Bostra. "Who are these three?"

Bostra scowled at the man and said nothing.

Kasix didn't hesitate. He leveled his Talon at Bostra's chest and fired. The burst of energy shattered the admiral's torso, bringing instant death. His lifeless body fell forward to the floor in a heap at the feet of Kasix. Gasps of horror filled the bridge. Daeson saw Raviel turn away. Tig was anxious to make a move, but Daeson shook his head.

"Bring her here," Kasix pointed to the officer at the sensor station.

A burly Reekojan marine grabbed the officer's arm and yanked her to stand before Kasix. He smiled down at her. Her stoic countenance could not hide the fear in her eyes.

"Before I kill these three, I need to know who they are and why your leader has them in fetters."

Kasix walked over to Daeson and jammed the end of his Talon up under his chin while eyeing him closely.

"This one is about to tell me about some fanciful treasure you have, and I need to know if I should believe him." Without removing the Talon, he looked over at the stoic officer. "And you can tell me that. So...who are these three, why do you have them as prisoners, and why are they on your bridge? Talk and I'll spare your life."

The young female officer lifted her chin in defiance.

"Very well," Kasix said. He dropped the Talon from Daeson's chin and aimed it at the officer instead.

"Wait!" shouted Vice Commander Orlic.

Daeson saw the quick exchange between the sensor officer and Orlic.

"Ah...someone finally willing to speak." Kasix glanced from Orlic to the sensor officer and then to one of his marines. "This is leverage, sergeant...watch."

Kasix walked to Vice Commander Orlic. "You have feelings for her. You will answer every question I ask truthfully, and I will let her live. If I suspect a lie, you will both die. Understand?"

Orlic looked toward the comm officer and nodded.

"These three arrived five days ago," Orlic began. "We don't know who they are or why they have come to us. Genetic scans show them to be Raylean, but Admiral Bostra didn't trust them."

Kasix slowly walked back to Daeson.

"And why did Bostra think they had come?" Kasix asked without taking his gaze from Daeson.

"Admiral Bostra believed them to be ravagers…thieves," Orlic replied. "This is why they're in fetters and held as prisoners."

"Now we're getting somewhere," Kasix said as he glanced toward his sergeant. "You see what a little leverage can do, sergeant?"

He turned back to Daeson.

"Now that I've established your purpose, you will speak, prisoner. What valuable possession?"

Daeson eyed Kasix closely. The man was nothing more than a merciless, murderous monster, but even men like him had ambitions. Daeson smiled. "The jewel of the galaxy of course. Haven't you heard of the Rayleans' possession of Immortal technology called the Protector?"

Kasix squinted at Daeson.

"I speak the truth. It's why we're here," Daeson said. "With my help we can both benefit."

Kasix held his gaze for a moment.

"I don't need your help," he scoffed, turning back to the communications officer. He put his charged Talon to her head.

"Is he telling the truth?" he asked Orlic.

Orlic's face filled with pain. "Yes. It's our most prized possession, but it's of little value to you."

The eyes of the murderer filled with wonder. "I'll be the judge of that. Where is it?" he asked without moving the Talon.

Orlic hesitated.

"It's the vambrace on Admiral Bostra's forearm," Raviel blurted out.

Kasix snapped his head toward Raviel then to the corpse of the admiral. The Protector was mostly covered by the admiral's cape.

"Bring it to me," Kasix ordered his sergeant.

The marine kicked Bostra's body onto his back, revealing the gleaming Protector still formed to his arm. It took the marine a few attempts, but after one solid pull the Protector released its grip and came free. The sergeant stood and held it with a look of wonderment in his eyes. A subtle glint of blue-flamed energy shimmied up and down the inlaid jewels. The mesmerizing display captured the attention of every single occupant of the bridge, especially Kasix. The marine slowly handed the vambrace over to his commander.

"So, it does exist," Kasix said with awed wonder. "Hiding in plain sight all this time. We had only heard mythical stories of such a thing."

Daeson swallowed hard. He couldn't imagine what Sovereign Ell Yon would do, but allowing such power to rest in the hands of this tyrant seemed unlikely.

"What you are holding, I'm told, is an instrument of boundless power," Daeson warned. "Admiral Bostra didn't understand what he had or how to use it. He who wields it is connected to unlimited power...power to rule," he said enticingly, suspecting the man had ambitions Prefect Verdok might not be aware of.

Kasix's eyes darkened with an insatiable lust for power. He grabbed the Protector and was about to push it onto his arm.

"Commander, I would be careful about that," his sergeant warned. "The legends say that only one with Raylean blood can wear it, and then only one that is worthy."

Kasix hesitated then scoffed. "Worthy? Ha!" He eyed the Protector closely...hesitating. "Do you believe all of the myths you hear, sergeant?"

The entire bridge waited—no one sure of what would happen. Finally, Kasix let his arm drop to his side. He held the Protector out to his sergeant.

"You put it on."

The sergeant's eyes widened in fear.

"Please...no commander!"

Kasix's eyes became fierce.

"Do it!"

The sergeant swallowed as he contemplated his options. One thing was certain—death awaited if he chose to disobey

Kasix. He slowly took the Protector and held it above his forearm. Kasix pointed his Talon at his sergeant.

"Betray me and I'll kill you."

The sergeant's eyes narrowed. Steeling himself, he pushed the Protector onto his forearm. Kasix and the rest of his men looked on in wonder as the Protector enveloped the man's arm. His eyes filled with brilliant and frightful illumination as the Protector seared his synapses with the power of Ell Yon. There was one brief moment of jubilant understanding, followed by a swelling visage of utter terror. Within seconds, the sergeant began to scream and claw at the Protector, but it would not yield. All at once, the Protector enveloped the man in a powerful surge of blue energy that evaporated the body of the sergeant to nothingness. The Protector fell at the feet of Kasix, remnant wisps of power surging until it was silent and still. Kasix stepped back in horror as did all of his marines. He gawked at it as he carefully knelt down and reached for it. He stood smiling with delight.

"Immortal power!" he whispered as he held the Protector once more.

He looked around the room, taking in the faces of horror on everyone in the bridge, especially his marines. They all looked away from his gaze, afraid he was about to pick another victim on whom to test the Protector. At last, his eyes fell on Daeson.

"You see, we can both benefit. I have a buyer that will pay handsomely for—"

"Buyer?" Kasix sneered. "Sell the most powerful Immortal technology to a buyer?"

He walked slowly toward Daeson, smiling sadistically. "I think not. This is perfect. They don't trust you, so that is in my favor, yet you have Raylean blood. This will work. You will be my weapon to rule Reekojah! I control you, and you control it."

Daeson feigned a look of fear. "That's not—"

Kasix jammed his Talon against Daeson's head and nodded to one of his marines. When the marine hesitated, Kasix grew angry. He turned to face the rest of his marines.

"Follow me, and I will make you all powerful officers in my regime."

Kasix looked back at the marine near Daeson. The man nodded, then cut the fetters that bound Daeson's hands. Daeson rubbed his wrists while looking at Kasix.

"Put it on!" Kasix said, handing the Protector to him while resuming his Talon's aim at Daeson's head. "At the slightest hint of betrayal, I will blow you to pieces...is that clear?"

Daeson took the Protector from Kasix. "Perfectly."

The Protector began to arc with ribbons of blue energy as he positioned it over his arm. He glanced toward Raviel and Tig. Both looked utterly stunned. They stepped back, as did Kasix and the rest of his marines. Vice Admiral Orlic's face was indeterminate...perhaps pity for the fate of even an enemy.

Daeson slid the Protector onto his forearm and his mind flooded with the glory of something supernatural once again. Only Raviel could begin to fathom what joining with Sovereign Ell Yon through the Protector was like. He closed his eyes and grimaced as he fought to focus and align the overwhelming intellect and power the Protector was channeling through him. It was as if a thousand years of power was waiting...anticipating this moment in time. And then everything synchronized. He opened his eyes, and the world changed.

He looked at Kasix as he opened his hand toward him. Before Kasix could react, the Protector exploded with a burst of energy that threw the man clear across the bridge and up against the main forward displays. He crumpled to a heap. Every Reekojan marine fired their plasma rifles at Daeson, but a sphere of protective energy surrounded him, and the shots were returned perfectly to their origins, eliminating every Reekojan marine instantly. Within less than five seconds, it was over.

Daeson gazed throughout the bridge, scanning for any missed threats. Every Raylean left alive on the bridge gawked in expectant impending death as they tried to retreat from Daeson and the power of the Protector. He pointed at the remaining security guard.

"You, release them," he said, nodding toward Raviel and Tig, at which the guard promptly obeyed.

Raviel and Tig then quickly armed themselves with plasma rifles while the bridge crew waited. Raviel handed Daeson the Talon used by Kasix as the *Liberty* shook again—the destruction of the Raylean colony continued. Daeson went to the admiral's seat and scanned the faces of his new crew.

"Vice Admiral Orlic, I am assuming command of this fleet."

Orlic found the courage to approach Daeson, his eyes fixed on the pulsing power of the Protector.

"Fleet? This isn't a fleet. It's a colony of a dying race of people."

Daeson glared at the man. "Not anymore! This is the fleet of the Raylean people...the people of the Immortal Sovereign Ell Yon." He then spun the Talon in his hand end-for-end and handed it to Orlic. The man took the offered weapon, eyeing Daeson closely. Daeson then turned to the rest of the bridge officers.

"Everyone, arm yourselves. Our first order of business is to retake this ship and shut down the attack on our fleet."

They hesitated, glancing toward Vice Admiral Orlic. He nodded, and every officer reacted quickly. Daeson went to the injured chief master sergeant who was struggling to gain his feet. Daeson reached for him. Chief Bern took his arm and eyed Daeson, a measure of humility gleaming in his gaze. Vice Admiral Orlic, Tig, and Raviel joined them.

"I'm here because Sovereign Ell Yon put me here. If we're going to save his people, I need leadership and trust. Are you with us?"

The chief and Orlic nodded.

"Very well then...let's do this!"

Daeson pointed at the com officer Verdok had threatened.

"What's your name, ensign?"

"Watts...sir."

Daeson nodded. "Watts, keep the bridge secure and stay in contact with us. We'll split into four details. Orlic, you lead a security team to the armory and gather recruits along the away. Raviel, you and Chief Bern secure engineering. Tig, take your detail along the port corridor. Find Kyrah and Rivet. I'll take the starboard. Meet up at the docking bay so we can launch our Starcrafts...if they're still there. The quicker we can get to them, the quicker we can turn this thing. Any questions?"

Hope seemed to pour into the souls of the Rayleans as Daeson organized and dispatched them to their duties. Before Chief Bern and Raviel were dispatched, Daeson grabbed her hand.

"Are you up for this?"

She smiled with that familiar fire in her eyes and charged the plasma rifle in her hands.

"Let's move!"

Daeson smiled back. *Be careful,* he mouthed then turned to his new crew.

"Sir," ensign Watts called out. "We're being hailed from the scitech lab."

Tig went to the com station.

"Bridge...this is Sergeant Antos...is anyone there?"

"Kyrah...this is Tig. What's your status?"

Daeson joined Tig.

"Your bucket head busted us out of our cell once the attack started. We've secured the scitech lab but need reinforcements. I can't find Avidan!" Kyrah exclaimed.

Daeson stepped forward. "Kyrah, this is Daeson. I need you and Rivet to move toward the docking bay and secure our Starcrafts. We're on our way."

"Copy. Hurry...it's a bloodbath down here!"

Daeson turned to the teams he had assembled and led them to the bridge doors. "Let's move out!"

As soon as the bridge door opened, six Reekojan guards turned to fire on them. One broad blast from the Protector instantly cleared the corridor. Deck by deck the Rayleans fought back and gained strength as they went. Daeson was eager to get to his Starcraft, hoping the fighters were still intact and not destroyed. He considered the fact that Verdok had planned to return with the *Liberty*, so the odds were in his favor that most of the transport would have limited damage, including the docking bay and its contents.

The fight was brutal and many good men and women were lost, but the Reekojans didn't expect such a fierce fight. Verdok had already departed and was on his way back to Reekojah with many of the prisoners, and with their commander missing, the remaining Reekojan marines had no command and control to lead them.

After fifteen minutes of fierce fighting, Daeson and Tig made it to the docking bay. They joined with Kyrah and Rivet to finish fighting the remaining marines.

Kyrah immediately went to Tig. "I can't find Avidan...I have to find him," she pleaded.

Tig grabbed her arm. "We will," he said. "One way or another we will find him...I promise."

Kyrah seemed to draw comfort from his words.

"Tig, we've got to launch now," Daeson instructed.

Kyrah nodded and backed away.

"Go," she said, then turned to join forces with those fully securing the rest of the ship.

"Rivet...backseat," Daeson ordered.

Daeson and Tig quickly surveyed the condition of their Starcrafts. With relatively little damage and fuel tanks nearly half full, they launched into a fray with the odds grossly against them. The few remaining Raylean security vessels were fighting valiantly, but they were outnumbered and outgunned. Once Daeson and Tig opened fire on the Reekojan vessels in a merciless, skilled counterattack, the Raylean security vessels renewed their fight. Rivet was instrumental in helping Daeson prioritize threats and eliminate them. Two Reekojan boarding frigates were still anchored to larger transports. Daeson's enhanced Starcraft unleashed a barrage of plasma cannon fire on each of them and breached their hulls. In seconds the ships were incapacitated.

"Raviel, what's your status?" Daeson radioed during a pause in the fight.

"Engineering secure. Our team is expanding to secure other sections of the ship. We'll have this locked down in another fifteen minutes."

"Roger that. When able, get back to the bridge and help Watts coordinate our attacks from there."

"Copy, you two be careful out there," Raviel returned.

From the bridge, Watts offered a steady stream of updates to Daeson and Tig as she monitored the progress of the battle. It helped them to coordinate and focus their attacks on the most critical areas of the fleet. Thirty-five minutes later, the Reekojans began disembarking and fleeing. At least one-half of the Reekojan vessels had been damaged or destroyed, but the cost to the Rayleans was even greater. Daeson grieved as he and Tig performed a battle damage assessment of the fleet in their Starcrafts.

"This is bad, Admiral," Tig radioed.

"Yes," Daeson replied soberly. "I can't imagine how many lives were lost this day."

After one more sweep of the hardest hit vessels of the colony, Daeson led the way back to the *Liberty*.

"We have a lot of recovery to do," Daeson radioed. "I guess we'd better get to it. Let's take care of our wounded first."

"Copy that."

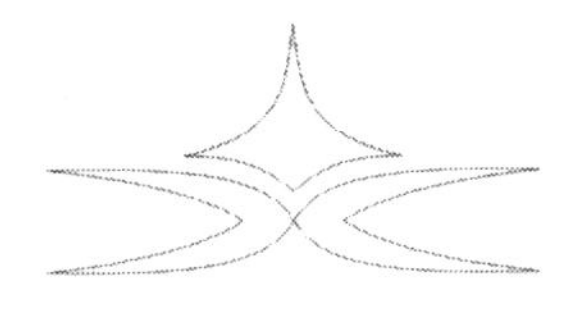

CHAPTER 11

A New Hope

The aftermath of the Reekojan marine attack was soul-crushing—tens of thousands had died and tens of thousands had been taken as slaves. Never before had the Raylean colony endured such immense tragedy. It changed them...all of them. Many of the ships and much of the colony infrastructure had been destroyed or severely damaged. Thankfully, the *Liberty* was mostly intact since it was to have been taken as a Reekojan prize. Daeson, Raviel, Tig, Kyrah, Orlic, and the chief, along with the clan leadership, worked tirelessly for weeks to recover their people and as much of their fleet as was humanly possible. Avidan had not been found, and Kyrah shed tears of anguish for him, his fate unknown. Her only hope was that he had survived the attack and been taken along with many of the other Raylean youth. In spite of her grief, Kyrah rose up to fulfill her duties as a leader among the people, even reconciling with a repentant Chief Bern. Rivet, once Raviel had repaired him, became a maintenance hero among the people, working tirelessly to assist and repair external damage in ways that humans could not.

Daeson's reconnection with Sovereign Ell Yon through the Protector was just as soul-piercing as he had remembered. The whispers in his heart helped him serve his people in ways that at times seemed supernatural. Instructed not to reveal his former identity, Daeson became known simply as Navi, a messenger from Ell Yon. He and his team quickly won the respect and admiration of a people desperate for hope and leadership. Once the threat to their survival had diminished, Daeson worked with Vice Admiral Orlic to convene a meeting of the clan chieftains and fleet leadership. The arena was used as the venue for this benchmark step for the Raylean people. Additional seating spilled onto the arena floor to allow for as many people as possible. For those who could not attend, the arena cameras were used to broadcast the gathering to the rest of the colony. A small space in the center of the arena allowed for a platform from which the two men could address the people. Nearly three thousand people had gathered, and another three hundred thousand watched via monitors across the colony.

"Good people," Orlic began. "We stand here as survivors. We stand here as the chosen people of the Immortal Ell Yon. Although we have suffered great loss, we are not abandoned. I am here to testify that a messenger of the Sovereign is here to lead us. I have seen the power of Ell Yon through his use of the Protector, and I submit to you the justification and validity of his right to lead our people. Without him and his valiant companions, we would not be here today. I therefore put before you a recommendation to commission Navi as Admiral of the Raylean colony."

Orlic stepped aside and held out his arm. Daeson gripped it tightly and nodded his appreciation. He then turned to face the people. "Mighty people of Ell Yon...all you have ever known is the harshness of life in this colony in space. Our hearts are broken...our children have been taken from us, our treasures robbed, and our future destroyed. What hope is there now, you ask? Who in all the galaxy even cares about our plight?"

Daeson looked out into the sea of despairing faces smudged with the pain of loss and suffering.

"I have been sent by Sovereign Ell Yon to tell you that he cares…that you are not abandoned. Today your lives change. Today we reclaim our future. You are the generation of Rayleans that will inherit the promise of a homeworld. And in this quest, through the power of the Immortal Sovereign Ell Yon, we will find and deliver our people from bondage."

Daeson could see a few of the people lift their heads, the beginnings of hope.

"Listen to me…the Reekojans didn't come to destroy us because we are consuming their resources. They came to destroy us because they fear us and more than that, they fear the one to whom we belong. And they should—Kayn-4 is our promised home by Sovereign Ell Yon himself. It is time to fulfill our destiny and establish our homeworld of Rayl!"

The clan chieftains began to murmur and nod their approval. Slowly the people seemed to come to life.

"There is much work to do…much to prepare. Vice Admiral Orlic has graciously given to me his endorsement of leadership. I will not accept the commission as admiral of the Raylean *colony*…no, but I will accept the commission as admiral of the Raylean *fleet*. For from this day forward, we are no longer a *colony*. We are a *fleet* of ships on a mission to our homeworld. The only mission of a colony is to survive. We are a fleet with a mission to advance to our homeworld, recover our people, and commission Kayn-4 as our new home…Rayl! This is our promise from Ell Yon…this is our destiny as a people through which the galaxy will be saved. We are one under the Sovereign!" Daeson shouted.

Orlic stepped up beside Daeson and joined in the rallying cry.

"One under the Sovereign!" shouted the people. Soon the entire arena reverberated with the chant of Ell Yon.

"One under the Sovereign…one under the Sovereign!"

Daeson lifted his right arm high into the air in concert with the voices of his people. The Protector began to shoot ribbons of blue energy in the air above him in a brilliant display of righteous power. The energy spilled out and over the people in affirmation that Ell Yon's Navi would lead them home. It lifted the people out of their despair and filled them with hope and courage.

"One under the Sovereign!"

Raviel, Tig, and Kyrah stood, and soon all three thousand Rayleans in the arena and another three hundred thousand spectators joined in the rousing cry to rise up and free their people from the clutches of the evil Reekojan regime.

At last, two hundred and seventy-one long years later, Daeson delighted in the unified hearts of all the people. That evening a battered and bruised fleet of Rayleans closed their eyes with hope in their hearts for the first time in many years...hope in the mighty Immortal who had neither forgotten nor abandoned them.

In time, Daeson came to believe that he could rely on the support of each of the clan chieftains. As had always been the case, the chieftains expressed differences on how some things should be accomplished, but it was the first time that he didn't feel animosity from them or toward their mission. For some of the key decisions, he relied on his inner circle of trusted leaders—Raviel, Tig, Vice Admiral Orlic, Kyrah, whom Orlic had promoted to lieutenant, Chief Master Sergeant Bern of the forcetech guild, who had humbled himself before Kyrah with an incredibly awkward apology, Master Gilzan of the medtech guild, Master Corbin of the scitech guild, and Master Skylin of the aerotech guild. Such was the case for the initial planning required to invade Kayn-4. This team became known as the Strategy Council.

"It's going to take many months to recover, train, and prepare our forcetech and aerotech forces for an assault on Reekojah," Daeson began. "I'm calling on you to help develop a strategy and timeline. I have the promised support of each of the clan chieftains, so you will each be working closely with them to accomplish our preparations. Sacrifice and grit will be required to get us ready. Thankfully food supplies continue to arrive through the gateway, but we are going to have to be extremely resourceful in acquiring and manufacturing the weapons and technology that will be needed. Our scitech guild is strong; it just lacks resources. Our forcetech and aerotech guilds need personnel, training, weapons, and spacecraft."

Daeson stopped and stared down at the table in front of him. He looked up and saw the faces of committed soldiers staring back.

"Speaking it makes it sound daunting...perhaps impossible. But you need to know and to not doubt...Ell Yon has promised it...the Protector has spoken it...and it will be done. Our first priority is securing and protecting the fleet so that we can ward off any future attacks. We were able to acquire many weapons from the last Reekojan attack, but we'll need more...many more. Tig, Raviel, and Kyrah, I want you working closely with Chief Bern and Master Skylin to develop training programs to get them up to speed as quickly as possible. Let's use the arena for something productive, shall we?"

Daeson turned to Master Corbin. "I want the scitechs working around the clock to improve and enhance all weapon designs. We're going to start sending trading teams to all planets in the Medarra Cluster. We may not have much to trade in the way of resources, but what we do have is technology, and we have the best scitechs in the galaxy. Technology and knowledge are our resources, and that is how we will acquire what we need to prepare. It will be slow at first, but our preparedness will grow quickly."

Daeson stopped and smiled as the Protector whispered. "And you might find a surprise or two in the next few deliveries through the gateway."

Master Corbin's eyes lit up with anticipation.

"Admiral," Vice Admiral Orlic interjected, "we do have a lot of preparation to do, but we also need to know what we will be facing when we go up against the Reekojans."

"Agreed," Tig said. "We have very little intel on their region or the rest of the planet."

Daeson looked at Orlic, Kyrah, and the chief. "What *do* we have?" Daeson asked.

"Not much," Orlic offered. "The Reekojans, all of Kayn-4 for that matter, are ruthless and brutal, as you well know. Our people have tried to stay away. Traveling to Kayn-4 and especially Reekojah is usually a one-way ticket for a Raylean."

"The only way to really know what we need in order to take the fight to them is to have someone on the inside," Kyrah said.

"Kyrah is right," Raviel agreed, leaning forward. "We need to send a reconnaissance team into the city to gather information. It will mean the difference between victory or defeat. We can gather intel concurrently with our war preparations and training."

Daeson's eyes furrowed as he glared at her. He knew what she was thinking. Raviel opened her mouth to speak.

"I volunteer," Kyrah interrupted.

Daeson glanced her way, somewhat relieved until he realized what her motivation was. Kyrah was eager for the job...too eager. Her perceived failure to protect Avidan was clearly motivation for the mission. However, in hoping to find him, she might become reckless and jeopardize the mission because of it. Daeson couldn't blame her—he himself had walked in her shoes.

Tig caught Daeson's attention. One fraction of a side movement of his head told him that Tig agreed with Daeson's analysis. Raviel waited, watching Daeson closely. Daeson's mind began racing to find an answer.

"Kyrah, your courage is admirable, and you're an excellent soldier, but I can't allow it," Daeson decided.

"Excuse me, Admiral, but why not?" Kyrah's eyes ignited with anger.

"Because as a soldier you know that emotions cloud judgment and can jeopardize mission success. Forcetech is going to need you here to train and lead them. Besides...I don't need a soldier—"

"You need stealth," Raviel interrupted, glaring at Daeson. "You need a spy. I must be the one to go."

Daeson shook his head. "Absolutely not! You've barely recovered from the slipstream disaster."

The room fell silent with the unbearable weight of the truth. "No one in this fleet has the training I've had," Raviel rebutted. "I've spent most of my life preparing for this. You of all people should know how good I am at it," she added with a subtle smile. "It's what I do, Admiral."

Daeson pursed his lips. Everything inside him rejected her proposal, but the logic was insurmountable. He scrambled for a way to deny her request but found none.

"Then I will go with you," Daeson stated.

It was an absurd response, and everyone knew it. The fleet needed him at the helm and no place else. But Daeson couldn't bear the thought of losing her again, and he believed he was the only one that could truly protect her.

"Admiral, that would be unwise," Orlic said. "Forgive my boldness, but you just lectured Lieutenant Antos on the peril of actions governed by emotion."

"I volunteer to go with her," Tig said. "I know weapon systems and leadership structures. With Raviel's espionage skills and my military training, we will be successful."

Tig looked Daeson in the eye. "And we will return with the intel needed," Tig added.

Daeson became numb with the overwhelming logic of having to put his Raviel in harm's way once again. And this scenario was as threatening as it could get. He would be sending her into the heart of a ruthless enemy. The occupants of the room waited in silence, their gazes convincing him of the role he knew he had to play…that of strong leader. Not finding the courage to speak the words he knew he must, he slowly nodded. Anger swelled within him. The others became uncomfortable as they witnessed the anguish of their commander.

"That's enough for today," Tig said. "We'll reconvene tomorrow at the same time."

The room quickly emptied…all except Daeson and Raviel. She stood up and walked around the table, carefully resting her hand on his shoulder.

He put his hand on hers but turned his head away, hiding the eyes of a leader in fear. "I can't lose you again," he said softly. All of the emotions of those dark months without her crashed in upon his emotional shore, and the tears welled in his eyes. "Do you know what I went through, believing I had killed you...perhaps abandoning you to a dark, cold, lonely death in space?"

A tear trickled down his face as he thought of having to bear such pain again. He felt so weak...so vulnerable. He was supposed to be the fearless leader that was going to conquer a world, yet here he was, paralyzed with the fear of potential loss. Raviel circled to the front of his chair, knelt down on one knee, and pulled his face toward hers. He tried to steel himself, but it just wasn't there. "I'm not strong enough for this," he whispered.

Raviel's eyes glowed with admiration. "Yes, you are, Daeson, because I'm coming back. Our love brought you to me when I was lost in space, and it will bring me back to you."

Daeson gazed into Raviel's beautiful soul once more and found the courage to move forward. He pulled her into his embrace and held her tightly. "If anything goes wrong," he whispered in her ear, "I'm coming for you, and nothing in this galaxy will stop me."

Raviel sank into the arms of her bonded. Daeson's quiet words of promise filled her soul with contentment, for she could not deny the fear that lingered in her heart. She knew she needed to be strong for Daeson, even if it meant denying her own apprehensions. She held on tightly to him, not yet daring to look into his eyes. As bonded, they often could discern a need of the other before they themselves knew the need. He would know if she faltered in her courageous act. He might already suspect her fears, and perhaps it is why he spoke those words. Whatever his thoughts, she needed to hear his words of promise.

Rationally, Raviel knew that she had only been trapped in space for just a few hours while traveling at near-light speed, and she had been unconscious for most of that. But somewhere in the recesses of her mind, it felt like she had lived three hundred years in isolation. She couldn't explain it. Daeson had been without her for months, but she had been without him for centuries...alone and adrift. The quantum anomaly that Avidan had described had changed her, and she didn't dare tell Daeson. There were moments when she felt like she was slipping away again. Was it real or was it the lingering shadows of psychological pain? She couldn't tell, nor could she describe it. She just knew that something was broken inside her and might never be fixed.

She donned a countenance of strength once more and pulled back from Daeson. He reached for her cheek. His eyes were different now...stronger.

"You're an amazing woman, Raviel Starlore."

She stood and lifted him up with her. She rested her head on his chest. "You just keep telling yourself that," she said with a smile.

After leaving Daeson, Raviel searched out Tig and found him talking with Kyrah.

"Am I interrupting?" Raviel asked.

"Nope," Kyrah said, flashing a quick smile her way. "Just discussing training requirements for forcetech. I'm meeting the chief, so I'll catch you two later."

Raviel watched as Kyrah disappeared through a corridor hatch. "Is she upset?" Raviel asked.

"Yep," Tig said. "But she's an officer and she'll be okay. She can't get over not protecting Avidan."

Tig looked over at Raviel. "How's he doing?" Tig asked.

Raviel wagged her head. "He'll be fine. He just needs some time to accept it." She looked over at Tig. "You ready for another adventure?"

Tig laughed. "Let's just hope this one turns out better than the last. I don't think there would be any restraining Daeson if something goes wrong this time."

Raviel nodded. "I'm afraid you're right. Let's get to planning, shall we?"

Tig held out his arm, pointing down the hall to the mission planning room.

"Lead the way."

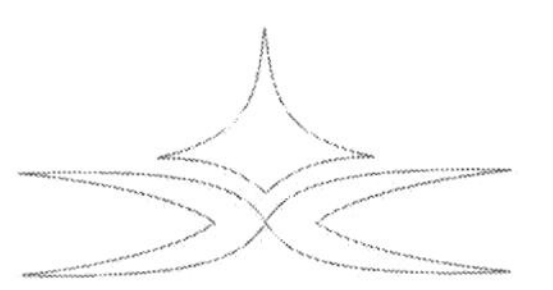

CHAPTER 12

Spies in a Land of Terror

In spite of the ever-present sorrow that many of their people were suffering under the bondage of slavery by a ruthless tyrant and his wicked people, an energy filled the hearts of every Raylean in the fleet as they worked toward the common goal of restoration and deliverance for their people in chains. Daeson, Tig, and Raviel began training pilots in earnest as Orlic, Kyrah, and Chief Bern began a massive arms and weapons training program for every able-bodied Raylean.

Hundreds of trading expeditions were sent forth into the Medarra Cluster. Just as Daeson had surmised, their gain was slow at first, but with each trade and return to the fleet, the scitechs exploited and advanced their technology prowess as the traders discovered what was in highest demand. Within a few weeks, the fleet had made remarkable progress in repairing and equipping their ships. Some of their most remarkable technology came from the Immortals through the gateway. One small but incredibly advanced power cell might spawn hundreds of other developments. The scitechs would then exploit and maximize the application of this new tech to advance their leverage in the next round of trades.

Perhaps the most significant Immortal contribution was a sophisticated tech design that allowed the scitechs to perfect their replicators. With the right elemental resources, they were able to reproduce and replicate any device or weapon, and trading for natural resources was accomplished with relative ease compared to trading for weapon systems. Larger components and craft were beyond the scope of replicating, but within a couple of months, the value of the trades had escalated to small fighter crafts and critical engine parts for repairing their transports. They found it necessary to venture beyond the Medarra Cluster to gain access to such resources and weaponry, but the Raylean traders did so with great courage and success. Kayn-4 remained unreachable, for word had begun to spread of the growing influence of the Rayleans in the region. Prefect Verdok became wary, knowing that many if not most of his slaves had come from this growing threat. Security on Kayn-4 and in particular the region of Reekojah was increased and tightened. Daeson knew it was time to send Tig and Raviel before their window of opportunity had closed for good.

One evening, Daeson asked Raviel to meet him on the observation deck. It was the place he had come to mourn so many times...so long ago and not so long ago. Raviel was met at the door by Rivet, who was wearing a waiter's coat with a napkin draped over his arm. Raviel burst into laughter.

Rivet stared at Raviel for a few seconds as she continued to laugh, his ever-steady android countenance unchanging.

"This is me smirking," Rivet said, then lifted his hand to point the way. "Welcome, Lady Raviel. Your table is ready," the android added.

"Rivet...you still have a sense of humor!" Raviel exclaimed.

"I'm glad you approve...please come with me."

Rivet led her to a cloth-covered table positioned in front of the gloriously brilliant view of the entire Aurora galaxy. Daeson smiled as he pulled out her chair.

"Had I known, I would have worn something more appropriate that I absolutely don't have," she said with a sly smile.

She sat down and waited for Daeson to sit across from her.

"Dinner will be served in 3.2 minutes," Rivet stated then left.

For a moment they just looked at each other. Daeson wanted to remember every detail of her face. Her mission could be a long one.

"This isn't necessary, you know," Raviel said. "I'm going to be all right."

"I know," Daeson acknowledged. "But technically, I've missed two hundred and seventy-one anniversaries of our bonding, and I thought I should try to start making them up."

Raviel laughed, and Daeson loved to hear it.

He reached out his hand, and she took it as he shook his head. "Do you remember on Mesos...when I almost died and you nursed me back to health? I yearned to hold your hand and couldn't."

Raviel squeezed his hand.

He looked into her eyes. "Please don't take any unnecessary risks when you're down there," Daeson pleaded. "Promise me."

Raviel pierced his heart with eyes that warmed his soul. "I promise...I'm coming back to you...I promise."

"Dinner is served," Rivet announced.

For the rest of the evening, Daeson and Raviel put aside the relentless and immense burdens of the fleet and allowed themselves a brief but joyous time of respite.

The next morning Daeson, the captains, and Rivet gathered to send-off Raviel and Tig.

"Are you sure about having us take Viper One?" Tig asked. "It's by far the fleet's strongest fighter for defense."

"Perhaps," Daeson replied, "but with Verdok on the watch, Viper One may be the only craft that can get near to their capital. We haven't been able to duplicate its cloaking technology yet, so...she's yours."

Tig nodded and asked Daeson to verify the Starcraft's upgraded specifications as Rivet approached Raviel.

"Lady Raviel, please be careful...I don't want to have to take care of him by myself."

Raviel laughed. "Rivet, even now, I don't think I will ever stop being amazed by you."

"Nor I by you, my lady," Rivet said with a bow. "May Ell Yon be with you."

Each of the other captains, in turn, shook their hands and wished them well. Daeson pulled Raviel aside to have a private moment with her. He kept it brief, not wanting to let the goodbye ruin him. As Raviel stepped away, he saw Tig reach for Kyrah's arm.

"I'll find Avidan," Tig said quietly to her.

Kyrah looked as if she were about to break down. She swallowed hard and nodded her thanks, then steeled herself.

Tig and Raviel climbed aboard Daeson's Starcraft and started up the engines. Once the docking bay was clear, the doors opened. With a final salute from both, Tig pushed up the throttles, and they were gone. Daeson's heart hurt. For him, time didn't seem to heal this pain...it only made it worse. At least he would be in constant communication with them via the quantum entanglement communicator. It was small compensation.

Raviel felt nearly whole again. The thrill of the mission helped to keep her focused, especially knowing just how critical their intel would be to the fleet. She and Tig had spent weeks planning and identifying goals for the mission.

From the little they did know about Kayn-4, Reekojah was the most fortified and protected region. The capital city and a portion of the surrounding land were protected by some sort of energy field dome. This would be their primary objective—to discover its power source, its technology, its strengths and its weaknesses. Finding a way to disable or destroy the energy dome would be critical if they were going to gain access to the city and free their people. As they approached the first gateway, Raviel began to tremble, remembering the horror of nearly losing her grip on this spacetime. Tig seemed to sense her apprehension and slowed the Starcraft.

"Are you okay, Raviel?" he asked.

Raviel took a few deep breaths, trying desperately to get on top of her growing dread as the gateway drew nearer and nearer. The pain and the cold were a very real terror to her. "Yeah…I think so," she finally called back.

Tig hesitated, giving her another few seconds. "Roger."

He punched the throttles, and just as she was about to ask him to stop, the gateway swallowed them. Raviel's stomach rose to her throat. She squeezed her hands into fists, and closed her eyes. The pain would be her first indication, but there was none. Slowly she opened her eyes and beheld the beautiful display of streaking stars flying swiftly past their canopy. She steadied her breathing and relaxed.

"Exit gateway in ten seconds."

They exited the gateway on the fringe of the Kayn System, and Raviel felt completely whole. She took a deep cleansing breath, knowing she was going to be all right for the rest of the journey. *Got that over with…now I can focus on the mission,* she thought.

As soon as they exited the gateway, Tig immediately engaged the Starcraft's advanced cloaking tech and set coordinates for Kayn-4. Tig approached the planet cautiously.

"Looks like they have at least a dozen patrols in orbit to welcome us," Tig spoke over the com.

"Yes, I see that. I sure hope this cloak is bullet-proof," Raviel returned.

Tig made a gentle entry through the atmosphere, trying not to leave too much of a traceable heat signature. The landing required more fuel than usual, but the mitigation of risk was worth it. They arrived at their predetermined landing site, a small clearing in a secluded, forested landscape. No habitations or roadways were nearby, so the Starcraft should remain safe, but there was a price to pay for such security...it was a full day's journey to the capital city of Reekojah through unknown country.

Raviel quickly connected the extra power cell they had brought and energized it so that the Starcraft's cloaking tech could remain on for the two weeks they would be away. They finalized their packs, checked the charges on their weapons, and set out for Reekojah. Tig was carrying a plasma rifle and Raviel a Talon. Although the rifle was a bit more conspicuous, Tig remembered some frightful stories about the predatory creatures that roamed the uninhabited regions of the planet from his earlier visit with Trisk, and Daeson had insisted they take a weapon with enough punch to ensure their protection.

Although the forest was dense, the undergrowth was minimal so that the land was still navigable. Both Tig and Raviel were stunned by the sheer size of some of the trees. One particular species averaged 50 feet in diameter and nearly 400 feet tall. Coarse ribbons of dark brown bark with diamond-like patterns ran from the roots up as far as they could see. The lofty branches sported thick green and blue foliage creating a beautiful lush canopy that nearly obscured all sunlight. Often, they became mesmerized by the tree's luminous seeds that would slowly spiral down on umbrella-like structures from the tree's lofty limbs. Later they discovered this species was called Magalla Lumen. Woodland creatures of all sizes and shape scurried away from them as they trespassed through their home. Raviel stopped to catch an umbrella seed in her palm just as a distant alien screech filled the walls of the forest. Some of the traders had brought back stories of huge flying creatures called Terridons that supposedly inhabited this region. Occasionally Raviel had seen gashes across the trunks of the massive trees that left no doubt as to the existence of such fabled winged creatures. Chills flitted up and down her spine as she and Tig looked at each other with wide eyes.

"Let's make sure we make the city before nightfall, shall we?" Tig said

"Agreed!" Raviel returned. She blew the luminous seed off her palm and quickened her pace.

Although the forest was a bit daunting for them to travel through, it did afford good cover for nearly three-fourths of their journey to Reekojah. By midafternoon, Tig calculated that they were nearing the edge of the forest.

"Let's take a break and get some food and water in us before we tackle the last leg," Tig said as he swung his pack off and set it up against one of the massive trees.

Raviel was thankful for the break, but she also didn't like being pampered.

"You don't need to go easy on me, Tig," Raviel said with a grin. "I'm one hundred percent now."

"I understand," he replied. "It's just wise to be refreshed and alert when we enter enemy territory."

Raviel nodded and sat down next to her pack, leaning up against the rough bark. She lifted a canteen of water to her lips and swallowed the cool liquid with delight. Tig remained standing but reached for his canteen and drank heavily as well. He wiped his lips with the back of his hand.

"Our biggest challenge is going to be making entrance through Reekojah's main gate," Tig said screwing the lid back on his canteen. "They're going to be looking for us."

Raviel finished with another long swig.

"No doubt," Raviel agreed. "I still think our best bet is to become familiar with the gate markets on the outside, then figure out a way to get inside. It may take us a few days, but our patience will pay off." Raviel pulled a protein stick out and ripped a piece off with her teeth.

Tig nodded. "I hope the tech you've packed will—"

Just then Raviel felt the ground rumble all around her. Deep, guttural sound oscillations pounded through the air, rattling her from the inside out. She flung an arm through one of the straps on her pack, and Tig reached out a hand to her. She took it, as he nearly catapulted her up and away from the trunk of the tree. When Raviel turned back around to see what was happening, the coarse, dark-brown bark of the tree began to move. Tig grabbed his pack while simultaneously charging his plasma rifle.

A second later the air around them erupted with an ear-piercing screech that would have paralyzed normal people. Raviel drew her Talon and charged it as Tig joined her in a sprint away from the tree. Raviel chanced a look over her shoulder and saw a Terridon unwrap its wings from around the tree, shedding its perfect, dark-colored, diamond-shaped camouflage. They had unwittingly stopped to rest right beneath a slumbering Terridon with its foot-long talons imbedded into the tree. What frightened Raviel the most was the horned head that was now fixing its fiery eyes on them from above. The creature looked like a giant lizard with wings. Raviel had seen similar hand-sized creatures back on Jypton, but they weighed much less than six hundred pounds. The Terridon released its grip on the tree, spread its twenty-five-foot wings and began a frighteningly swift dive upon them.

"Ninety-degree split!" Tig shouted.

They each planted a foot, turned ninety degrees from each other, and began sprinting at right angles from the attack azimuth of the Terridon. This forced the creature to choose one or the other...it chose Raviel. In spite of its size, the monster was quite aerodynamically agile. With one powerful beat of its muscled wings, it turned midair and was nearly on Raviel within just a couple of seconds. Raviel felt as if the Terridon was about to swallow her whole, so she dove behind the trunk of one of the giant trees just as she heard Tig's plasma rifle discharge. The Terridon responded with an angry screech, turning its horny head towards Tig.

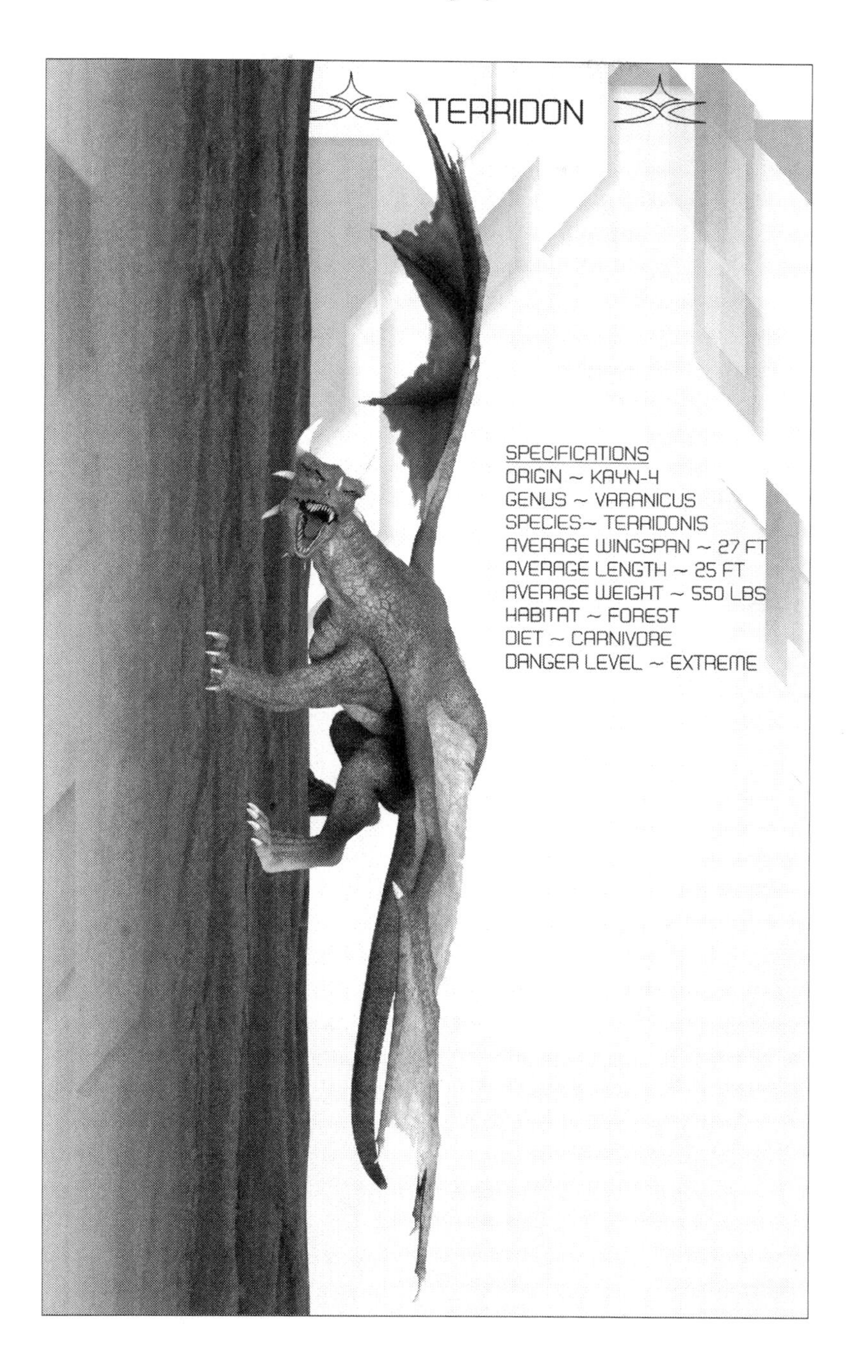
TERRIDON
SPECIFICATIONS
ORIGIN ~ KAYN-4
GENUS ~ VARANICUS
SPECIES~ TERRIDONIS
AVERAGE WINGSPAN ~ 27 FT
AVERAGE LENGTH ~ 25 FT
AVERAGE WEIGHT ~ 550 LBS
HABITAT ~ FOREST
DIET ~ CARNIVORE
DANGER LEVEL ~ EXTREME

The Terridon made a tight turn around the tree where Raviel was hiding, zeroing in now on Tig. He shot again while Raviel shot two rounds from her Talon from behind the creature. Two of the three hit their mark. The angry Terridon seemed confused and frustrated by food that fought back so painfully. It beat its wings twice more, changing its flight path upward at a near vertical trajectory. Within seconds, it had pierced the lofty green and blue canopy and was gone. Tig and Raviel rejoined, both breathing heavily.

"Are you okay?" he asked.

"Yeah...you?"

Tig nodded, trying to catch his breath. "Well, that was terrifying. I guess we'd better be a little more aware of the trees now that we know where they rest."

They resumed their course toward Reekojah, exiting the edge of the forest by late afternoon. The upper portion of the dome was visible even from fifteen miles out. The closer they got to the dome, the more dwellings and people they began to see. At ten miles out they caught their first clear view of the shimmering dome that protected the massive city of Reekojah and thousands of acres of outlying land. With each mile they traveled the spectacle of this technological wonder became a marvel to behold. Raviel wondered if Tig felt as intimidated by it as she. The sheer size and power of such a massive energy field was staggering to behold. A mile out they stopped and just gawked at what they saw. A perfectly half-spherical energy dome comprised of honeycomb subfields glimmered in blue and orange hues left to right from horizon to horizon. Its base was a solid fifty-foot-tall wall that must have housed the energy transmitters, not unlike the arena back at the fleet except on a scale that was a thousand times larger.

"Can you imagine the power station required to generate a field like this?" Raviel said.

"It must be massive," Tig remarked.

"I'm guessing it's smack dab in the middle," Raviel said. "Look there."

Raviel pointed to the center of the slightly obscured outline of the city within the dome. The cityscape was as grand as any other with aero-craft scurrying from one part of the city to the other. They could see a stream of unending energy fountaining upward from one tall structure in the middle of the city. The beam of energy rose up hundreds of feet into the air meeting the top of the dome.

"Ah...yes," Tig said. "That must be its power source and the perimeter wall must house the energy directional antennas."

"Exactly," Raviel said. "The scope of it is incredible. It must be nearly 10 miles in diameter."

Tig glanced over at Raviel.

"A little overwhelming, isn't it?" he asked.

"Yes...yes, it is," Raviel replied. "But inside are tens of thousands of our people."

"And Ell Yon is with us," Tig reminded.

Raviel smiled. "I see the gate...shall we take a closer look?"

Tig nodded.

Something in the back of Raviel's mind bothered her—just how crafty and devious was Prefect Verdok? How much did he already know? Did he have the ability to crush the Raylean rescue before it began?

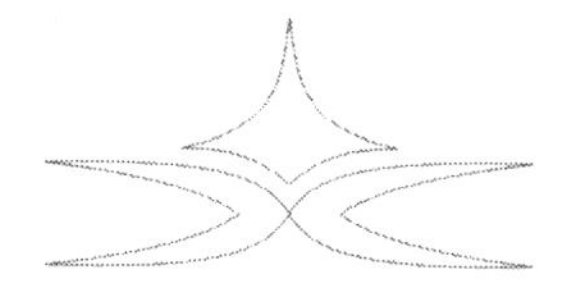

CHAPTER 13

The City of Glass

As Raviel and Tig approached the main entrance, they once again stood amazed. The city of Reekojah was centered under the dome, but buildings, dwellings, and farmland were scattered throughout the encapsulated perimeter. Many buildings and structures were built right up next to the edge of the dome. High up on the solid portion of the wall where the energy dome antennas were mounted, buildings meshed with the solid wall and even bordered the energy field itself. The domed habitat had four entrances. Each entrance allowed flying traffic to enter through a carefully controlled break in the dome's energy field, while also allowing grav vehicles and foot traffic through a passageway in the solid wall below. Raviel and Tig observed a steady stream of both aero and ground traffic through the larger main entrance. On either side of the roadway leading into the gate, shops and trading stalls enticed travelers to buy their wares.

The gate itself exhibited an extreme level of security and patrols. Tig and Raviel considered traveling to one of the other entrances, but the distance was so great that it would have been dark before they arrived. When Raviel and Tig approached the main entrance via the open market shops, they became immediately aware of watchful eyes and decided to turn back. They back-tracked to a small village, where they were able to secure a room and purchase a meal to eat. Posing as tech-traders, they continued to play their roles even when isolated in their room, until Raviel was able to scan for any listening devices. She gave Tig a thumbs-up and pulled out their QEC. Daeson would be waiting for a situation report or SITREP. She would have to compile the data and make their report quick—the adrenaline rush of the day and the lingering fatigue from her quantum anomaly event, though she admitted this to no one, were taking their toll.

Daeson paced back and forth on the bridge of the *Liberty*, waiting for Raviel and Tig's first SITREP. Letting Raviel go on this mission into the heart of enemy territory was one of the hardest things he'd had to do as a leader thus far, especially after having just rescued her from the quantum peril that had flung her two hundred seventy-one years into the future and nearly taken her life. He tried to occupy his time with the pressing duties of returning the fleet to operational status, but he could not keep his focus.

"Sky Guardian, this is Nighthawk." Raviel's voice burst through the QEC Daeson was holding. Although the QECs were completely secure since these two communicators were quantumly linked only to each other, it was decided that they would use call signs in case Tig and Raviel had been compromised or captured and the QEC fallen into enemy hands.

"Nighthawk, this is Sky Guardian. What's your status?" Daeson responded eagerly.

"We've made it to the perimeter of the dome. Access is proving to be difficult. Will attempt tomorrow once we've gathered more information."

Daeson wanted to ask how she was doing but knew exactly what she would say, regardless of the truth.

"I am transmitting images and logs now," Raviel continued.

Daeson went to his chair and set the QEC in its cradle.

"Ensign, put the data on screen," he said to his communications officer.

A few seconds later, images of the dome appeared on their main monitor as meticulous log notes appeared in a sub-window. The entire bridge was mesmerized by what Raviel had recorded.

"That entrance into the city looks quite large," Daeson commented. "Are you sure flying your cloaked Starcraft in wouldn't work?"

"We considered it." Tig's voice was now being transmitted. "But we're pretty sure they have extremely sensitive heat signature detectors that might give us away. Besides that, we didn't know if there was a secure place to set down. I believe ground entry or by one of their shuttles is the only way."

"Copy that, Nighthawk. Be careful when attempting that entry," Daeson said unnecessarily.

"Will do, Sky Guardian," Raviel's voice returned. "Our next transmission will be in twenty-four hours. Nighthawk out."

It was difficult for Daeson to end the transmission.

"Sky Guardian out."

Daeson lifted the QEC from its cradle while staring at the massive dome protecting their enemy's grandest city...a wall that kept his people as prisoners. As technologically marvelous as the dome was, it made him angry. He could only imagine the plight of his fellow Rayleans, and many of them so young. An urgency welled up inside him that fueled his desire to accelerate their training and preparations. He called for a meeting of the captains and chieftains to discuss their progress. Ultimately their success in defeating the Reekojans lay in the intel that Raviel and Tig were gathering and hoped to yet gather. Their success could very well determine the future of the Rayleans.

After the meeting adjourned, four of the chieftains asked to meet with Daeson privately.

"Admiral Navi, we would like to know your thoughts on something we've been talking to Master Scitech Olin about," Chieftain Porl began.

"Okay...regarding what exactly?" Daeson asked.

The four chieftains looked back and forth to one another, apparently a bit sheepish about their request.

"With our replicator technology nearly perfected because of the Malakians, we feel it would be prudent to consider replicating—" the man hesitated, which frustrated Daeson immensely.

"Replicating what?" Daeson urged.

"The Protector."

Daeson blinked, speechless. The Protector? Were they serious?

"I see," he finally responded. He looked down at the Immortal tech on his forearm. Though at first it seemed like an appalling idea, their concerns regarding its preservation were indeed valid. "But it's Immortal technology...from the hand of the Sovereign himself. We don't even understand how it works."

"That's true," agreed one of the other chieftains. "But Master Olin tells us that we don't need to understand it to replicate it. The replicator simply repeats and builds what is already there."

"Hmm," Daeson voiced as he stroked his chin. "I need to think this over and petition the Sovereign for any guidance. Give me until tomorrow."

"Yes, Admiral...of course. Thank you," Chieftain Porl replied.

Early the next morning, Daeson met with the four chieftains and Master Scitech Olin. "I haven't received any guidance from the Sovereign in regard to your request, so

I've come to the conclusion that you're welcome to try. It makes sense that we should have a backup…if possible."

The four chieftains appeared relieved, and Olin looked delighted.

"It will take my team and me a few hours to analyze its composition and then a day to replicate it," Olin explained. "We can return it to you after the analysis, however."

"Very well," Daeson agreed as he pulled the seamless technological marvel from his arm and offered it to Master Olin. He held it as if it were a treasure of immeasurable worth—and it was.

By late afternoon of the following day, Daeson, the four chieftains, and Master Olin and his scitech team had gathered in the scitech lab. Olin was smiling as he held out a case for Daeson to open. Daeson slid a metallic pearl-colored lid from off the case to reveal what looked like a perfect replica of the Protector he was wearing on his arm. He lifted the replica out of the case and inspected it closely.

"Remarkable!" he exclaimed. "You were able to completely replicate every detail."

Master Olin's smile faded. "All but one constituent, but it's 98.3 percent complete."

"Which constituent?" Daeson asked as he pulled the original Protector from his arm and handed it to Master Olin.

Daeson took the replica and held it over his forearm. He pushed it downward, and it yielded, forming perfectly around his arm just as the original had.

"Omeganite," Olin stated as they all looked on with amazement.

Daeson held out his arm and inspected the replica, testing its fluidic movement. It felt just like the original, but something was indeed missing. He waited for the synaptic interface, but it wasn't there. He pulled the replica off, and it yielded. He gave it back to Olin.

"It's quite remarkable, but he's not there," Daeson said bluntly. "The voice of the Sovereign is not there. I think you need the omeganite."

Scitech Olin frowned.

"Unfortunately, that's quite impossible," Olin replied. "Even in the smallest of quantities, it's deadly to us. We can't collect omeganite, nor could we infuse it into the protective jewel that the original Protector seems to use to encapsulate it."

Daeson took the original Protector back and pushed it onto his arm. The presence of Ell Yon immediately filled him.

"Now we know," he said.

The next morning, Tig and Raviel went to settle their room fee with the housing manager.

"We're new to Kayn-4 and are interested in doing some tech trading in Reekojah. Are there any shuttles that can take us there?" Raviel asked.

The housing manager hesitated, eyeing them suspiciously. Tig slipped three extra credits on top of the requested fee.

"Shuttles leave the dispatch station every hour…it's just a mile up the road. Takes you straight to Market Street."

Raviel and Tig turned to leave.

"Hey," the man called out. "They'll be scanning for weapons, so you'd better mind that," he said, nodding to Tig's plasma rifle. "Secure storage lockers are located along the way. I'd check 'em or you'll lose 'em."

"Thanks," Raviel said.

They made their way toward the dispatch station and found a secure storage facility just a short distance away. Although they were both leery about leaving their weapons, they certainly couldn't afford any undue attention. They wondered what else might be required to board.

A few minutes later they arrived at the dispatch station. They stood in a short line, waiting for a Reekojan sentry to scan them. A second sentry was at a table operating a glass console.

"Insert your IDs and state your intentions within the city." The sentry at the table didn't look up as he spoke the words, like he had already said them hundreds of times that day.

"Tech trading," Tig said as they inserted their IDs. They had worked closely with the traders back at the fleet to acquire fake IDs they said would pass on Reekojah.

"How long will you be in the city?"

Raviel held her breath as the device scanned their IDs.

"Ten days."

A few seconds later, the green "PASS" light illumined. Raviel quietly recovered her breathing.

"Any profit-yielding trades must be claimed and fees paid before departure. Step through the bio scanner...next!"

Tig stepped through the scanner and cleared without incident. Raviel stepped through, and a red alarm blared. The sentry by the scanner pulled her aside to an area with a table. This sentry was fully engaged—Raviel began to sweat.

"Empty your contents," the sentry ordered.

After a few minutes of rifling through her pack, he sorted out two of her devices...the QEC and a miniature Malakian power cell.

"What are these?" he asked, hard blue eyes staring through her.

"A bio scanner and a power cell."

The sentry scowled. He took the QEC and scanned it with a hand-held device. He threw it back onto her pile of devices. He then scanned the power cell, and an alarm on his hand-held went off.

"The energy level of this power cell doesn't fall within the dimensionally acceptable range," the sentry stated coldly. "I'll have to report you and confiscate this device."

"That's why it's so valuable for tech trading." Raviel leaned in toward the man. "We have a source for these that will make us and whoever is willing to invest rich." Raviel let a subtle smile cross her lips.

The sentry's countenance eased slightly as he glanced toward the other sentry who was busy processing more passengers thirty feet away.

"How rich?" the sentry asked.

Tig stepped forward, blocking the view from the other sentry. He laid a generous number of credits on the table.

"This rich," he said quietly. "And more on our next trip."

The sentry swallowed. He took one more quick glance toward his occupied counterpart then scooped the credits off the table and shoved the power cell back into Raviel's bag.

"You're clear to board," the sentry said tersely, returning to his station at the scanner.

Raviel quickly finished gathering her devices and boarded with Tig. They found two seats away from any other passengers and sat down. Raviel's heart was pounding. That was close...too close.

"I guess bribery goes a long way here," Tig said softly.

Raviel took a deep breath and exhaled, calming herself for the next encounter.

The ride on the shuttle through the dome's main entrance was revealing. They took note of every detail, capturing as many images as possible without appearing too suspicious. After a twenty-minute flight, the shuttle settled onto another dispatch station's landing pad. This station was large, with over thirty landing pads designed for shuttles traversing the city in all directions and through each of the four dome entrances. Once they exited the shuttle, the perceived beauty of the majestic city of Reekojah disappeared in an instant. Within the walls of the city, the evidence of harsh slavery was everywhere. Bio-collars with amber lighting were secured around the necks of every slave, and there were many. Even though it was still early morning, an atmosphere of debauchery permeated the city, which could only be explained by a culture-wide overdose of Deitum Prime. The wealthy of the city were garishly clothed in brightly colored fabrics that often clashed in a painful display. High-collared shirts and blouses, painted faces, and jewel-festooned fingers and necks left no doubt as to who the elite of Reekojah were. The traders most often were arrayed in drab long coats or functional work attire, but occasionally traders from more prosperous planets could be identified by their more professional dress.

Although their true goal was to recon the city structure itself and in particular the dome's energy field, Tig and Raviel needed to sell their cover as traders, knowing that their IDs would be monitored for any trades made. Market Street was in and of itself its own grand spectacle of commerce—food, clothing, spices, exotic materials, small machinery, specialized tech devices, and even weapons, although every weapon sold was disabled and without power cells in accordance with city trading ordinances. The market spanned dozens of thoroughfares and was nothing short of managed chaos. Although the fabulous metal and glass towers of the city were always visible from any avenue, the shops and buildings on Market Street were comprised of moderate modern architecture meshed with vestiges of mud and earth structures from a trade industry centuries old.

Raviel and Tig spent most of the morning getting familiar with the market's layout and expected trading practices. Every shop, stall, and thoroughfare cascaded a continual digression of spirit for Raviel, and she sensed the same for Tig. The gleeful lust for money, pleasure and power in the Reekojan citizens contrasted with the sorrowful faces of the enslaved was unbearable. The two friends knew that many—perhaps most—of these slaves were their Raylean brothers and sisters. Even though Raviel and Tig were "new" to their people in this time, there was no loss of emotional sympathy for the wretched condition of their people. Raviel found herself continually trying to quell her anger so that her cover would not be ruined.

After three hours of navigating through the square, they found an eatery to stop at for a meal. They found a table in the corner that provided some privacy. Both she and Tig sat in silence for a time, processing everything they had seen.

"Can I take your order?"

The quiet voice of a young girl jolted them out of their musings. Raviel looked up into the somber countenance of the girl, her eyes echoing the ache of bondage. Raviel knew that look all too well. She had seen it for twenty years on Jypton, but here it was even worse. The amber ribbon of light pulsed on her slave collar. Raviel tried to smile but felt foolish for even trying.

"What's good?" Tig asked.

The girl looked his way, struggling to appear cordial. She glanced back toward the kitchen, where the burly owner was watching with scornful eyes. The girl pasted on a fake smile.

"I recommend the turion steak with our special spices."

"That sounds perfect," Tig replied. "We'll take two and something mild to drink."

The girl nodded and returned to the man in the kitchen. Raviel noticed that their order seemed to please him, which gave the girl great relief. A few minutes later, the girl returned with their drinks. As she placed them on the table, Raviel looked up at the young lass.

"Where are you from?" she asked.

The girl looked stunned. She glanced again toward the kitchen, but the man was fully occupied in preparing their food. Her chin dropped and her gaze fell to the floor. She hesitated.

"I am from the Raylean colony in the Ianis System." Her voice was nearly imperceptible. She momentarily made eye contact with Raviel before turning to leave.

"Wait," Raviel said. "How long have you been here?"

The question nearly ruined the girl. "Just over six months," her voice quavered, then she quickly turned and left.

"Be careful," Tig said quietly.

"I know…I just—"

"I get it," Tig said. "It hurts to see, but that's why we're here…to put an end to this horror."

Raviel nodded.

When the girl returned with their food, Raviel said nothing, even though the girl lingered a bit and looked directly at Raviel's face more than once. It tore Raviel's heart in two. Although the meat dish was truly delicious, Raviel could hardly eat it. When the girl returned to collect the money for the meal, she looked once more toward Raviel, a yearning for the smallest shred of hope. When Raviel said nothing, the girl reached for the credits Tig had placed on the table. Raviel reached out and touched the girl's hand.

"Ell Yon has not forgotten you…don't lose hope."

The girl's grave countenance shifted to one of astonishment, then timid hope, her eyes brimming with tears. Raviel lifted a finger to her lips, and the girl nodded. She fought to compose herself as she collected the last few credits. Pushing the moisture to the corners of her eyes, she took a breath and turned away.

Raviel looked at Tig, knowing what she had just done was foolish. He stood, and she followed. Outside the eatery, they walked in silence. Once clear, Raviel looked over at Tig again.

"I'm sorry…I know that was foolish. I just couldn't leave her in such despair."

Tig nodded. "It's okay. She needed that reminder, and so did I," he said with a smile. "We'd better make a couple of trades today so we don't look suspicious."

They walked toward the specialized tech market, which was nearly half a mile long. Reekojan patrols were now a consistent presence throughout the market, so they did their best to avoid them. As they passed one market stall, they overheard two men talking about the patrols.

"Never been this many in the market before," one gruff voice commented.

"Yeah. Word has it they're on the lookout for someone."

"Ha! Don't think they'll have much luck in this rabble."

Raviel and Tig walked on, looking for a stall where they could make a trade at that wouldn't draw any attention.

"Hey…take a look at these gems," one stall owner called out. "We've got non-invasive micro genetic scanners…no one else in the Medarra Cluster has these."

A barrel-chested man threw a crooked smile their way. His eyes gleamed with anticipatory delight at the prospect of a sale.

Raviel and Tig walked to see the device. The man handed it to Raviel, understanding in an instant by the look in her eyes that she was the one to engage. Raviel eyed the sleek instrument, turning it over multiple times as she analyzed it. She was impressed with the technology, but it would do them little good.

"It is impressive, but what we need are hydronic pulse purifiers and compact O-2 reclaimers. Have you got anything like that?" she asked handing his device back to him.

The man's face soured in an instant. "I specialize in bio-tech. How about a sub-dermal augmented endorphin implant or a retinal image capture implant? I can even perform the insertions myself."

Raviel winced a smile then shook her head. "Not what we're looking for today."

The man grunted his disapproval. Raviel turned to join Tig.

"Hey…you might find a reclaimer over there," the man said, pointing a short distance down the thoroughfare. "Tell him, Faldon sent you…and that he owes me!"

Raviel nodded, then she and Tig made their way toward the market stall he had pointed to. This particular thoroughfare was quickly becoming crowded, and they found themselves weaving between other traders to make their way. They passed by a slender but striking woman with dark red hair, toting a grav-cart, but the push of the crowd caused Raviel to stumble into the woman.

"I beg your pardon," Raviel said, trying to recover and to avoid being tongue-lashed by another arrogant Reekojan.

The woman looked slightly older than Raviel. She lifted her chin and glared at Raviel first, then Tig, her eyes narrowing to slits as she scanned them up and down. Raviel instantly became nervous.

"Come," Tig said, grabbing Raviel's arm. "Our trade is this way."

Raviel quickly moved beyond the woman.

"I don't know if I'm just paranoid or if everyone here is actually on the lookout for us," Raviel whispered to Tig.

When they arrived at the stall the other trader had pointed to, a slender man with unnatural purple-colored eyes glared at them from behind a counter laden with a variety of tech devices, including power cells. Raviel found it difficult to make eye contact with the man because of his unusual visage. She wondered what peculiar optic modifications the man had acquired for his eyes. Unlike their previous encounter, this man appeared quite apathetic toward Raviel and Tig.

"We're looking for an O-2 reclaimer. Faldon said we might find one here," Raviel said.

The man hesitated.

"I see you deal in power cells," she continued. "We've got a revolutionary power cell that will give you twice the power in half the space."

Raviel hoisted her pack on the counter and presented him with a down-graded version of the Malakian power cell the scitechs had created for her. The man did a precursory inspection of the power cell, and his eyes brightened.

"Let me see what I have," he said then disappeared into the shop behind him.

Raviel and Tig waited for what seemed to be too long. They became anxious and were just about to leave, but the man then reappeared carrying a small case.

"I have what you're looking for," the man said as he put the case on the counter. He smiled for the first time, but it only lasted a second. His eyes grew wide as he quickly pulled the unopened case off the counter and set it out of sight.

"Show me your identification."

A stern voice jolted Raviel and Tig from behind. They turned to see a sentry standing right behind them. His right hand was resting on the stock of his plasma rifle, which was hanging from his shoulder on a sling.

Raviel and Tig produced their IDs for the sentry.

"Is there a problem?" Tig asked.

The sentry scrutinized each of them as he scanned their IDs with a device he had removed from his belt. He looked at the results on his scanner then clipped it back onto his belt. He smirked at Tig.

"Yes, there's a problem. Your IDs don't check out. You need to come with me to the security complex." The sentry tightened his grip on his plasma rifle.

Raviel swallowed. She wondered what action Tig was considering.

"Our IDs were already scanned at the dispatch station, and they cleared just fine. There must be some kind of mistake," Tig said, taking a small step toward the sentry as he pointed at the IDs still in his hand.

Raviel recognized Tig's posture. She prepared herself, knowing this was going to end badly no matter what happened. Discovery meant the end of their mission and certain execution.

"This way...now!" the sentry said, pointing to their left with his plasma rifle.

Just as Tig was about to make his move, a voice startled them all.

"There you are!" The red-headed woman Raviel had stumbled into earlier came from behind the sentry and grabbed her arm.

"I told you I would give you the best deal in the market for that power cell. You should know better than to make a trade with this skug!" the woman said, scowling at the purple-eyed man.

He sneered back.

"Don't interfere, Hara! I'm taking these two in for interrogation. I've never seen 'em here before," the sentry interrupted.

The woman put her hands on her hips and glared at the sentry.

"Look here, Jabril, I'm not about to let you ruin one of the best trades I've made in months. I've been working on this a long time."

The sentry shook his head. "Go back to your shop and mind your own business. Let's go!" he started to shove Tig with the broad side of his rifle.

"How is Sulla enjoying her new implant I gave her?" Hara asked, her voice dripping with intent. "Be a shame to have your partner exposed to unnecessary scrutiny, don't you think?" she continued.

The sentry froze then turned to scowl at the woman, his face red with anger. He lifted a finger to point at Hara, but she reached out and gently put a hand on his, lowering it.

"Listen, Jabril," she said lowering her voice and turning him away from Raviel and Tig. "This deal is very important to me. Just walk away, and I can make it worth your while...I promise."

Her words seemed to abate the sentry's anger, but he still hesitated.

"Trust me...Sulla will be very pleased as well."

The sentry drew in a deep breath, let his plasma rifle hang back down to his waist and walked away. Hara turned back toward Raviel, Tig, and the purple-eyed man.

"Bosra," she called out. "What were you going to offer for the power cell?"

The man squinted. Raviel and Tig continued to watch and wait, not knowing this woman's intent. The man lifted the case back onto the counter and opened it. He spun it around to show them.

"A portable class one O-2 reclaimer...brand new," the man added.

Raviel inspected the unit as Hara stepped up beside her. Tig kept his eyes outward, now wary of other sentries potentially surprising them.

"It's a fair trade," Hara said. "I'd take it if I were you. I don't have a reclaimer to offer."

The purple-eyed man tilted his head. "What you got up your sleeve, Hara?"

"I don't need the power cell. The other tech she's got...that's what I'm after, so hurry up and make your deal."

"What other tech?" the man asked.

"Ah, ah, ah," Hara taunted. "That's mine. Now finish up."

Raviel and Bosra exchanged tech, then he scanned her ID to register the trade with the Reekojan regional trade center.

"It's been a pleasure doing business with you," the man said with a sly smile.

"Yeah, yeah," Hara urged. "Now let's get on with my business."

She turned and motioned for Tig and Raviel to follow, moving quickly up the thoroughfare without waiting for them. Raviel looked at Tig with a raised eyebrow. He shrugged.

"She got us out of a very dicey situation, so what have we got to lose?" he concluded.

Raviel nodded and followed after Hara. After traveling for thirty minutes, it became apparent that Hara was not taking them to her market street shop. Raviel hurried to catch up.

"Where are we going?" she asked.

"My dwelling," she replied, looking over at Raviel and Tig. "Any longer for you two in the market, and you were bound to be taken in. You stick out like a sore thumb."

Raviel frowned. Her response was alarming to say the least...for multiple reasons. Why would this woman risk her own security for two foreigners she had never met before? They continued on in silence. Hara eventually led them to the edge of a city garden.

"Wait here," she said then disappeared into a large building that looked like it housed thousands of grav vehicles. A few minutes later Hara arrived, driving a grav vehicle large enough for all three of them to ride in. When they entered, Hara held a finger up to her lips. Raviel and Tig sat in silence as Hara skirted through a throng of traffic and eventually to the outskirts of Reekojah. As they continued their journey, they neared the edge of the dome-protected section of the city where the dwellings were fewer. Hara turned into one that welcomed them with an opening bay door on one side. As was the case with other dwellings in this region, Hara's was nestled up against the lower solid wall of the dome, and the upper portion of the dwelling used the energy dome itself as part of the southern outer wall. Once the grav vehicle entered the bay and its door was shut, Hara led Raviel and Tig up two flights of stairs and into the sitting room of her dwelling. She held up a device and activated a small button on one side. After a few seconds, she clicked the button again and set the device down on the center table. Hara then turned to face Raviel and Tig. She eyed them once again, much like she had when they had first seen her.

"Why did you save us from that sentry?" Tig asked.

"Because if he had taken you in, that would have been the end of you," she replied. She crossed her arms. "You are from the Raylean colony, are you not?"

Tig looked over at Raviel.

"The entire city is looking for you," Hara continued. "We know the Rayleans are planning to invade, and I think that Prefect Verdok is actually quite afraid. There are...stories about the Immortal that protects you. Those stories make many of our people very anxious." Hara paused. "So, are you or are you not from the Raylean colony?"

Raviel and Tig still remained silent. Denying the accusation seemed foolish now, especially after having hesitated for more than a few seconds. But what if this was a trap by Verdok to get an easy confession from two Raylean spies.

"Why did you give the power cell trade to the other tech trader?" Raviel asked. She surmised that this answer could give her the insight she was needing.

"Because without a trade, your entrance into the city would become very suspicious. It wouldn't take long for Verdok to suspect you were here to spy on us. I gave the trade to purple-eyes because if I had made the trade, the sentries might put two and two together and begin to search for you here. For a few days, this should be reasonably safe as long as you're not being tracked."

Raviel looked over at Tig. He gave a subtle nod.

"Yes, we're from the Raylean colony, and we are grateful for your help."

Raviel wondered if she had just condemned their mission, but on the other hand, if Hara wasn't deceiving them, her aid would be invaluable.

"Well, in that case let me introduce you to someone," Hara said with a smile.

Raviel and Tig tensed as Hara pressed a com button on her wrist bracelet. Raviel instantly regretted her confession, realizing that she had already violated the number one rule the Plexus had taught her back on Jypton...trust no one!

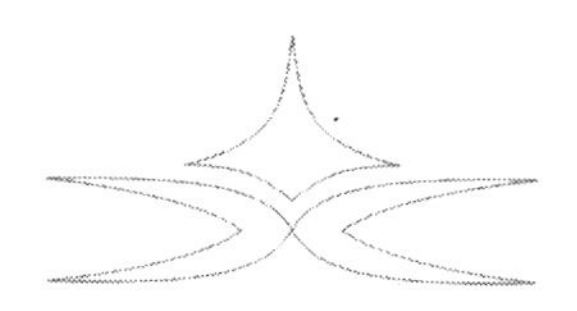

CHAPTER 14

The Horrors of Reekojah

Daeson immersed himself in the work of preparing for war in order to keep his mind occupied. Whenever he dwelled too long on Raviel, he would convince himself that he had made the wrong decision to send her. What if her recovery from the quantum anomaly was temporary? What if she had an incident in the middle of Reekojah? There would be no way he could get to her in time. Such anxious thoughts bred irrational responses, so he filled his days with activity instead.

With both Tig and Raviel gone, the training of pilots fell primarily on his shoulders. Two pilots in the aerotech order, Makson and Fi, had distinguished themselves early on in the training. Daeson focused on qualifying them as instructors as quickly as possible, knowing that delegation of training was absolutely necessary. He just had to make sure that the quality of training was not diminished in the throes of rapid preparations. Although Makson's and Fi's flying skills and even their weapon deployment were quite satisfactory, what they lacked was the ability to coordinate their flying with other craft. Once Daeson was able to demonstrate the advantages of coordinated attacks and flight teamwork strategies, their skill as fighter pilots reached a whole new level.

When Daeson wasn't conducting flight training, he was organizing and managing resource acquisition and leadership training for each of the other tech orders. He also continued to work closely with the scitechs to ensure they had a significant technology advantage over anything they might see when proceeding to battle with Reekojah and the other forces they would encounter on Kayn-4. In spite of his fervent activity, Daeson could not help anticipating the QEC call from Raviel each night. Hearing her voice gave him the courage to move into the next day.

After pressing the com button on her wrist bracelet, Hara looked toward one of the doorways. Raviel looked toward Tig, wondering if they should make their move before it was too late.

"Mommy!" shouted the squeaky voice of a child. Raviel nearly jumped out of her skin.

A little girl ran into the room and into the arms of Hara, who knelt down to catch her. In just a few seconds, the woman had transformed from shrewd tech trader to tender mother. Right behind the girl came a little boy who looked to be about six. And behind him entered an elderly woman with silver-streaked hair who bore a striking resemblance to Hara.

Hara hugged the little girl, a broad smile on her face. The little boy leaned into Hara and added his arms to the hug.

"This is my family," Hara said proudly. "This is Zee and this young man is Vander." Hara looked toward the older woman. "This is my mother Aubrin." She then looked at Tig and Raviel, her countenance sobering. "I will help you with whatever you are trying to accomplish here in Reekojah on one condition...when your people come, you must spare my family."

Raviel walked over to Hara and knelt down so she could see the children eye to eye.

"Hi, little ones," Raviel said gently. She fought back her emotions as she thought of Petia.

"Hello," they both replied.

Raviel looked up at Hara. "Is there anyone else?" she asked.

"My husband died two years ago, but I have a sister and her family is not far from here."

"You and all of your family will be spared. In the name of Sovereign Ell Yon, you have my word."

Hara looked up at Tig.

"On the day of our return, be sure you are all here in your home," he added.

"Very well then. Let's talk," Hara said.

Aubrin took Zee and Vander out of the sitting room as Raviel, Tig, and Hara rested in comfortable chairs. A few minutes later, Aubrin brought them a cool drink and some fresh fruit. Raviel and Tig began sharing their mission objectives with Hara. She was able to answer many of their questions without them having to embark on any immediate clandestine operations. But the design of the power station for the dome's energy field was something she didn't have access to.

"Your dwelling looks like it is almost in contact with the energy dome," Raviel said.

"Yes. I paid a handsome price for this location," Hara replied. "I wanted to be able to see beyond this prison wall."

"You can do that?" Tig asked.

"Sure...come with me."

Hara took them up a couple of long staircases that ended up on the roof of her dwelling. Here, Hara had constructed a small haven amidst the Reekojan horror. A pergola decorated with beautiful flowering plants and a number of small trees created a serene and peaceful retreat. But Raviel hardly noticed any of it as she immediately went to the southern edge of Hara's dwelling where the soft hum of the city's energy dome was dutifully in place. Just inches away from Hara's haven was what many considered a technological marvel. Raviel held up her hand, tempted to touch the dome to see if the force was reactive to an object or if it simply functioned as a passive shield. Tig joined her to gaze at the dome.

"I wouldn't do that," Hara warned.

"Why...is it a reactionary energy field?" Raviel asked, retracting her hand. "That would be even more remarkable, considering the power it would take to accomplish that instead of a simple passive shield." Raviel had a hard time believing the Reekojans could accomplish such a thing as she mentally calculated the power approximations necessary for such a feat.

"Oh...it's reactionary to be sure. It's a stasis field," Hara revealed.

Raviel gasped. Slowly she and Tig backed away.

"Surely not!" she exclaimed. "That's impossible! The power...the tech...it's just not possible!"

Unlike a typical energy field that both repelled physical objects and focused energy weapons away from whatever it was protecting, a stasis field disintegrated whatever came in contact with it. This attribute of the stasis field technology is what made it so useful for the cutting edges of certain weapons like the Talon. It was difficult to generate a stasis field much larger than what was useful for handheld weapons, which is why a complete city dome stasis field was such a marvel. As far as Raviel knew, the largest stasis field that had been successfully generated and maintained was for a mining blade back on Jypton. And even then, it was just along the fifteen-foot edge of the mining blade. The power requirements made the machine virtually unjustifiable. But then she remembered that they were now living in a time two hundred seventy-one years later.

Hara grabbed a small branch that had fallen from one of her trees. She went to the dome and pushed the end of the branch into the stasis field. Raviel and Tig watched in horror as the branch disappeared into vapors, punctuated by sizzles and pops. Raviel lifted her hand to cover her mouth.

"How can this be?" she whispered. The burden of their mission and the scope of the Rayleans' challenge to defeat Reekojah instantly became overwhelmingly daunting. She stared ahead in wonder. When they had seen enough, Hara led them back to her sitting room.

"We need to get close to that stasis power generator," Raviel said. "I must see if there are any weaknesses we can exploit."

"Agreed," Tig said.

Hara sat back in her chair and took a sip of her drink.

"That section of the city is under high security for obvious reasons. The only way I can think of to get you close is if you were to pose as sentries."

Raviel looked toward Tig and then back to Hara.

"Is that possible?" she asked.

"There is a chance I could pull off one sentry ID with one of my contacts, but two—" Hara shook her head. "The risk is too great. Only one of you can go."

"That will be me," Raviel said.

Tig sat forward. "No. I'm sorry, Raviel, I'll not let you go in alone." Tig looked at Hara. "Are there any other options? What if one of us posed as a slave under escort?"

Hara's gaze fell admiringly on Tig. "Yes, I suppose that might work. There is a continual replenishment of slaves used to clean the reactor cores. I already have a slave collar that I could adapt to appear authentic." Hara offered a brief smile to Tig.

Tig nodded. "Perfect. Are you good with that?" he asked, looking toward Raviel. Although slightly perturbed at his insistent protection, she fully understood it. Tig had watched the torture Daeson had lived through for months while she was lost in space. He was protecting all three of them.

"Yes, that will work," she replied.

"How quickly can we get a sentry ID and uniform?" Tig asked Hara.

"The ID will take a few days, but I already have the uniform."

Tig tilted his head, one eyebrow slightly lifted.

"You need to understand something about me," Hara said, glancing toward Raviel and then back to Tig.

"In order to survive in this city of corruption and depravity, I have had to resort to, shall I say, questionable activities. In many instances, I`ve had to play their games and be better at them than they."

Hara looked directly at Tig. "Like you, I will do anything to protect my family."

Raviel noticed Tig's countenance soften toward Hara.

"I have connections in Reekojan's dark market. What we need can only be acquired there at significant risk and at significant price."

Tig looked over toward Raviel. Hara was putting everything on the line for them, and Raviel understood that it was only possible because of Hara's complete belief in the power of Sovereign Ell Yon and his demonstrated favor toward the Rayleans. Such faith would humble the best of their own people. Raviel pursed her lips.

"Hara, we understand and are grateful," Tig said, looking deep into Hara's eyes. "Our promise to you stands as sure as the Sovereign reigns."

Hara seemed lost in thought for a moment, then nodded.

"What can we do to help?" Raviel asked.

Hara broke her gaze from Tig and looked her way.

"Continue trading in the market so as not to draw attention." Hara smiled. "Although there are a few things I need to teach you in that regard."

Raviel smiled back. "Fair enough."

"There is one more thing we could use your help with," Tig said. "Do you have access to a database of slaves that are held here?"

Hara looked his way and shook her head. "No. If there is such a database, I've never heard of anyone obtaining access, not even in the dark market. Who are you looking for?"

"A young man named Avidan," Tig replied. "He was taken from the colony on the most recent raid."

Hara's face became somber. "Although most of the slaves do end up here in Reekojah, some are sent to other cities on Kayn-4, and some are even traded off-world."

Tig and Raviel were silent as they considered Avidan's possible fate.

"He is someone special?" Hara asked.

"Yes," Raviel replied.

Hara slowly nodded. "I'll carefully ask around and see what I can find out. Please don't be too hopeful though. Prefect Verdok's perspective on the slaves of Reekojah is uniquely dreadful. There's no telling what he may have done with his last acquisitions. The arena he's constructed for the Games is often the end of many."

"The Games?" Tig asked.

Hara's gaze fell to the floor. "His regime is the most bloodthirsty I've ever witnessed. Beasts and reprogrammed droids prey on slaves in a massive arena in the center of the city simply to satisfy the people's thirst for violence and blood."

Raviel felt anger rising up within her. She looked toward Tig and saw the fierce fire in his eyes ignite as well. If ever they had doubted their cause, there was no doubt now. Hara seemed to sense their shift.

"I'll ask and let you know. Tomorrow you must do your best to blend."

Over the next few days, Raviel and Tig made multiple trades and found numerous opportunities to recon much of the city's infrastructure. They were also able to obtain accurate estimations of military strength and armament. Hara helped them identify thirty-six plasma cannon emplacements around the perimeter of the city. These were placed to ensure no craft were able to fly in the no-fly zone above the stasis field dome. Any metallic object or weapon structure larger than a Talon was locked on to and immediately destroyed. After a thorough analysis, both

Raviel and Tig were duly discouraged because of the impenetrable defenses Reekojah seemed to have in place.

Late in the afternoon of their fifth day in Reekojah, Raviel and Tig entered the market to make another trade before plotting out their route into the heart of the city for reconnaissance on the stasis field generator.

"Last night I was talking with Hara," Raviel said as they walked toward a market thoroughfare they had not been to before. "She asked about you."

"Oh?" Tig replied.

"She wondered if you were attached to anyone," Raviel said with subtle smile.

Tig walked on in silence. Raviel felt a bit awkward but pressed forward. "I asked Daeson about Zee'la. I know you had feelings for her, Tig, and I can't help but carry a sense of—"

"It's okay," Tig interrupted.

"But it's not," Raviel said, grabbing his arm to talk with him face to face. She took a breath then struggled with her next words. "I've never met someone as devoted and loyal as you, Tig. Daeson and I owe you our lives and our love. I just want you to know that you deserve someone as amazing as you. You deserve to know how special it is to be bonded to another, and your commitment to Daeson and I should never stand in the way of that."

Tig turned his gaze away from Raviel for a moment then back. "Okay. I understand. Thank you."

"Really?" Raviel pressed.

Tig laughed. "Yes…really. Now, can we get on with the day?"

Raviel laughed as they started walking again. "So…what about Hara? She's pretty amazing."

Tig shook his head and laughed again. "In my time, and in my way."

Raviel looked over at him. "All right. I'll not say another word."

As they walked through the city, they became aware of a stream of grav vehicles and pedestrians making their way to one of the largest structures in the city...a massive arena with giant columns surrounding the perimeter. This was the place of horror of which Hara had told them—the Games of Reekojah. The cheers from within were already deafening. They ventured closer, and as they did, Raviel increased her pace. But Tig pulled back on her arm.

"Is it necessary to see it?" he asked.

Raviel's jaw was already set firm, her eyes aglow with the fire of justice. "Yes, it is," she countered. "Look around, Tig. Behold the decadent beauty of this place for it will not stand much longer. Sovereign Ell Yon has already judged this evil man and his evil city. I don't want a single corner of my heart to hesitate in being his arm of justice to accomplish it."

Tig relaxed his grip.

"Let's go," he said, leading the way.

Three hours later, Tig and Raviel emerged with tear-filled eyes from the horror of watching Reekojan entertainment at the cost of Raylean blood. Raviel's heart cried out with inconsolable pain against the abject atrocities she had just witnessed. Stunned by the creative ways Verdok had fabricated technology to incite such violence upon fellow humans was simply unbearable.

They walked in silence back to Hara's dwelling. The experience had changed them both. Whatever the future held, Raviel fully understood that this bastion of evil could not be allowed to stand.

Over the next couple of days, Raviel and Tig executed their mission of discovery and reconnaissance with renewed zeal. And although Hara had tried to find some information as to the possible whereabouts of Avidan, she had come up empty.

On the ninth day of their mission in Reekojah, Raviel and Tig were ready to launch the final, most risky investigation—evaluating the stasis field generator complex in the heart of the city. Hara had acquired the ID they needed, and she had also prepared the slave collar that Raviel would wear so that they might gain access to that section of the city. They would have to penetrate security, evaluate a massive and complicated power generation system, and then make their way out of the city, all without being detected.

One final preparatory observation trip near the complex brought them to a section of the trading market through which they had never traveled. As they feigned a few more trade negotiations, Raviel stumbled onto a piece of information that got their attention—a tech slave in one of the shops that could presumably repair any device, no matter its origin of technology or its level of sophistication. That evening, as they discussed the final preparations for the mission, Tig insisted they take time to investigate their new lead.

"It has to be Avidan," Tig insisted.

"It's possible," Hara agreed. "But there's risk in exposing yourselves. So far you have been able to avoid any suspicion. If it is him, you don't know how he'll react to seeing you. One false move now and you're done."

Tig frowned and Raviel remained silent.

"How important is the lad to you?" Hara asked.

Tig looked at Raviel. Her gaze fell to the floor as she remembered awakening from the nightmare of the quantum anomaly that had terrorized her. She looked up at Hara.

"He risked everything to save my life. We can't leave here without trying."

Tig looked satisfied. "I made a promise to Kyrah, and so far, this is the only lead we have on his potential whereabouts. If we can locate him and let him know we're coming, it would mean everything to her."

Raviel nodded. "Agreed. Let's see what we can find out."

Hara didn't look convinced.

"I would recommend taking your O-2 reclaimer and asking for him to replace the phase inverter and calibrate it. There are very few who could do that on Kayn-4. If the shop owner has a slave like that, he would be priceless. He probably won't even let you see him."

"Very well," Raviel said. "We check this out tomorrow morning, then on to the stasis generator station. We leave after that."

The next morning, they travelled to the shop in question. It was on the eastern edge of Market Street. A shrewd-looking older man eyed them suspiciously as they approached. Raviel and Tig had become experts at playing their parts. She glared back at the man with just as much scrutiny.

"I need an O-2 reclaimer repaired and calibrated, and I'm willing to pay handsomely for it," Raviel stated as Tig set the reclaimer on the table before the man. Raviel's eyes narrowed as if to be evaluating his abilities. "I'm told you are the one to talk to. Is this true?"

The man lifted his chin and sniffed. "I am the *only* one to talk to if you want it done right."

He reached for the reclaimer, but Raviel slammed her hand down on top of the case.

"I need to supervise the work," Raviel demanded.

The man glared back at Raviel. "No. I work in solitude. It's delicate work, and you'll only distract me."

Raviel didn't move. She glared back at the man. "What's the hysteresis frequency offset for the modal reclamation calibration sequence?"

The man's eyes widened as his gaze darted from the case back up to Raviel's icy-cold stare.

"I...ah...it's—"

Raviel sneered and pulled the case away. "Let's go," she said, turning to Tig. "This man's a fraud."

"No...wait," the man exclaimed, offering a sheepish smile. "I have a tech who does my work...the best work in the city." The man turned to the doorway of his shop. "Drudge!"

Raviel's visceral reaction to hearing that word was impossible to hide. She reached for the dagger at her hip, but Tig grabbed her arm, shaking his head.

"The time will come...not now!" he whispered.

Raviel took a deep breath, squeezed the handle of the dagger, then let it stay in its sheath. Her anger abated once the form of Avidan appeared in the doorway to the entrance of the shop. His eyes quietly conveyed the full measure of his hopeful heart as he looked first to Raviel and then to Tig. All three of them had to play their parts well. Raviel continued to glare with a skeptical countenance.

"This is your tech...a boy?" she exclaimed.

"He's as skilled as any of Reekojah's techs," the man replied.

"Twenty-eight point four gigahertz," Avidan said as he approached them. "The hysteresis offset frequency."

Raviel's eyebrow lifted as she allowed her skeptical gaze to diminish.

"Very well, but I will still supervise the work," she demanded.

"Two hundred credits and nobody knows about the boy," the man countered. "And I keep the O-2 reclaimer as collateral on our arrangement."

Raviel hesitated. "Deal. We'll be back later this afternoon to supervise the work." She looked at Avidan. "Be ready."

One corner of Avidan's mouth lifted ever so slightly. He nodded. Raviel and Tig turned to walk away, and it was the hardest thing she'd had to do since she had entered the city. The tyrannical machine of Verdok's armored city demanded patience. She would oblige for now...but not forever.

"We can't leave him here," Raviel said quietly once they were far enough away.

Tig looked over at Raviel. "I know."

They made their way toward Reekojah Central and found a place to don their mission outfits—Reekojan sentry and Raylean slave. When Tig locked Raviel's slave collar in place, she had to suppress buried emotions from her twenty years as a Jyptonian Drudge. Tig looked her over.

"Everything looks good except your eyes."

"My eyes?" Raviel responded.

"There's nothing about them that says you're a slave," he said with a crooked grin.

Raviel huffed. "There never was."

Tig nodded. "I believe that. It might work in our favor. Don't try to fake it."

"You look the part," Raviel said after inspecting him. Hara had even been able to acquire an official sentry plasma rifle. It wasn't functional, but hopefully they wouldn't need it to be.

"You ready for this?" she asked, putting her hands out for him to bind.

He put composite fetters around her wrists, clenched his jaw, and forced his eyes into a hard, fierce gaze. "Yes."

The transformation almost frightened her. Today they would be exposing themselves to the very breath of this ugly dragon. Raviel hadn't even dared tell Daeson what they were planning...he would have forbidden them both, but they needed this intel. They stepped out into the street as master and slave.

They set their course directly for the stasis field generator complex. It would be a thirty-minute walk through two security checkpoints, and perhaps an undefined number of random checks as well. The first checkpoint was less formidable, but it would tell them instantly if their ruse had any chance of success.

Tig shoved Raviel in the back with his plasma rifle toward the waiting guards. She looked over her shoulder at him and sneered.

"Slave transfer to the reactor core sanitation detail," Tig said with a measure of indifference.

The two guards eyed them closely. "Nobody told us about a slave transfer today."

"Didn't find out myself till this afternoon. Guess one of 'em didn't last very long," Tig replied.

At that the guard smirked. "Yeah...that's why they send the feisty ones," he said with a smug glance at Raviel. "It's always the lookers too," the guard added with a leering gaze. Raviel wanted to take a Talon to the man's disgusting heart.

"So, we good? The station master wants me back ASAP," Tig urged.

"Yeah. I'll let Bravo checkpoint know you're coming."

"Obliged," Tig said, pushing Raviel forward with the muzzle of his rifle. "Move, Drudge!" he added.

Once they turned the corner to the next thoroughfare, Raviel breathed a sigh of relief. It was just the start, but at least there didn't appear to be anything too obvious about their ruse. The second checkpoint was even easier since they were expected. They made their way into the underbelly of the city, eventually arriving at the stasis generator station. Once inside, they were careful to try to avoid any more interactions with guards. They maneuvered clear into the power generation chamber without incident, but that was about to change.

"Hey! What are you doing in this sector?" a voice behind them shouted.

They both turned abruptly to see a sentry approaching with his plasma rifle leveled at them.

"Slave transfer to the reactor core sanitation detail," Tig replied.

"I don't think so," the sentry replied, stopping a few paces away, his rifle at the ready. "That's an entirely different sector. Neither you nor the slave is allowed access to this sector. What's your ID number, sentry?" he demanded.

Tig reached for his ID as he took a step toward the sentry. Raviel understood in an instant that Tig was attempting to close the gap. There would be no peaceful way out of this.

"ID 378-13," Tig said, holding out the ID as he took another step.

The sentry lifted his rifle to shoulder level.

"Don't move!" the sentry exclaimed as he reached to press the com button on his forearm.

Tig was still three paces away, too far to risk an attack.

"I'm just following the station master's orders," Tig said. He let his mock plasma rifle dangle harmlessly at his side as he shrugged his shoulders. Tig turned and pointed to Raviel, managing to move a half step closer while doing so. "You want to take her the rest of the way, be my guest."

The sentry's eyes diverted to Raviel for just a second, and Tig made his move. With no margin for error, he dove below the muzzle of the rifle and into the sentry's lower midsection. The sentry was able to get a first shot off that barely missed Tig and almost took Raviel's head off. The plasma round exploded into a metal support beam behind her, adding to the momentary chaos. Raviel dove to the ground to avoid being hit by two more rounds as Tig desperately wrestled with the man on the ground for control of the weapon. Three more rounds went off, and this time the first round blasted into Raviel's pack, obliterating their QEC. The second round grazed Raviel's shoulder. She screamed as the searing pain enveloped her. The smell of burnt fabric and of her own skin filled her nostrils as she rolled to avoid the last shot.

For just one wisp of a moment, a terror enveloped Raviel that shook her to her core...the same terror that had held her prisoner to a spacetime quantum anomaly. She fought back to maintain a grip on this time...this reality. Paralyzed by the moment, she was frustrated at hearing the deadly fight just a few paces away. Two more wild shots were fired, then Tig briefly released his grip on the weapon in exchange for a hard elbow to the sentry's head. It momentarily dazed the man enough for Tig to gain control. He swung the butt of the rifle upward into his opponent's jaw, which knocked the man nearly unconscious, then deftly flipped the rifle and fired one shot into the man's chest. Tig rolled away, clearly exhausted by the encounter. It had only lasted a few seconds, but for both Raviel and Tig, it had felt like minutes. Tig checked to make sure the sentry was dead while looking toward Raviel.

"You okay?" he asked.

"Yeah. I guess so," she said, slowly feeling like she was fully back in time. She winced when she tried to move her arm.

Tig came to her, inspecting her wound. He shook his head. "That's gotta hurt."

"I'll be okay. Let's finish up and get out of here," she said. "Did he get a radio call off?"

"I don't think so, but we'd better move fast just to be sure," Tig recommended, exchanging his mock plasma rifle for the sentry's real one.

As they did their best to hide the body of the sentry, Raviel struggled to mentally let go of her episode with the threatening quantum anomaly. She realized that something was different this time—the ice-cold temperature was absent, but that thought did little to alleviate her anxiety about what had just happened. *Would it happen again?* she wondered.

Raviel and Tig had been able to collect incredibly valuable information about the operation of the generator station and about the defensive measures in place to protect it. Two hours later they had recovered their previous clothing and were back near Market Street, making their way toward the shop where Avidan was serving as a slave.

The shop owner led them into his repair lab, where Avidan was waiting. The O2 reclaimer was resting on the lab bench in front of him.

"All right, Drudge, calibrate it and be quick about it," the shop owner said with a sneer.

"Hey, mister," Raviel said, tapping the man's shoulder.

When the man turned, she cold-cocked him, and he fell to the floor unconscious. Tig kneeled down and rolled him over to put fetters on his wrists.

"Satisfied?" he said with a grin as he looked up at her.

Rubbing her fist, she smiled. "Yeah."

Avidan jumped up from his seat and hugged Raviel.

"Don't worry, we're going to get you out of here," she said, returning the hug.

Raviel pulled a device out of her pack. "This is an instrument a friend gave us to remove your collar," Raviel said, lifting it to a place near the back of his neck. "We have to disable it before we remove it."

Avidan reached up and grabbed her hand. "Unless it's set to the right code, it will kill me."

Raviel froze. She carefully removed her finger from the instrument's activation trigger.

"That, I didn't know. What now?" Raviel asked.

Avidan took the device from her hand. "I've already ascertained my collar's code. I just need to see if I can set it in this instrument."

While Avidan worked, Tig and Raviel dragged the shop owner to a back closet, gagged him, and locked the door.

"That should buy us enough time to get out of the city," Tig said.

When they returned, Avidan was standing with his disabled collar in his hand. "I guess it worked," he said without emotion.

Raviel took a big breath.

"Okay...let's move."

As soon as they exited the shop, alarms began to sound all across the city.

"That's not good," Raviel said. "They must have found the body of the sentry."

Dusk was fast approaching as Reekojah went into lockdown. The next thirty minutes were filled with one stressful near-encounter after another as they stealthily made their way back to Hara's dwelling. She greeted them at her door, her countenance filled with angst.

"I thought you had been captured...quickly!" she urged, ushering them into her home. "I've received word they're coming here. They must suspect you and have tracked you to my home," she explained as she led them up the stairway to the upper lever.

"Hara, we shouldn't have come back here. We've put you and your whole family in jeopardy," Raviel said, hesitating on the stairway.

"We'll be okay, but you have to hurry...come!"

They followed but did not go completely up to the roof where drones would soon be watching. Instead, she led them to a room arrayed with shelves of all sorts of devices, including tech Raviel had never seen before. Hara opened a panel in the wall and pressed a button. The wall up against the city's protective dome retreated away to the left and to the right, revealing the inner surface of the stasis field. Raviel could hear the gentle buzz of the dome in its technological power. Raviel took one more moment to stare at the beauty of such raw power. Standing this close to it was mesmerizing and terrifying at the same time. She held her hand a few inches away, knowing full well that touching it would incinerate that portion of her hand.

Outside they could hear sentry craft approaching with sirens blaring. Raviel turned around.

"What now, Hara?" Tig asked. "There's no place to hide here. We're trapped!"

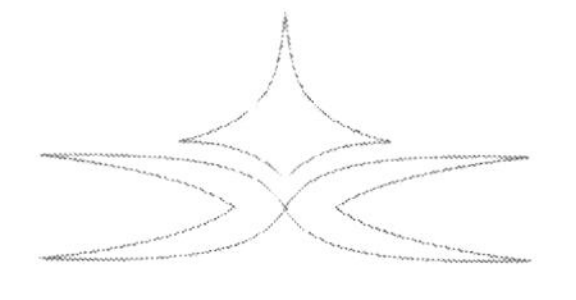

Chapter 15

Escape from Reekojah

Raviel searched for an access door or something that might give them a last chance at escaping the Reekojan sentries. She looked at Hara who let a wry smile cross her lips. Raviel couldn't help but wonder if after all of her help, this might be an elaborate ruse just to lead them here to be captured. Hara pulled back the sleeve on her shirt and pressed a sequence on an electronic wrist band. Another section of an adjoining wall slid away as a shelf slid out that held a number of devices whose function they could only guess at. Avidan's eyes opened wide with excitement.

"I knew this day might come for me, so I've been working on an escape plan, equipping with tech from the dark market."

"But there's no way through," Tig said. "Nothing can penetrate a stasis field."

Hara grabbed a large three-foot circular device with the most unusual array of levers and mechanisms.

"Except another stasis field," Avidan offered.

Hara smiled. "Exactly. This is a stasis field interrupter. The problem is...I never dared to test it for fear of drawing attention. Let's hope it works!" She motioned toward Tig. "Quickly, but keep your hands clear of the inner ring!"

Hara pressed a couple of buttons, and the interrupter came alive. Lights flashed around its perimeter as the power module energized the unit. The device had an outer solid structural ring and what looked like a collapsible inner ring patterned after the iris of an optical lens. It was closed now with just a pin-point opening. Once the device was at full power, a four-inch needle-like column of pink energy protruded outward from the pin-point opening in the iris.

"Help me lift this to the dome," Hara said. "We must be very careful to keep it stable. This stasis needle should be able to penetrate the dome stasis field."

They held the interrupter up to the dome stasis field, careful not to touch it. When they pushed the needle stasis column into the dome, violent arcs of resistant energy pushed back against the column, unyielding to the attempt to penetrate the field. Hara and Tig pulled the device back.

"Curses," Hara exclaimed. "We might be finished after all."

Raviel thought of Hara's family and what would surely happen to them.

"What if we just need more power," Raviel offered, reaching into her pack to reveal her last Malakian modified power module.

"I think I can tie into the source," Raviel said as she inspected the power module interface port.

"It's worth a try," Hara replied.

A few seconds later, Tig and Hara made one more attempt. This time, in spite of the dome stasis field's resistance, the interrupter's own stasis needle pushed completely through the field.

"Now what?" Tig asked.

"Now we rotate the inner ring," Hara announced.

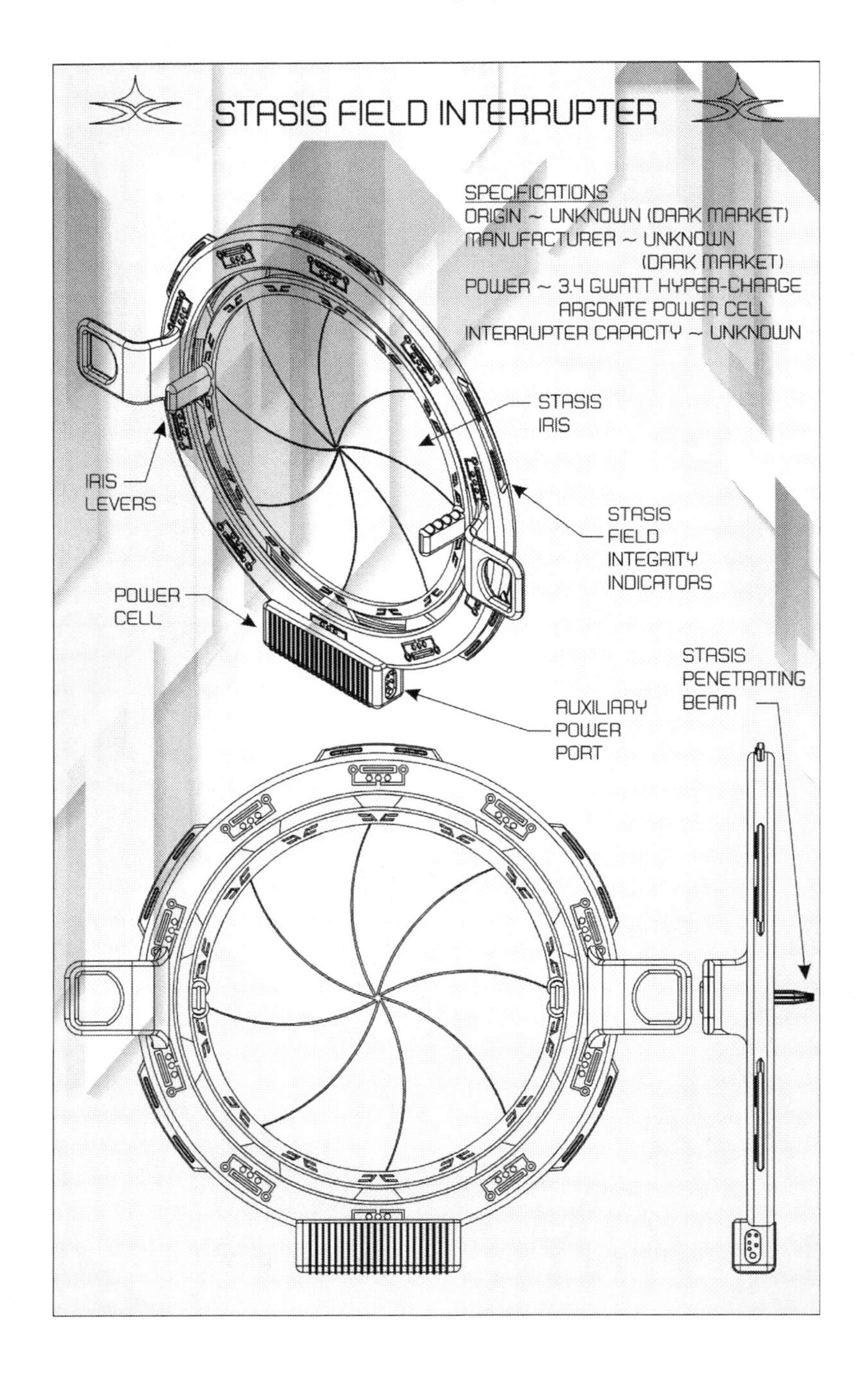
STASIS FIELD INTERRUPTER
SPECIFICATIONS
ORIGIN ~ UNKNOWN (DARK MARKET)
MANUFACTURER ~ UNKNOWN (DARK MARKET)
POWER ~ 3.4 GWATT HYPER-CHARGE ARGONITE POWER CELL
INTERRUPTER CAPACITY ~ UNKNOWN
STASIS IRIS
IRIS LEVERS
STASIS FIELD INTEGRITY INDICATORS
POWER CELL
STASIS PENETRATING BEAM
AUXILIARY POWER PORT

Raviel took Tig's place, holding one side of the interrupter while Hara held the other. Tig grasped the two handles that controlled the opening of the iris and began rotating them in a clockwise fashion. At first the iris didn't budge. Tig added more force to the levers, then slowly it began to open. The needle-like column of energy expanded outward with the iris. One inch...two inches...three inches. Agonizingly slow, Tig forced open a hole in the dome's stasis field. The larger the hole got, the harder it was to turn the lever and open the iris. Avidan joined Tig, and all four of them put all their strength into opening the iris fully. Hara engaged the lock, and the moaning interrupter became nearly silent. Each of them slowly let go, then stood back in amazement to see what they had done. There before them was a thirty-inch hole in the dome's stasis field.

"Remarkable," Raviel whispered.

Hara went back to the sliding shelf and grabbed three of the four remaining devices. They were smooth, elliptical devices about the size of a small melon, with a stem and handle protruding out the bottoms.

"Here," she said, handing one to each of them. "These are anti-grav floaters. Set your weight here," she said, turning a dial. "Then extend the anti-grav pods and jump. Get a run because your forward momentum is the only thing that will carry you away from the city wall."

"But you...your family!" Raviel exclaimed.

They could hear shouts and banging down below them as the sentries demanded entry.

"Not enough time...or floaters. Just get out of here, and I'll handle the sentries," Hara replied.

Raviel grabbed Hara and hugged her. "Thank you," she said quietly.

Tig put a hand on her arm. "We'll be back for you...I promise," he said.

Hara smiled sadly. "I know."

Raviel pushed her pack through the interrupter first, then the floater. She hesitated just a second, looking the device over once more before stepping through with her left leg, followed by her head, torso, and right leg. Once on the other side, she breathed a sigh of relief.

"Come on, Avidan!" she called.

Avidan followed. Now it was Tig's turn.

He shoved his bag and plasma rifle through. As he handed his floater to Raviel, the interrupter jilted. Raviel's power supply arced, and the iris shimmied as if it were about to collapse.

"Hurry!" Hara and Raviel both said at the same time.

Tig put his left leg through, and the interrupter jilted again, this time with threatening quavers in the iris. He ducked his head through, followed by his body. As he began to pull his right leg through, the interrupter completely collapsed. The dome stasis field instantly severed his right leg just below the knee. Tig screamed out in pain as his severed leg fell with a thump amid arcs of stasis energy and shattered parts of the interrupter. The amputated limb left no blood since the searing edges of the collapsing stasis field cauterized both sides of his leg. Raviel reached for Tig as he fell to the ground writhing in pain.

Hara stood stunned on the other side of the now impenetrable stasis field with eyes wide and mouth open. The sentries were coming up the staircase, having forced their way into her dwelling. She grabbed Tig's severed leg, threw it onto the sliding shelf alongside the shattered pieces of the interrupter, and pressed the button to retract the shelf into the wall. She then took one last look at Raviel and pushed the button to close the wall, separating herself from the three fleeing Rayleans.

"We have to jump," Raviel said to Tig as he fought to regain his equilibrium.

Tig took three deep breaths. "Okay...help me stand up," he said, grabbing onto her shoulder.

Raviel and Avidan lifted Tig up as he hobbled on one foot. He grabbed the plasma rifle, strapping it across his shoulder.

"You'll have to jump with my bag," he said to Avidan. "Add forty pounds to your floater weight."

Avidan nodded, his face pale from watching Tig lose his leg.

They each set their weights. Then they helped Tig stand on the edge of the twenty-foot-wide wall. He held on to the floater's handle and pressed the button to extend the anti-gravity pods. A rod with smaller elliptical modules extended outward left and right of the main module. The device immediately lifted Tig's arms up above his head.

"Ready," he grimaced.

Raviel and Avidan counted to three before pushing Tig outward off the wall. After floating outward, he moved downward at a gentle angle as he held onto the protruding handles of the floater. Raviel and Avidan backed up to get a running start, then activated their floaters' anti-grav pods. They both ran to the edge of the wall and jumped. Raviel could still hear the muffled sirens of Reekojah as they gently floated away under the cover of darkness.

When they landed nearly half a mile away from the city's wall, Raviel and Avidan went to help Tig. Raviel supported him on the right as they journeyed farther from the city as quickly as Tig could handle. Once they made it to the edge of the small village, Raviel left Avidan with Tig while she retrieved their weapons from their secure storage locker. When she returned, she inspected Tig's leg.

"How are you doing?" she asked.

"I'm good," he lied. "Once they discover we're not in the city, they'll expand their search. We need to get to the Starcraft."

Raviel felt Tig's leg and lifted up her hand. It was covered in blood.

"The exertion of our run has opened up your wound," Raviel said. "I need to put a tourniquet on it."

Tig nodded.

Avidan held a light so Raviel could apply a make-shift tourniquet, which helped stop much of the bleeding. Raviel wished they had stopped earlier since Tig had lost quite a bit of blood.

"Are you sure you can travel? We still have a long way to go."

"Then we'd better get moving," Tig responded with a grimace, followed by a forced smile.

It took them a few hours to make it to the edge of Titan Forest. Inside the walls of the forest, they felt somewhat safe from the Reekojan sentries, but now they would have to contend with the Terridons. They could only hope the creatures weren't nocturnal. Hours later when they finally made it to the Starcraft, Tig was exhausted. The entire time they traveled, Raviel had been wrestling with an insurmountable logistics problem—all three of them couldn't travel in one Starcraft.

They set Tig up against a nearby tree to allow him to rest.

"Give him some water and some food," she instructed Avidan, then quickly set about preparing the Starcraft for launch.

Once the craft was ready, she came to Tig, and he opened his eyes. The water and food seemed to help revive him.

"Give them my coordinates...I'll be waiting," he said with a smile, setting his plasma rifle across his lap.

Raviel looked at this incredible man. He was the truest version of a friend there could ever be. He had sacrificed everything in his life for Daeson and now for Raviel, journeying across centuries to honor the promise of his word. He possessed the mettle of a true follower of Sovereign Ell Yon.

"No, Tig. You're going to fly Avidan back to the fleet," Raviel said. "You need immediate medical attention, or you won't make it."

"I—"

"It's not up for discussion," Raviel interrupted. "Are you able to pilot the Starcraft? And don't lie to me."

Tig struggled to answer. "Yes," he responded flatly.

"Good," Raviel replied.

"Raviel, I can't allow this...I won't allow this!"

"There's no other option," Raviel insisted as she and Avidan helped him stand and then walk to the Starcraft. "We both know that this is the only logical solution. Your wound will draw the Terridons in, and you'll have little to no ability to fight them off."

Raviel extended the cockpit ladders, then she and Avidan helped Tig into the front cockpit. Raviel then helped Avidan strap into the rear cockpit. When he was set, she gave him a thumbs-up and stepped over to Tig's ladder to make sure he was ready to launch. Tig looked up at her with a pain in his eyes that she had never seen before, and it had nothing to do with his amputated leg. She placed a gentle hand on his arm.

"You haven't failed me…or Daeson. You've given so much. Save Avidan, and get a rescue team back here as quickly as possible. You have the coordinates. I'll make it…I promise."

Tig's eyes grew moist. He offered one subtle nod.

Raviel smiled, then jumped to the ground. She retracted both ladders, stepped back and gave a snappy salute. A few minutes later, Tig and Avidan lifted off the forest floor in their Starcraft, leaving Raviel in the wash of their launch wake. She watched them until Tig engaged the cloaking device then turned her attention to the forest. The utter silence closed in and threatened to steal away any pretense of courage she had demonstrated for Tig's sake. If Tig were to make it safely back to the *Liberty* without incident, she figured a rescue team would be here no later than tomorrow afternoon.

"One night in a forest haunted with giant winged reptiles…shouldn't be so bad," she said softly. She scanned the walls of the forest as they closed in around her. The first thing she needed to do was to put some distance between herself and the blood trail left by Tig. As she turned to plot her course, a low guttural rumble shook the ground beneath her. Was she already too late?

The QEC remained silent well past Raviel's check-in time. Daeson found it impossible to sit in the captain's chair for any length of time as he waited. The entire bridge crew felt the tension as Daeson occasionally paced from station to station. No small part of the reason for his apprehension at sending Raviel to Kayn-4 was the fact that he knew she would take risks to get the information the fleet needed to be successful—and at her own peril. He feared that this was exactly what had happened. Six hours had passed, and she was never late with her report.

"I want to know the instant anything comes through that gate," Daeson demanded from his sensors officer.

"Aye, sir."

Another hour ticked by...nothing. Daeson began thinking about how to initiate a rescue mission, a nearly impossible task without some information as to what might have happened.

"Starcraft exiting the gateway!" the sensors officer reported. "It's Viper One," he added.

"Thank the Sovereign!" Daeson said, feeling the tension in his entire body lessening.

"*Liberty*, this is Viper One," Tig radioed. He sounded tired.

"Viper One, this is *Liberty*...welcome home!" Daeson radioed.

There was a long pause. Something about it unsettled Daeson.

"*Liberty*, we have a situation," Tig came back. Daeson's heart stopped. "I have Scitech Avidan on board. We will be docking in sixty-five minutes. Recommend assembling a search and rescue team immediately."

Daeson's mind instantly went wild with speculation.

"Com, give me a private channel."

Daeson put a com transceiver in his ear as he walked to the aft section of the bridge.

"Tig, what's happened...where is Raviel?"

"She's still on Kayn-4. We need to get a rescue team to her as fast as possible."

What have you done? Daeson thought, anger quickly rising against his friend for the first time since he'd known him.

"Is she hurt?" Daeson radioed back. "Is she captured?"

"No, she's not hurt or captured." Tig was slow with details, which further angered Daeson. "She's hiding in the Titan Forest, but the Reekojans know we were there and are looking for her," Tig replied. "Circumstances—" he began but did not finish.

Daeson couldn't imagine any circumstance where Tig would allow such a thing...to abandon Raviel by herself as the enemy closed in. He trembled with fear and rage.

"I'm sorry, Daeson. I—"

Another unfinished sentence. He could feel Tig's shame, but it did nothing to help.

"Get that ship here now!" Daeson ordered.

He turned back to the bridge. Every officer sat or stood perfectly still...waiting. He couldn't send a full search and rescue team. It would only draw attention and potentially destroy their entire plan, as well as put Raviel in greater harm's way.

"Get two mechtech crews ready to receive Viper One," he said to his operations officer. "I want that ship refueled and ready to launch twenty minutes after it docks. Is that clear?"

"Yes, sir!" the officer snapped back.

"You have the bridge," Daeson said then exited.

He went to his quarters and quickly donned his flight suit. By the time he made it to the docking bay, most of the mechtechs were already there. Five had suited up and entered the docking bay so they could keep working as Viper One entered and docked. Within a few minutes, a medtech crew had arrived also. His ops officer must have thought it a good precaution.

"Is it true?"

Daeson turned to see Kyrah approaching the docking bay door.

"Do they have Avidan?" she asked, coming toward him.

"Yes."

Kyrah's face lit up. Daeson turned to look through the door's window, anticipating Viper One's arrival, but also to hide his frustration at the sacrifice Raviel had obviously made to get Avidan home. Harsh words for Tig filled his mind.

Focus on saving Raviel...then deal with Tig, he reminded himself.

Kyrah stayed quiet, seeming to understand what must have happened. A few minutes later, the alarm sounded, alerting all that the docking bay door was opening. Tig's approach was slow and sloppy which irritated Daeson further. Didn't he know that time was of the essence?

When the outer door finally closed and pressure was restored, the rest of the mechtech crew was first in, followed by Daeson, Kyrah, and the medtech team. As Daeson approached his Starcraft, he heard the engines winding down. Only the rear canopy began to lift. Tig's canopy didn't lift until the crew platform was seated up against the fuselage and one of the mechtechs activated the external lever. Daeson looked up at Tig, but he didn't look down. He was slumped over, as if he were reaching for something below him. The mechtechs extracted Avidan first.

"He needs help!" the lad shouted. "Get the medtechs here!"

There was a flurry of activity as mechtechs and medtechs jockeyed for position to help get Tig out of the cockpit, off the crew platform, and onto a gurney. Daeson met him on the floor.

"Tig! What—"

That's when Daeson saw Tig's blood-soaked clothes and his missing leg. Tig reached a weak hand out for Daeson, tears in his eyes. "I'm sorry, Daeson. I'm so sorry!" His words were heavy and slurred, unconsciousness closing in fast.

Daeson grabbed his hand, utterly ashamed for his ill-thoughts toward his friend. "It's okay, Tig. I'll bring her home."

"Coordinates locked into the nav..." Tig's eyes closed as his hand went limp.

Daeson looked at the lead medtech. "Make sure he lives!"

The medtech nodded then whisked him out of the docking bay. As Daeson prepared for launch, he was barely aware of the joyful reunion between Kyrah and Avidan. Minutes counted, and everyone knew it. Strapped into the cockpit, he conducted a quick pre-launch check while spooling up his engines. He motioned for the mechtech crew to evacuate the bay. Then his eye caught sight of Kyrah. She snapped a sharp salute, and Daeson returned the same. Minutes later he was accelerating full speed to the gateway for his jump to the Kayn System, hoping against hope that Raviel was still alive and safe.

Raviel sprinted on a course ninety degrees off from the route she, Tig, and Avidan had travelled to the Starcraft, using only a soft glow light when absolutely necessary to navigate the dark forest. Occasionally a break in the canopy overhead allowed the light of one of the two moons to penetrate onto the forest floor in patches. Additionally, the luminescent seeds of the Magalla trees created a near fantasy-like forestscape that helped her navigate her midnight sprint.

The Terridon's low guttural rumblings weren't far away. Raviel's best guess was that the smell of blood was the prime draw for the Terridon. Keeping an eye upward, she ran with the speed and agility of a cat until she came to a small stream. Hoping to disguise her own body odors to evade the Terridon's acute sense of smell, Raviel took a few moments to slather mud and moss over her entire body and then resumed her sprint. After another fifteen minutes of separating herself from Tig's blood trail, she found a rocky outcropping surrounded by low-growing brush and trees. She was winded but felt quite certain there were no

Terridons in pursuit. She had her pack, but without the QEC, there was no way to contact the fleet until a rescue team was within the atmosphere of the planet.

Once she recovered from her sprint, she began constructing a temporary shelter, but if a Terridon spotted her, there would be little she could do to defend herself, and her makeshift shelter would offer little to no protection. The two plasma rifles Tig had left behind held only partial charges, but hopefully they would last for a few good shots. Evasion was her best play. It was during times like this that she was extremely grateful for her training as a Plexus spy back on Jypton. Much of the training had focused on mental fortitude that required one to keep calm in spite of very tense circumstances. She channeled that training now, for the monsters of a dark forest had a way of shattering one's confidence and strength.

Daeson engaged the Starcraft's full cloak just before exiting the Kayn System's slipstream gateway. He entered the atmosphere a bit aggressively, pushing the limit of what he knew was a safe approach to avoid detection. Dawn was just breaking over the treetops of the Titan Forest. He quelled the horrid thoughts of Raviel's possible demise—captured by the ruthless Reekojans or eaten by a ferocious Terridon.

"Nighthawk, this is Sky Guardian, do you copy?"

Please respond, Raviel...please!

Nothing.

"Nighthawk, this is Sky Guardian, do you copy?"

Daeson wondered if perhaps he wasn't yet within range of her standard tactical radio.

"Sky Guardian—" followed by static. "—need help!"

Daeson's heart began to race. It was difficult to make out most of what she had said, but the word 'help' was enough for him to know that she was in trouble!

"Nighthawk, state coordinates," Daeson replied.

With each mile he flew, the radio transmissions grew clearer.

"Three miles southwest of the original site. Terridons coming. Hurry!"

Daeson threw caution to the wind, accelerating to full speed and leaving a fiery heat signature behind him for all of Reekojah to see as he closed in on her position. He saw one Terridon skimming just above the green canopy of the forest, ready to dive through a slender opening. He would never make it through the opening with his Starcraft.

"Call me in…when am I overhead?" he radioed. He flew to the spot where the Terridon had descended. Just a few hundred yards prior, she called.

"Overhead now! Two Terridons closing in!"

Daeson scanned for a place to set down, but the only place open enough was nearly a mile away. He considered blasting an opening in the forest, but he might waste precious time and not be successful. Besides, he couldn't be perfectly sure what effect this might have on Raviel's safety. He made for the clearing, landing in a fraction of the normal time it took to safely set down. He sprinted toward Raviel's last known location.

"On the ground…coming your way, Rav!" he radioed.

There was no reply, but he heard multiple discharges from a plasma rifle. Altering his course, he ran as fast as he could in her direction. Another round of distant blasts and a forest-piercing screech filled his veins with adrenaline. He could see the ruckus through the towering Magalla trees. Raviel was pinned between two massive trees that offered protection on her right and left, but she was vulnerable from either her front or back, depending on which of the two Terridons was attacking. The one to her rear seemed slightly injured and hesitant to attack, but the one to her front was full of fury and heading right toward her.

"Raviel!" Daeson screamed.

He saw her point and fire, but the rifle discharged a mere fraction of its normal energy. It did nothing to thwart the attacking Terridon. The creature lifted itself up on its two hind legs and spread its wings wide, preparing for a final lunge. Daeson paused, took aim, and fired his own plasma rifle. The plasma burst passed just in front of the creature, missing him but getting his attention just the same. The Terridon turned its head to discover what had disturbed its hunt. Daeson continued his final hundred-yard sprint toward Raviel and into the jaws of this winged eight-hundred-pound monster. He took aim again, this time planning to fire on the run, but his rifle instantly powered down when he pulled the trigger.

Perfect time for a malfunctioning plasma rifle! he fumed.

With the Terridon coming at him and with no time to power the rifle up and try again, Daeson drew his Talon and fired two shots. The Terridon charged right through them, its scaly hide offering enough protection that although the shots did not penetrate, the fury of the creature was intensified. Two more Talon shots rang out, this time from behind. Raviel had left her cover and began working her way toward Daeson.

At this moment, the second Terridon looked as if it had resolved to try once more for its meal. The situation was turning from bad to worse quickly, and Daeson couldn't imagine how they were going to survive. They alternated Talon shots and dodged from tree to tree, working their way towards each other. After a few harrowing evasions, they were finally able to take cover behind a massive fallen Magalla tree. Both were breathing hard and nearly exhausted from the fight.

"No one else coming?" Raviel asked.

"Only one ship has cloak," Daeson returned, checking the charge on his Talon. "What's your charge level?"

"Thirty percent," Raviel replied. "But these are just pea-shooters against these creatures."

Both Terridons had taken flight to position themselves for a final attack, and there was nothing Daeson and Raviel could do to stop them. Daeson frantically looked for some way out as he scanned the heights of the trees, watching the monsters zero in on them. A screech filled the air as both

Terridons dove at them from above. Daeson and Raviel aimed their Talons, but before they could fire, a deeper pulsating, ear-piercing screech penetrated through the lofty Magalla trees and shook the ground upon which they stood. A Terridon nearly twice as large as their attackers swooped down from some secret perch, grabbing one of the Terridons with his talons and casting it aside as if it were a plaything. The other attacker turned abruptly in an attempt to avoid the same fate.

Daeson and Raviel were stunned with no idea what to do next. Their Talons were utterly useless against a Terridon of this size. Daeson gawked as the creature flew past them making a wide arc around three huge trees before turning back.

"Okay...this is not good," Daeson stated flatly.

"The locals say there's always an alpha in any inhabited region. This must be him," Raviel acknowledged.

The twelve-hundred-pound creature made a graceful landing just fifty feet away, never taking its fierce yellow eyes off of them. It roared its pulsating screech once more, standing on its two hind legs with wings spread wide, preparing to pounce. The sight was terrifying.

"Let's focus our shots at its heart. Perhaps our combined firepower will have an impact," Daeson whispered to Raviel. He aimed his Talon at the creature's torso where he speculated its heart would be.

"Ready..." he said quietly, seeing out of the corner of his eye that Raviel was already poised to shoot. His finger began to press down on the trigger.

Hold, the whisper came. Daeson tried to ignore it.

Hold! This time an unmistakable command.

The Terridon charged.

"Daeson!" Raviel exclaimed.

"Hold!" Daeson returned. In just seconds the beast would be upon them.

Daeson dropped his Talon and held out his right hand. He heard Raviel gasp, but she didn't fire. The Terridon continued its charge with jaws open wide, unhindered in any way.

"Daeson!" Raviel shouted again, retreating a few steps.

At the very last moment, the Protector came to life, but it didn't burst forth with a powerful disintegrating beam of energy as Daeson had hoped. Instead, a broad aura of blue emanated from his hand, enveloping the Terridon in its mesmerizing power. The beast skidded to a halt just inches from Daeson's hand. It clamped down its salivating, four-inch, razor-sharp teeth like a trap, nearly taking Daeson's hand as it did so. Confused, the creature opened its jaws again and tried to devour its prey, but it could not advance one more step. This seemed to enrage the creature to near madness as it snorted and fumed, shaking its head as if trying to rid itself of some hypnotic spell. Being this close to a fearsome monster designed to devour anything and everything that it pleased was nearly more than Daeson could take. His hand trembled as the Protector continued to flow with an inhibiting influence on the Terridon.

"Wha...what now?" he heard Raviel softly ask from behind.

"I have no idea!" Daeson replied.

At the sound of Daeson's voice, the beast renewed its efforts to eat its prey, gnawing and thrashing the air around itself. One of the other Terridons drew close, apparently in an effort to do what the alpha could not, but once it came within striking distance, the alpha Terridon turned on the smaller creature and clamped its vicious jaws around its neck, shaking the smaller Terridon like a rag doll until it hung lifeless in its grip. Dropping the carcass to the ground, the alpha turned back to Daeson, ribbons of blood now drooling from its mouth. Daeson nearly faltered as it tried once more to take his arm off but failed. After a few more seconds of frustrated fury, the creature stopped and looked Daeson straight in the eye. Finally it snorted, splattering Daeson with droplets of red saliva, then turned and took flight, screeching its frustration to the forest. The Protector slowly fell to silence. Daeson was frozen in place, his arm still stretched out to nothing but the empty space that just seconds earlier had been occupied by a monster that inhabited nightmares. Slowly he turned his arm inward so he could see the final whisps of Ell Yon's power dissipating.

"Why?" he nearly shouted as he wiped splatters of Terridon blood from his face. "Was that really necessary?"

He immediately regretted his outburst as images of the powerful Ell Yon filled his mind. Raviel stepped up beside him, and they both stood in silence for a moment, trying to regain a portion of their composure. She leaned into him, and he wrapped an arm around her.

"That wasn't much of a rescue plan," she quipped.

"True, but if I had taken any time to come up with one, you might not have been around to rescue," Daeson jabbed back.

"Touché!" Raviel said, looking up at him. "I love you," she added.

Daeson leaned his head against hers. "I love you too. Let's get out of this place."

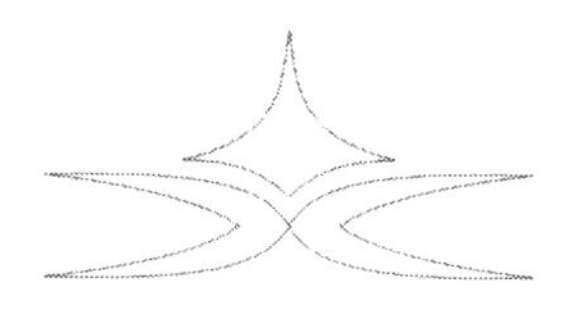

CHAPTER 15

Preparing for Battle

Ground Effect Principle – Ground effect is the reduced aerodynamic drag that an aircraft's wings generate when they are close to a fixed surface such as the ground. An airfoil, such as a wing, passing through air increases air pressure on the underside, while decreasing pressure across the top, thereby enabling a craft to attain flight with considerably less energy.

Once Daeson and Raviel returned to the *Liberty* and exited the docking bay, they headed straight for the medtech facility to see Tig. They were greeted at the entrance by Master Medtech Gilzan.

"How's he doing?" Daeson asked.

"He's going to be fine," Gilzan replied. "I gave him two pints of blood, and he's been resting."

"Can we see him yet?" Raviel asked, looking past Gilzan to the bed where Tig was lying.

"Yes," came a groggy voice. "Please come and get me out of here!"

Gilzan smiled, stepping aside. "And when you're done, I'll be treating that shoulder wound before it gets infected," he added.

Raviel smirked as she and Daeson stepped up beside Tig's bed.

"Hey, partner…how are you doing?" Daeson asked.

"I'm good," Tig replied with a weak smile. "I see you were successful."

Raviel reached for Tig's hand.

"I'm glad to see you made it back, my lady," Tig added.

Raviel shook her head. "I'm sorry this has happened to you, Tig. I wish—"

"Nothing to be sorry for," Tig interrupted. "Our mission was a success, and we even rescued Avidan from that place of horrors. Nothing to be sorry for at all."

Raviel squeezed his hand and smiled.

"Besides, I hear Avidan is already working on a neuro-linked prosthetic. Knowing him, it will probably be better than the original."

They all laughed, knowing that he wasn't far from the truth.

"Excuse me, am I interrupting?" a quiet voice called from the entrance.

Daeson and Raviel turned to see Kyrah standing there. Raviel immediately went to her, and the two women embraced.

"I'm so glad to see you're all right," Kyrah said as they parted.

Raviel smiled. "Come," she offered, pulling Kyrah toward Daeson and Tig.

Kyrah went to the far side of Tig's bed. Her eyes glanced down at his missing leg then up to Tig's face. There was a brief moment of awkward silence as Kyrah seemed to search for the right words. Her military demeanor softening with each passing second.

"I didn't get a chance to thank you," she said, glancing up at Raviel, "both of you, for saving Avidan. I can't tell you how tortured I've been, not knowing if he was even alive." She stopped and looked back at Tig. "I promised him I would take care of him, and when I couldn't, you helped me keep that promise."

Kyrah's pale blue eyes brimmed with tears as she looked down at Tig's missing leg again. "And at such a high cost to you."

Tig fumbled for words with which he could respond.

"I…ah…" He looked to Daeson and Raviel for some help, but as he did so, Kyrah put a hand on his arm, bent down, and kissed his cheek. She then promptly turned and left, her emotions of gratitude and sympathy threatening to undo her carefully fabricated tough personae.

"Well," Daeson said, trying to dispel some of Tig's uneasiness, "as soon as you're up for it, I'd like you two to give a briefing to the Strategy Council, the clan chieftains, and a few other key personnel.

"Of course," Tig replied. "I'll be ready by tomorrow."

"No…you won't be," Gilzan interrupted. "Not if you plan on keeping the rest of your leg." He turned to Daeson. "I need three days minimum before I can be reasonably sure he's out of danger."

Daeson shrugged his shoulders. "Sorry, Tig. We can wait. There's a lot going on right now, so let's make sure you're both ready."

"Besides," Raviel interjected, "I need to prepare my notes and specification models for the briefing. That will take some time, so just rest up."

Tig frowned. "Can't stand people gawking and making a fuss over me. How about two days?"

"Three," Gilzan replied firmly. "Now let's take a look at you, Raviel."

Daeson stayed by her side while Gilzan disinfected and bandaged her wound. He wasn't ready to leave her, not even for a moment. Gilzan then scanned her entire body. He stared at the results longer than he should have.

"Your vitals are off a bit," Gilzan finally said. "How are you feeling?"

"I'm feeling fine," she quickly replied.

Daeson eyed her closely, and when she refused to look him straight in the eye, he put a hand on her arm. "What is it, Rav? What aren't you telling us?"

Raviel squirmed, then rotated her injured arm as if to test its usage. When she didn't answer, Daeson gently put his hand on her cheek. Gilzan slipped quietly away, preoccupying himself with other duties. Raviel finally looked up at Daeson, her dark eyes holding back something of great importance. Daeson waited.

"When I got shot," she began, gently touching her injured shoulder, "I felt as if…as if I might slip away again."

Shivers flitted up and down Daeson's spine as he recalled the horror of those first days in this new time. He stood motionless as he processed what she had just said.

Raviel reached for his hand, pressing hers against his. "I'm sure it's nothing," she said. "Just an aftereffect of my ordeal."

He wanted that to be true but didn't quite dare believe it.

"We have to bring Avidan here to check you out," Daeson said, turning his attention to Gilzan.

Gilzan caught the signal and returned. "I'll call him right away."

Over the next two hours, Avidan and Gilzan conducted a thorough examination of Raviel to determine if there was any indication that her quantum anomaly might return. When they were through, Avidan wore a look of concern.

"But it was different this time. The freezing cold was absent," Raviel insisted.

"That's because you weren't in space when it happened," Avidan explained. "The moment your cells began to experience the time-slip, for lack of a better term, there was no ship to give you any protective environment. That's why your bodily pain was so horrific. If we hadn't been able to stop your body from slipping into the future, you would have materialized hundreds or perhaps thousands of years into the future, but you would have been immediately frozen by the coldness of space. For your most recent episode, you were on the planet in a warm atmosphere."

"But the planet is traveling through space too," Raviel rebutted. "Wouldn't I still materialize in space…where the planet used to be?"

Avidan shook his head. "We know that space, time, and gravity are all interconnected in a relativistic relationship. Although we are in unchartered physics here, I theorize that the mass of the planet and its corresponding gravity well are able to keep you positionally stable, even through the quantum event. The fact that your experience was so vastly different is evidence that I'm right."

"Is she in danger now?" Daeson asked.

"Right now her cells have stabilized, but I don't know what might trigger another episode. Perhaps it was your injury, or perhaps it was just time because our solution wasn't enough to permanently stabilize your cells. There's a chance that what you experienced was just as you said—an aftereffect of our stabilization attempt—and may never happen again."

"Is that what you believe?" Raviel asked.

Avidan pursed his lips. "I don't know…honestly. But I do have an idea."

Daeson and Raviel leaned forward. It was the first glimmer of hope they had heard.

"Give me a few days to work on it, and I'll get back to you," he said, his mind already preoccupied with incomprehensible ideas and thoughts that average men would never comprehend.

Daeson and Raviel left the medtech bay with heavy hearts. At the doorway of their quarters, Raviel stopped and wrapped her arms around Daeson. "I say we don't waste a single minute of our time together bemoaning some random slim chance of a quantum catastrophe." Her smile soothed Daeson's concerns.

Daeson smiled, but the heaviness lingered in his heart. "You're right. And I bet you're famished," he added with a sly look as he stepped back from her. "I'll fetch some food while you..."

Raviel laughed. "You don't have to say it. I'll take a shower so you can stand to be around me again."

The next two days were filled with more fervent activity as stories of Tig's and Raviel's expedition were revealed. The horrors of the captives' conditions fueled the entire fleet's motivation to accelerate preparations for Liberation Day. On the third day, Tig arrived at the Strategy Council meeting a little less himself than Daeson was used to seeing. In spite of his determination to ignore his new handicap, the temporary prosthetic he had to wear for a while was difficult for him to get used to.

Daeson called the room to order and began by offering praise to Raviel and Tig for their courageous and successful mission of reconnaissance and rescue. They received a vigorous standing ovation which both attempted to quickly dismiss. Once the ovation subsided and everyone took their seats, Daeson turned the meeting over to the two of them. Tig looked toward Raviel, waiting for her to lead the briefing. Raviel wanted to choose her words carefully, but she also understood that every single person in this room wanted the blunt and untainted truth about what they were facing. She took a deep breath and began.

"Reekojah is a technological fortress," she stated bluntly before lowering her head. "The reports I've sent to you don't do it justice." She looked toward Daeson, noting the concern in his eyes and realizing that her tone and delivery could affect the morale and the initiative of the entire fleet. "And although we have yet to discover the weaknesses we are looking for, I know that Ell Yon will help us find a way. Here are the facts concerning the defense systems of Reekojah."

Raviel nodded to a tech controlling the 3D visual projector. The space in front of her immediately filled with technical specs and perfect three-dimensional holographic images of Reekojah and its protective dome.

"The dome is not your ordinary enhanced energy field like we have seen protecting smaller institutions, which are typically reflection fields that repel physical objects and energy weapons. Instead, it is a fully functioning domed stasis field on a colossal scale, similar to the micro stasis field used to protect the edges of a Talon's blade."

The response from the rest of the room was notable, especially from the scitechs who understood exactly what that meant.

"As most of you know, a stasis field cuts and/or disintegrates whatever it comes in contact with. There is no known substance that can molecularly withstand the impact of a stasis field, other than another stasis field. But the magnitude of Reekojah's domed stasis field is simply staggering."

"How were they able to shape the stasis field?" asked one scitech.

Raviel shook her head. "I have no idea. I wasn't able to study it in detail, other than to describe its capabilities. Avidan may be able to offer some insight on this." She glanced toward the lad and nodded.

Avidan stood and turned to address the room. He fidgeted at first as he struggled to find the right words.

"From what I have observed, and after analyzing Tig and Raviel's data, the dome's field antennas create a powerful secondary stasis energy boundary just inside the dome. The honeycomb visual that you see is that boundary field, not the actual stasis field."

The hologram displayed a visual depicting Avidan's description.

"Essentially, there is a double-layered energy boundary that creates the dome...one to guide the stasis field and another to offer the protective shielding. It's really quite remarkable." Avidan suddenly realized that admiring an enemy's technology at this time wasn't quite appropriate. He sat down.

Raviel looked around at the men and women as they considered Avidan's words. "One thing for sure, there's no going through it, and bombarding it with our weapons would be pointless. It must be disabled from the inside.

Disabling the stasis generator seems to be our best bet but—"

Raviel looked toward Tig. It was his turn.

"That will prove to be problematic as well," Tig acknowledged.

The hologram transitioned to show a fly-through of the Reekojan defense systems and locations.

"The generator is located in the central section of the city with an entire company of soldiers and guards protecting it every minute of every day. There are also auto-fire plasma cannons located around the periphery of the generator's housing base and weaponized drones that are constantly scanning this section of the city. Anyone without the proper identification is immediately killed...no questions asked," Tig explained.

Someone let out a low whistle.

"As far as I can tell, the one potential external weakness to the dome is at the very top center where the stasis field antennas are located," Raviel picked up the explanation. "The generator creates an energy beam that is projected upward toward the antenna platform. The platform is where the real tech-magic happens. It is suspended by eight anti-gravity engines, one thousand five hundred feet above the city center. Once the energy beam is received by a collector shield, the platform feeds each stasis antenna a portioned amount of energy that is converted to a stasis field and focused downward toward the receiving antennas at the base of the wall. There are thirty-six antenna pairs that create the dome. If the antenna platform could be destroyed, it would disrupt and disable the entire dome."

"That seems too obvious." Daeson sounded dubious. "What's the catch?"

Tig nodded. "On the wall near the base of the dome, there are class four plasma cannons positioned at each of the thirty-six stasis-field antennas."

"So we take out an entire section of plasma cannons on the base wall first, then fly in and destroy the antenna platform at the top of the dome," one of the fighter pilots offered.

"Won't work," Raviel said. "They also have four focused electromagnetic pulse devices that will disable any flying craft or electronic equipment that comes within twenty miles of the dome in any direction, except for the approved low-level flight corridors for traffic approaching the city gates. Those EMP devices are encased deep in the fortified lower sections of the wall. The lower wall would have to be completely obliterated before we dared to fly a single fighter or transport anywhere near the city."

The room fell silent for a long while. Raviel looked at Daeson apologetically. He slowly nodded, then came to stand beside her and Tig.

"The defenses of Reekojah are formidable, and we owe our gratitude to Raviel, Tig, and Avidan for risking their lives to bring us this critical information. Now it's up to us to find a way to bring this bastion of evil down. Thousands of innocent lives have been lost to Verdok and his treacherous people. As we speak, many more thousands of our brothers, sisters, and children suffer under their barbaric institutions of slavery and blood-thirsty entertainment. Though our challenge is great, do not forget that Sovereign Ell Yon has called us to this world, and he will be with us!"

"Hear, hear!" came unified shouts of approval.

"We are one under the Sovereign!" Daeson shouted.

"One under the Sovereign!" the people echoed in reply.

Daeson then broke up the assembly into four teams to evaluate their options and discuss possible solutions. Raviel, Tig, and Avidan floated between groups answering questions and providing input and additional information for any potential strategy. The meeting lasted hours as multiple plans were discussed, but at the end of the day, the only clear decision made was the need for a fleet of nimble ground assault vehicles once the dome was destroyed.

Over the course of the next few days, the forcetech and scitech guilds had designed what they dubbed an "A-65 Ground Screamer" marine troop carrier which utilized some anti-grav tech along with the aerodynamic ground effect principle. The design would allow the craft to carry up to ten soldiers at a hover height of up to thirty feet off the ground. Equipped with a class two medium plasma cannon mounted on a turret and two side-mounted phaser burst guns, the A-65 Ground Screamer would give them the agility, punch, and mobility necessary to gain quick access to the city. With Daeson's approval, they began fabrication of a prototype. Once that was approved, full manufacturing began.

Shortly thereafter, Avidan completed Tig's neuro-link prosthetic, which was nearly indistinguishable from his other leg. Daeson, Raviel, Rivet, and Kyrah were there when Avidan attached and verified its performance. Tig walked away from them then spun about and jumped up and down a few times. A wide grin spread across his face. He walked back and extended his hand to Avidan.

"Well done, lad. It works perfectly!"

Avidan took his hand and smiled back. "It's the least I could do in exchange for what you did for me. Thank you!"

Tig then turned to Kyrah who was smiling ear to ear as well, a slight blush in her cheeks.

"I never could dance much, but I think with this new technological marvel Avidan's made for me, I might be able to give it a try. Perhaps at the next monthly celebration you would be willing to accompany me?"

"I'd like that very much," Kyrah replied.

Rivet knelt down and began examining Tig's prosthetic closely. Even the skin looked real. He looked up at Avidan. "Could you fabricate synthetic skin for me?" he asked.

Avidan's eyes raised as he considered the request. "Well, I suppose—"

Raviel knelt down and looked at Rivet. "Rivet, why would you want such a thing?"

The android tilted its head. "Shouldn't it be my goal to look more human-like?" he asked as he stood and looked toward Daeson.

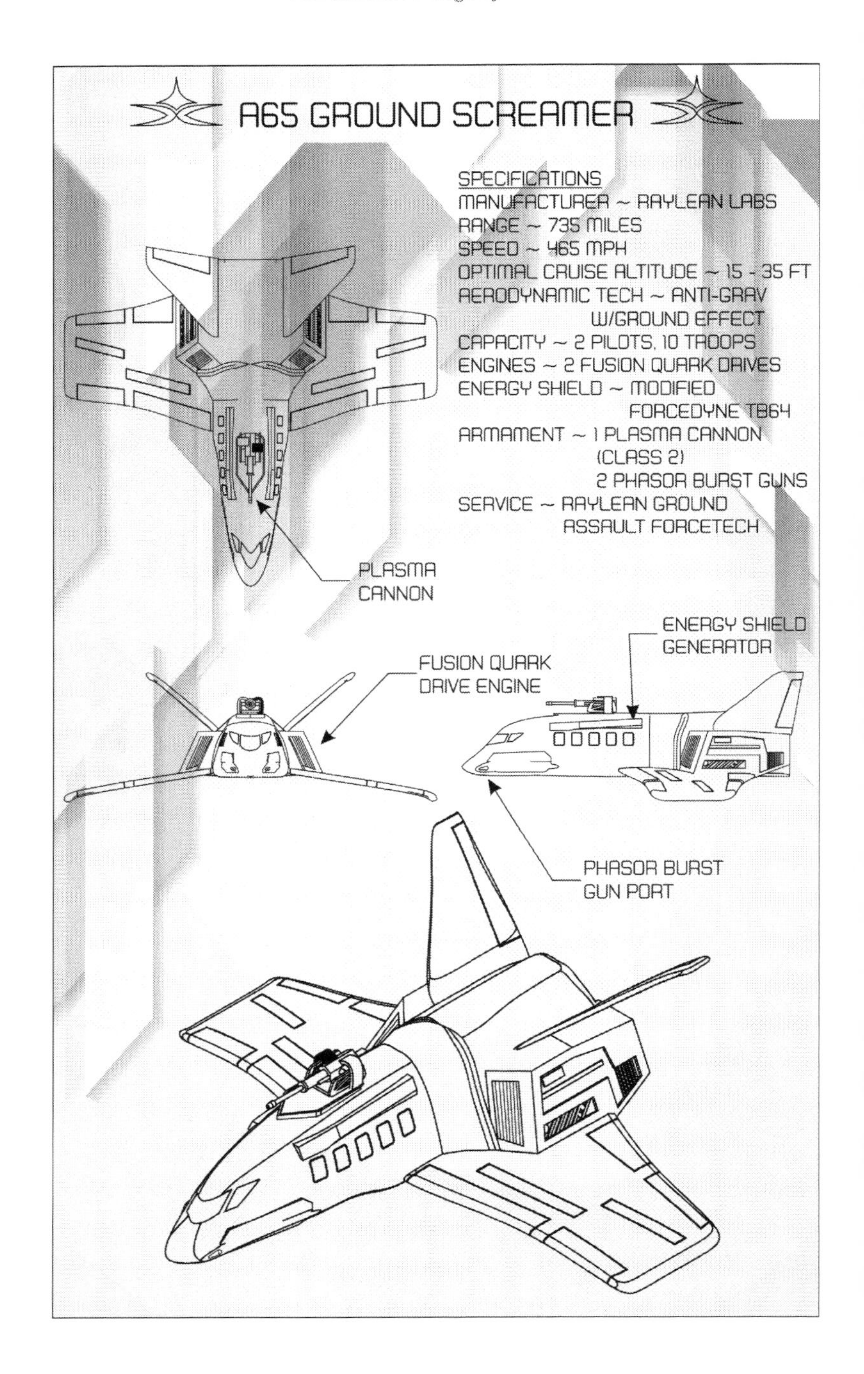
A65 GROUND SCREAMER
SPECIFICATIONS
MANUFACTURER ~ RAYLEAN LABS
RANGE ~ 735 MILES
SPEED ~ 465 MPH
OPTIMAL CRUISE ALTITUDE ~ 15 - 35 FT
AERODYNAMIC TECH ~ ANTI-GRAV W/GROUND EFFECT
CAPACITY ~ 2 PILOTS, 10 TROOPS
ENGINES ~ 2 FUSION QUARK DRIVES
ENERGY SHIELD ~ MODIFIED FORCEDYNE TB64
ARMAMENT ~ 1 PLASMA CANNON (CLASS 2)
2 PHASOR BURST GUNS
SERVICE ~ RAYLEAN GROUND ASSAULT FORCETECH
PLASMA CANNON
ENERGY SHIELD GENERATOR
FUSION QUARK DRIVE ENGINE
PHASOR BURST GUN PORT

Daeson crossed his arms and stared back at the bot. "No, Rivet. To do such a thing would put you in danger as an android. We need you just like this. Okay?"

Rivet nodded. "Yes, my liege."

Avidan then turned to Daeson and Raviel. "I also have something for you."

Avidan motioned for the two of them to follow him to another section of his lab. He retrieved a small black case and opened it. Inside was a thin black wafer. He lifted it carefully out of the container with a delicate instrument.

"Is this it?" Daeson asked. "Is this a device to stabilize Raviel's cells?"

"No, I'm afraid not," Avidan answered soberly. "I'm sorry to say that I don't believe there is a way to ensure that Raviel's cells will stabilize in this spacetime. But that doesn't mean you will have another incident either."

"Then what *is* this?" Raviel asked, nodding to the device he was holding.

"I've borrowed technology from our Quantum Entanglement Communicators and designed a spacetime locating beacon using the particle entanglement principle," Avidan explained.

The reality of what Avidan was implying sobered Daeson and Raviel.

"What you're saying is that if Raviel does time-slip again, I will be able to track her through time and find her."

Avidan nodded hesitantly. "Essentially, but it won't be quite that simple, and I must warn you that this is all just theoretical. We really don't have any way of testing this device, considering Raviel is the only person or thing, for that matter, that has ever experienced such a condition. We know that entangled particles remain linked regardless of distances, even hundreds of light years. In theory, this will be true even if one of the particles is experiencing extreme time dilation, like Raviel experienced when she time-slipped to this time period. I've devised an entangled transmitter," Avidan held up the device, "and a corresponding entangled receiver." He turned and reached for a small metal wristband. "If we implant the transmitter subdermally in Raviel, you, Daeson, should be able to track her through time and exit your own time dilation event fairly close to when Raviel restabilizes."

Daeson reached for the wristband, noticing the small display with a single number on it.

"That indicator tells you the time dilation delta...or in other words, how much more or less time dilation Raviel's transmitter has experienced. Right now, the number is zero because the two particles have been synchronized in this time. If you were to take the transmitter and travel at 90 percent the speed of light, the receiver would start indicating a positive number. If you then took the receiver on the same journey, the number would stop increasing until the transmitter decelerated to normal spacetime, at which point the receiver number would begin to decrease. When it reaches zero, both the transmitter and the receiver would have experienced the same time dilation and essentially arrived at the same spacetime...theoretically."

Daeson looked at Raviel then back to Avidan.

"What happens if the receiver overshoots and experiences a greater time dilation than the transmitter?" Daeson asked.

"The number on the wristband would become negative. Each number on the display roughly represents one month of time dilation." Avidan shook his head. "Even that is an approximation. We are venturing into uncharted territory." He looked up at Daeson and Raviel. "I know you were hoping for something more, but this is the best I have, at least for now."

Daeson put a hand on Avidan's shoulder. "It's amazing, Avidan. You are truly a remarkable young man."

"Yes, thank you!" Raviel added. "Where should the transmitter be implanted?"

"I would recommend under your armpit in the torso." Avidan pointed to the spot on himself. "The transmitter needs minimal power, so I use body heat to generate the few microwatts required. Also, it would probably be the most protected part of your body if you were ever in conflict. If it breaks—"

He didn't finish...he didn't need to.

"And you think a subdermal implant would be time-slipped with Raviel?" Daeson asked.

"I believe so," Avidan said. "It would explain why her clothes were so tattered during her last incident. It seems to me that anything actually in contact with her skin, the cells in quantum instability, experiences the same phenomena."

Raviel nodded. "I think I'll be wearing close-fitting undergarments from now on, just in case that theory is right. Can we implant the transmitter now?" she asked.

"Yes, I've told Master Gilzan—he's ready whenever you are."

Avidan put the transmitter implant back in its small black case and handed it to Raviel. She took the case then hugged the lad.

"Thank you, Avidan. You're my hero," she said then kissed his cheek.

Avidan blushed, turning away to tidy up his bench. Daeson locked the receiver wristband on his left wrist. "Now you can't get away from me even if you try," he quipped.

Raviel smiled, but there was a sadness behind it. Her life might very well never be the same. She could wake up one morning in a different century.

Over the next three months, incredible progress was made in preparation for their attack on the region and city of Reekojah. But there was still no solid plan to disable or destroy the dome that protected this impenetrable city. Daily Daeson sought the voice of Sovereign Ell Yon in this regard, but other than the command to advance, the Protector remained silent.

Finally, the day came when the A-65 Ground Screamers were complete, the air attack crafts had been acquired and weaponized, the pilots had been trained, ten transports had been adapted for battle, and the ground assault marines were fully trained and equipped. Daeson stood before his Strategy Council and the leaders of their attack force.

"All of our equipment and personnel are ready, Admiral," Chief Bern said as the meeting was called to order. "But we still don't have a plan for disabling the stasis dome. We also need a plan for staging the ground assault once the dome is down?"

"Yes," another added. "And our intel indicates that Verdok knows we're coming. I'm quite certain he's making preparations of his own."

Daeson remained quiet for a moment, thinking through all of the options and logistical challenges that such an assault from a space-faring people would face.

"Gentlemen, you are correct. Here's how we pull this off. Our first priority is to establish a forward operating base on Kayn-4 fourteen days prior to Liberation Day. The FOB will be fifty miles from Reekojah. This will be done under heavy protection from our aerotech fighters."

Daeson turned to the commander of the aerotech forces. "When Verdok's fighters attack that FOB—and they will attack—we don't just protect our FOB. We squash their offensive with overwhelming force. When they turn tail and run, we pursue and destroy them all the way back to Reekojah. Our pilots have superior training, and I want Verdok to know it. Commander, I want you to destroy every last one of their fighters. This will be our first message to this evil tyrant!"

"Yes, Admiral!" the commander exclaimed.

"Once the FOB is established and secure, we will begin transporting our A-65 Ground Screamers and forcetech assault personnel. From all of our intel reports, Verdok has been only marginally successful in garnering support from other Kayn-4 governments. I have a feeling that once we demonstrate our intentions with skilled and overwhelming force, that support will quickly dissolve. Tig, with an operational FOB, we should be able to establish communication with our contact inside the city. Any intel she can provide would prove invaluable in the days leading up to Liberation Day."

Tig nodded as Daeson continued.

"During the fourteen days leading up to Liberation Day, we will send scout ships through every slipstream gateway leading to the Kayn System to thwart any surprise attack from vessels that Verdok may be hiding. I want autonomous scanning probes sent to orbit every planet and every moon in the entire Kayn System that could hide any sizeable assault force. I don't want to be surprised by any clandestine operation Verdok might be planning. We will know where his forces are at all times."

Daeson looked at his intelligence officer. "I want a real-time map of every craft in the system and one slip-stream jump beyond, is that clear?"

"Yes, Admiral," the officer snapped.

"On Liberation Day, our attack sequence will be a simultaneous air attack by our fighters and ground attack by our A-65 Ground Screamers. We know that Verdok has a sizeable aerotech force...we've felt it here, so the battle for air superiority will be fierce, but we must win it quickly." Daeson looked once more at the aerotech commander. "I'll not lose a single troop transport! The lives of thousands of marines will depend on your assurance that we have air superiority and that all surface-to-air weapons in range of our transport landing site have been disabled."

Daeson turned to the chief. "Once the A-65 Screamers reach the city, we need a secure landing site for those transports ASAP."

"Roger that," Chief Bern replied.

Daeson scanned the faces of the leaders in the room. There was an anticipatory look of excitement as they waited for the one missing piece to his assault plan to liberate the slaves of Reekojah. He once more desperately listened for guidance from the Protector, but it remained silent.

Vice Admiral Orlic broke the silence. "What of the dome, Admiral? How do we destroy it?"

Avidan stood before Daeson could respond.

"And what of the slave-collar termination codes?" the lad asked. "Verdok could kill them all with the press of a button."

Daeson had no answer for either of the questions. Without warning, the Protector gently hummed, sending a wisp of power through Daeson's neurons. He hesitated, trying to recover from the overwhelming presence of his Commander's voice. *I will deliver Reekojah into your hands.*

Daeson recovered, straightening his back to address the assembly. He looked first to Orlic and Avidan, then to the rest of his people. "The Sovereign Ell Yon will provide. We must trust him. Tomorrow at 6 a.m. it begins. Prepare your people!"

Over the next fourteen days, all that Daeson had decreed had been accomplished. He also assigned Vice Admiral Orlic to command and to protect the fleet remaining in the Ianis System during the attack on Reekojah. Early in the morning on Liberation Day, Daeson addressed the entire fleet—ground assault forcetech personnel at their FOB on Kayn-4, as well as all aerotech pilots flying cover.

"Raylean people...this is our day, a day of deliverance, a day of hope, and a day to establish a future for our people. We are the people of the mighty Immortal Sovereign Ell Yon. He has promised us this world...a world of profound opportunity...a world of hope. Yes, there are giants and monsters to conquer and a dome to topple, but if Ell Yon is for us, who can stand against us? Choose today whom you will follow. I will follow Sovereign Ell Yon!"

At Daeson's declaration, every person stood with hands raised high.

"Sovereign Ell Yon!" came the shout of valiant unified voices.

"Sovereign Ell Yon!"

"Sovereign Ell Yon!"

CHAPTER 17

Flight of the Terridon

Daeson gave the order for the assault force to assemble and advance. Two hours later it was a sight to behold. Ten transports, which had been weaponized and converted into troop transports, and eighty-three fighter craft moved in formation to the slipstream conduit gateway that would take them into the Kayn System. Once through, there would be no question as to their purpose. Prefect Verdok would see his coming doom, and the rest of Kayn-4 would watch with fearful wonder. As Daeson had predicted, Verdok's attempt to rally an alliance of lesser governments on the planet to fight with him had utterly failed. They all feared that the Rayleans would then turn their attention to them and destroy them too. The outcome of the attack on Reekojah would dictate how these other governments would proceed in order to secure their future survival if the Rayleans were successful in toppling Verdok and his tyrannical power.

Chief Bern and Lt. Kyrah Antos were already on the ground on Kayn-4, ready to lead the Ground Screamer assault. Daeson and Raviel led the assault of the aerotech fleet in Starcraft Viper One with Tig and Rivet in Viper Two. Once it was confirmed that there appeared to be no secretive Reekojan aero forces either in the Kayn System or in other systems one jump away, most of the fighters entered the gateway first to provide arrival protection at the exit gateway. Then one by one the transports and remaining fighters made their journey to the Kayn System. The space here was eerily quiet—no trade ships, no transports, no traffic of any kind. In just a few hours, the fleet was entering orbit around Kayn-4.

"Continue scanning for any threats," Daeson radioed to his entire fleet. "They obviously know we're coming, and it's too quiet."

After confirming that there was no immediate threat, Daeson led the Raylean fleet in an atmospheric entry vector that brought them to Reekojah. They set up a wide circling pattern around the region with the transports at a safer distance. Even now there was no attempt to thwart their attack. Daeson waited for the Protector…nothing.

"They've buttoned up the region under the dome," Raviel said through her com link to Daeson. "The four gates are locked down."

"Copy that," Daeson replied.

The assault fleet circled the dome multiple times before setting down in an ancient siege-style position.

"Admiral," Rivet's voice called on the com link. "I'm picking up a broadcast from Reekojah. I'll pass it through to your monitor."

Daeson's glass monitor filled with images of horror as Verdok showed violent scenes from the games arena. The transmission ended with Verdok's scowling face. "Leave my planet at once, or I will execute every remaining Raylean in my city." The image zoomed in to reveal his twisted mind through darkened eyes. "I swear it!"

Daeson had seen those eyes before. Verdok was a willing puppet of the powerful archenemy of Ell Yon, Lord Dracus. As if to balance the galaxy, Lord Dracus was as evil and dark as Sovereign Ell Yon was perfectly good and full of light.

Chills of horror and anger flowed up and down Daeson's spine as the image of Verdok slowly faded away.

"The entire assault force will have seen this, Daeson," Raviel said. "We have to do something and soon!"

Daeson cleared his mind.

Mighty Ell Yon, your people are ready to hear your command. Speak and we will follow.

Daeson trembled as the whisper of the Immortal came. He dared not question the command of Ell Yon but could scarcely make his hands move. Although he didn't fully understand the plans of his Commander, he knew how it was to begin.

"Daeson?" Raviel queried.

"Hold on, Rav," Daeson said over the com link.

"Viper Two, have you established communication with our contact inside the city?"

"Roger, Viper One. She's monitoring for any slave termination code transmissions."

"Copy that. Remain here and ready the fleet. When Raviel returns, be ready to launch the assault. Once we've engaged, do whatever is necessary to protect our contact and keep me apprised of any intel she can provide."

"Copy, Viper One."

"And what did you mean, 'When Raviel returns'?" Raviel asked, the edge of her voice revealing her apprehension.

"I'm not exactly sure just yet, but I need you to come with me," Daeson replied. "Are you still strapped in?"

"Yes."

Daeson lifted off, and soon he and Raviel were skimming the treetops of the Titan Forest. He found an opening in which to set the Starcraft down. Once the cockpit canopies were open and they were on the ground, Raviel eyed him suspiciously as he led her a few paces away from the Starcraft.

"What's going on, Daeson?" Raviel questioned. "You know more than you're saying."

Daeson looked at her, his fear betraying his feigned attempt at courage. She came to him, putting a hand on his chest.

"What has he asked of you?" Raviel's eyes now mirrored his own apprehension.

He lifted the arm covered by the Protector into the air as a ribbon of blue energy emanated outward in all directions.

"We tried for months to find a way to take down the dome. There is none…except for one," Daeson said, his eyes scanning the horizon.

A shrill screech pierced the air around them, and then seconds later the alpha Terridon descended on them from above.

"No!" Raviel said, shrinking back from the frightening beast that was nearly upon them. "Surely not!"

The Terridon's wings pushed powerful bursts of air against them as it landed just a few paces away. It spewed a vicious hiss their direction. As if chained by some invisible tether, it tried to turn away but couldn't. Slowly it came toward them as Daeson held out his hand, the hypnotizing power of the Protector bathing the creature with subduing commands. Raviel and Daeson stared once more at the beast in near-paralyzing stupor. Slowly the Terridon unwillingly crouched down until its head was almost resting on the ground. Its eerie yellow eyes glared at Daeson the whole time. It snorted and shook against the power of Ell Yon, but it obeyed.

Without taking his eyes off the creature, Daeson turned his head to Raviel.

"You must take the Starcraft back to the assault forces and fly on Tig's wing for the attack. Tell him to be ready. I will fly on the back of this creature to the stasis platform. Because both it and I are organic, we should be able to make it through the EMP cannons and hopefully the plasma cannons as well."

Daeson felt Raviel's hand grip his arm. "I can't leave you here with this monster, Daeson. It looks like it wants to eat you at any second."

"I think you're right, Rav. But this is the only way," Daeson replied.

"Even if you make it to the platform...what then? How will you destroy the platform? How will you survive if you do?" Raviel asked.

Daeson shook his head. "I have no idea. I just know this is the command of Ell Yon. I'll deal with that question when the time comes. Please go and ready the forces. The longer the Protector keeps this Terridon under control, the more agitated it seems to become."

Raviel went to the Starcraft and climbed into the front cockpit. She donned her helmet then looked down at Daeson once more. Clearly torn by the difficult command of Ell Yon and her love for Daeson, she flipped down her visor as the canopy began to lower.

"Can you hear me?" Raviel radioed to his earpiece.

"Yes," Daeson replied quietly.

"Engines spooling up," she warned.

When the engines began to wind up, the Terridon nearly broke loose from the mesmerizing grip of the Protector. It snorted and screeched, trembling in power as it shifted to the left and rotated so it could see the Starcraft lift up and away. Once Raviel was gone, it turned its vicious yellow eyes back on its tormentor. Daeson slowly circled to the beast's left side. It opened its mouth wide and hissed, revealing rows of razor-sharp teeth. Daeson put a hand on its neck, and the Terridon trembled in defiance once again, but it allowed his hand to stay. Daeson's heart was racing, wondering if even a momentary interruption in the Protector's control would mean the end of him. He looked for a place where he could straddle the beast and found one section where the coarse scales might not be too painful. He tested his left foot on the creature's shoulder to see if it would react, but it stayed still. He put his weight on the muscled shoulder and lifted himself up and onto its neck.

Two spiny protrusions just aft of its neck made for decent handholds.

Daeson shook his head. "This is crazy!" he said quietly to himself.

When he felt as though he was set, he radioed Raviel.

"Viper One, do you have communication with Viper Two and the assault force?"

"Affirmative," Raviel replied. "Do you want me to tie you in?"

"Roger that." A few seconds later Daeson could hear Tig's voice.

"Viper One, this is Viper Two. What's your status?"

Daeson tried to position himself in order to get a firm hold on the creature. Once this ride began, he was quite certain there would be little he could do except hang on for his life.

"Viper One is en route to your location. I will be following shortly after. Prepare all ground and air assault teams for immediate deployment."

"Copy. We can be ready in fifteen minutes," Tig answered. "How will we identify your craft?"

Daeson could hear the confusion in Tig's voice and rightly so. Daeson hesitated with an answer, not sure just how to describe this bizarre situation. The Terridon shook its head and snorted once again, displaying its extreme displeasure as it waited impatiently for Daeson.

"I will be flying directly to the target on the back of a Terridon. When the dome falls, attack."

Seconds passed. Daeson could wait no longer. He gripped tightly to the Terridon's spines.

"Copy, Sky Rider. Ell Yon be with you!" Tig finally replied.

Daeson smiled at Tig's new call sign for him as he nudged the base of the beast's neck with the heels of his feet. That one motion catapulted him into the wildest ride he had ever imagined. The beast sprinted forward five paces, spread its massive wings, and launched into the forest air. Daeson's stomach churned as the ground disappeared from beneath him. It took every bit of strength and stamina he had to hang on. He nearly flipped around the side of the creature when it banked to miss a tree. Then when it launched itself nearly vertical, Daeson clung to its neck in desperation. This was the most painful, frightening experience he'd ever had in his life. The Terridon accelerated upward toward a break in the lofty forest canopy, and Daeson hung on for his life once more.

Once above the trees, the beast leveled out and began a flight path for Reekojah. The less aggressive maneuvering above the forest trees allowed Daeson to recover from his sheer terror and concentrate on finding a better position from which to ride. He discovered that if he placed his feet against the spot where the Terridon's wings attached to its torso, it provided significant stability. Though Daeson was well acquainted with flying of most forms, this was wholly unique. To feel the pulsing wings beneath his feet and the warm exhaust of the creature's breath was both frightening and spectacular at the same time. He was quite certain that he would have enjoyed the experience immeasurably more if he didn't feel as though the Terridon would rather eat him than carry him.

As he skimmed the tops of the Titan Forest, the Protector continued to radiate its powerful influence. All at once, the Terridon opened its massive jaws and bellowed a screech that would carry for miles. Without warning, it turned and circled back over the forest in a broad arc, screeching four more times as it did so. That Daeson was not in control of the beast's actions was quite evident. He wondered what had prompted the creature to circle back, until he saw movement in the canopy below. At first, he saw two Terridons rise up, then four, then dozens. The sight was terrifying.

Had the beast found a way to circumnavigate the power of the Protector? Over twenty flying monsters were headed his way, and there was nothing Daeson could do to stop them. But as the Terridons approached, they did not try to pluck him from the back of their reluctant leader. Instead, they flew in trail behind him. When all were gathered, the alpha Terridon resumed its course toward Reekojah, along with twenty-three more of its kind in a chaotic flock of giant flying lizards. It was then that Daeson understood what Ell Yon was doing. A Terridon was immune to any EMP burst weapon, but not to the class four plasma cannons. These creatures were large enough for the cannons to lock onto and take down. His winged escorts would be diversions so that he could hopefully reach the platform. The alpha began to climb high into the sky, flying over the tops of the Raylean assault fleet that had resumed its circling pattern around the city of Reekojah. Daeson shivered against the cold, thin air. He looked behind him to see the other Terridons still following.

"Vipers One and Two, I'm at your six o'clock high," he radioed.

"Copy, Sky Rider. We have a tally on your position. What's the plan?" Tig asked.

"Hold your position until the dome is down. Arm weapons hot," Daeson replied.

"Copy, Sky Rider. All units, arm weapons hot and hold your positions."

Soon they would be within range of the thirty-six plasma cannons that protected the airspace over the region of Reekojah. The Protector began to pulse bursts of energy, at which time the rest of the Terridons began to spread away from Daeson. The honeycomb glow of the city's stasis-field dome was now clearly visible.

"Sky Rider, be advised you are now within weapons range of the dome cannons," Raviel's voice chimed in his ear.

Daeson was too cold to respond. He was finding it difficult to even hang on. Then all at once, the beast tucked its wings and began a forty-five-degree dive toward the dome. The speed the creature was able to attain was terrifying. Daeson closed his eyes and ducked his head to reduce the force of the wind drag so he wouldn't lose his grip on the horny spines.

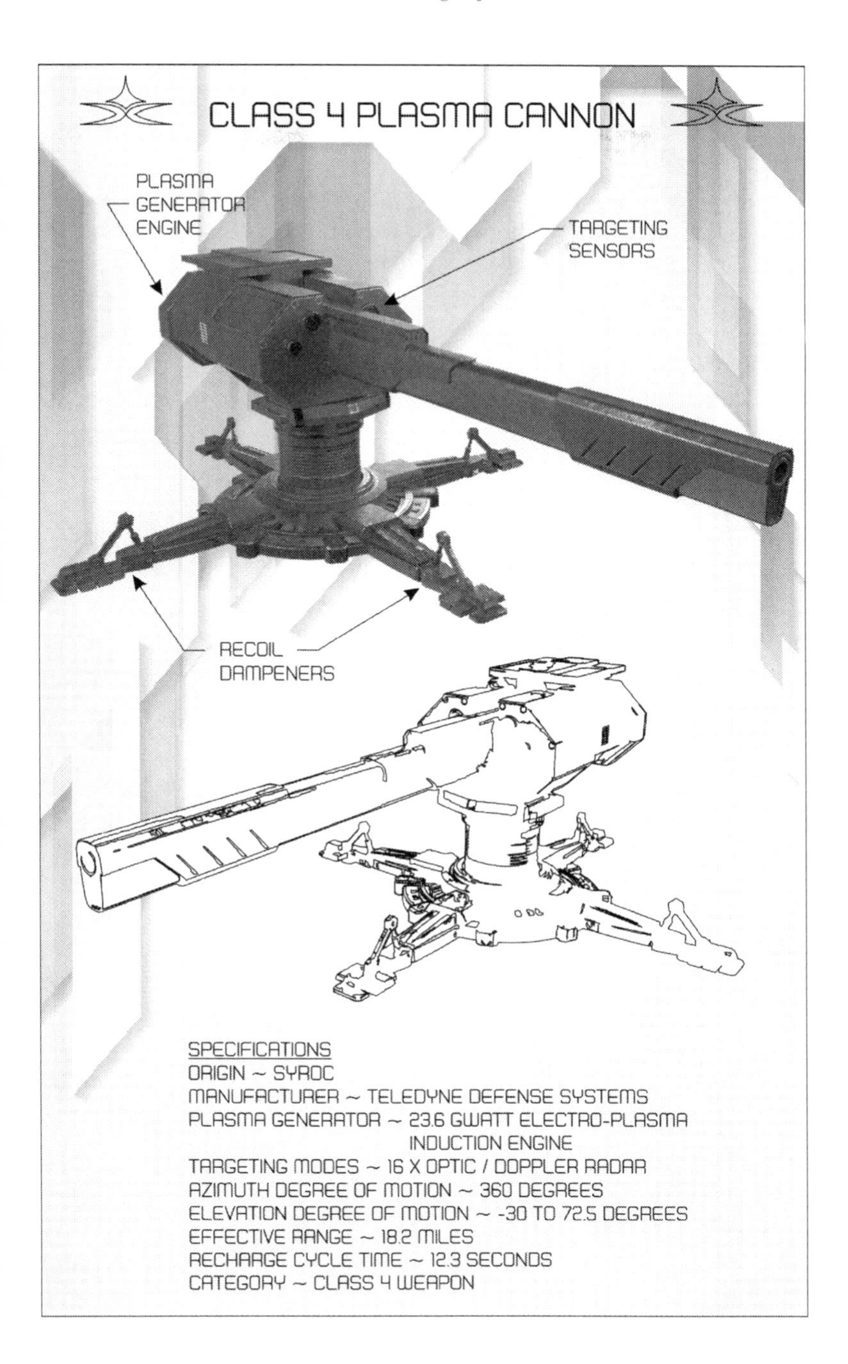
CLASS 4 PLASMA CANNON
PLASMA
GENERATOR
ENGINE
TARGETING
SENSORS
RECOIL
DAMPENERS
SPECIFICATIONS
ORIGIN ~ SYROC
MANUFACTURER ~ TELEDYNE DEFENSE SYSTEMS
PLASMA GENERATOR ~ 23.6 GWATT ELECTRO-PLASMA INDUCTION ENGINE
TARGETING MODES ~ 16 X OPTIC / DOPPLER RADAR
AZIMUTH DEGREE OF MOTION ~ 360 DEGREES
ELEVATION DEGREE OF MOTION ~ -30 TO 72.5 DEGREES
EFFECTIVE RANGE ~ 18.2 MILES
RECHARGE CYCLE TIME ~ 12.3 SECONDS
CATEGORY ~ CLASS 4 WEAPON

Daeson heard the rapid concussion of plasma fire far below, and he chanced a glance to his left and right to see the other Terridons diving at the dome as well. One of the creatures took a hit to its left wing and careened out of control, screeching as it fell. A moment later the beast impacted into the dome, which disintegrated the creature's carcass in a fraction of a second. Streaks of plasma fire swished past Daeson on his right and on his left as he felt the alpha Terridon maneuver with incredible agility in a ferocious dive to apparent destruction.

The closer they came to the dome, the fewer the number of plasma cannons there were to shoot at them, simply because of line-of-sight geometry. The dome itself had now eliminated the direct line of fire of all but three cannons. Another shot rang out, and the Terridon rolled so quickly to the right that Daeson nearly lost his grip. He felt the searing heat of the plasma as it passed by, narrowly missing him and the beast. Daeson struggled to regain his position and hold on to the creature. He remounted just as the Terridon pitched slightly upward, now just one hundred yards away from the platform.

Things were happening so fast there was barely time for him to react. One more cannon burst rang out, and the beast was too close and too slow to avoid it. The searing heat energy tore into the lower section of the Terridon's left wing. It screeched angrily as it tried to adjust its now erratic flying. Just thirty yards away from the platform, the plasma cannon fire stopped. The dome once again disrupted the line of fire, but the reprieve from Daeson's predicament remained precarious. The Terridon approached the platform with powerful vertical bursts of its wings, trying all the while to compensate for its injury. The creature was able to hover just a few feet above the platform, waiting for Daeson to jump. For Daeson, it would still be a ten-foot fall onto a hardened surface.

The creature screeched in anger, waiting. Daeson saw more landing area to his right than his left, so he flung his left leg over the neck of the creature and let go. He did his best to perform a parachute landing fall to keep from breaking a leg. He hit the platform with as much arc in his body as possible and rolled. The momentum carried him to the very edge of the platform where the unforgiving power of the stasis field was waiting to disintegrate him at his first touch. He teetered with his torso hanging just inches away from arcing death. Just below him he could see one of the eight anti-gravity engines pushing up against the platform. He reached behind him, trying desperately to get a hold of something to pull him back, but the smooth surface of the platform offered nothing. Ever so carefully and slowly, he regained his balance, finally turning and rolling away from the edge of the platform. Out of the corner of his eye, he saw the alpha Terridon swooping downward at great speed, skimming just above the stasis field toward the ground.

"I guess you're not my ride home," Daeson said. Then a sobering thought hit him...*What if there is no ride home? What if this is a one-way trip?*

Daeson stood, feeling the vibration of immense power beneath him. Were it not for the collector shield just a few feet underneath the platform, the beam of transmitted power from the generator far below on the ground would incinerate him in a microsecond. He looked around for something to make sense of why he was here. With the exception of multiple pie-shaped, segmented seams converging at the very center, the top of the platform was featureless. Yet within its construction was the powerful technology that converted the transmitted energy beam into stasis-field energy. Around the platform's circular edge were thirty-six antennas that directed the stasis-field energy downward toward the receiving antennas mounted on the perimeter wall far below. Daeson was eager to do something, but he had no weapons and no explosives.

"Sovereign Ell Yon, this is all by your hand. What am I to do?" he asked, calming himself under the power of the Immortal.

The Protector guided him to stand at a specific place, at a particular azimuth near the center of the platform. Daeson hesitated, knowing that his next action could mean the end of his life. Slowly he placed his hand directly over the center of the platform and opened his fingers wide. The Protector surged to life, its jeweled ribbons building blue arcs of Immortal power. Daeson readied himself, knowing deep within that whatever Ell Yon was going to accomplish through the Protector would demand his all. That emptying of body, mind, and soul took its toll, especially for one not thoroughly purged of Deitum Prime. Such power crushed mortals, undoing them because of their inability to be in the presence of such terrifying power.

The Protector's power amplified to such strength that Daeson felt as though he could not bear it. Then in a moment, it unleashed on the city of Reekojah. Uncontainable power exploded through the Protector and into the structure of the platform. At first a single burst of power seemed to push through the platform and into the deflector dish. Then over the next ten seconds, a rhythm of unstoppable power began to pulse across that platform in all directions except where Daeson was standing and directly behind him. Daeson felt the shudder of the platform with each harmonic pulse, building in intensity until it was apparent that something, perhaps everything, was going to explode.

Through the crescendo of the noise, Daeson barely caught a radio transmission stating that the slave termination codes had been activated, but apparently there was no effect on the collars all of the slaves were wearing. Daeson continued to hold the Protector as commanded but cringed as the inevitable was about to happen. How could he possibly survive this collision of energy fifteen hundred feet in the air? Perhaps Ell Yon was asking of him the ultimate sacrifice. Was he able to give it?

In a fraction of a moment, his contemplation came to an abrupt end. One final burst of the Protector's power was enough to tear the platform to pieces. First, a harmonic energy wave rippled outward from the platform into the stasis field in all directions except one. When this wave was received by thirty-four of the thirty-six antennas on the ground wall, the entire wall and plasma cannon abutments on the ground crumbled to rubble in seconds. Only a small segment of the wall remained intact.

Two seconds later, the platform on which Daeson was standing exploded with such force that it could be seen from twenty-five miles in all directions. Daeson was swallowed in the convergence of mighty power. The eight antigravity engines careened off on wild trajectories. The collector shield shattered in an instant, and the energy beam being transmitted from the massive generator station on the ground below exploded upward one hundred miles into the atmosphere. The dome of Reekojah was destroyed, and Daeson's world went black.

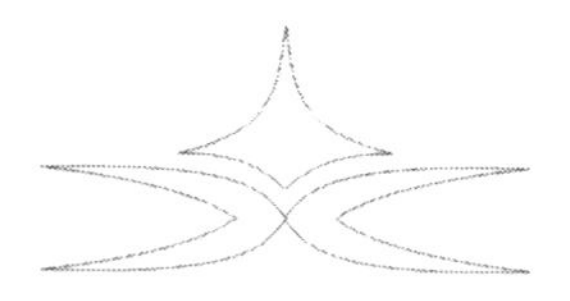

18

Attack!

Using the advanced optical imaging system of her Malakian-modified Starcraft, Raviel zoomed in to see the dome's floating platform. She watched in frightful anticipation as Daeson became a conduit of energy by which the Protector transmitted pulses of destructive power into the stasis-generating platform.

"Viper Two, are you seeing this?" Raviel radioed from her position in the circling line of assault ships.

"Yes, Viper One."

"He has no way down. When that thing blows—"

Tig didn't reply.

"I'm going in!" Raviel radioed.

She banked her Starcraft ninety degrees to the left, simultaneously pushing her throttles up to full speed.

"Assault force, hold position!" Raviel heard Tig radio as he attempted to join up with her, but her Starcraft quickly outdistanced him. Each flight lead acknowledged Tig's standing order.

Raviel's acceleration quickly brought her inside the weapons range of the Reekojan class four plasma cannons, but it didn't matter. Raviel gasped in horror as the entire dome rippled outward from the platform and down to the ground wall. The concussion obliterated the entire wall and cannon abutments in seconds, leaving a wake of rubble all around the city. Raviel immediately thought of Hara, her family, and the promise that she and Tig had made to them.

"Oh no!" she exclaimed, glancing to the southwest section of the city where Hara's dwelling had been located. She saw one small segment of the wall intact. Could it be? A couple of seconds later the unthinkable occurred—the platform on which Daeson was standing exploded. The resulting chaos was difficult to watch—anti-gravity engines swirling out of control, antenna fragments flying in every direction, and the platform itself turning into fragmentation projectiles that would take out anything in their path. The most horrifying of all for Raviel was watching Daeson being swallowed up in the generator station's immensely powerful energy beam, which shot up into the air for miles. The last image she had of Daeson was a blue cocoon of energy being flung upward in the direction of the energy beam.

Raviel was almost to the resulting chaos. She pitched her Starcraft straight up, not knowing if there was anything she could do.

"Aerial assault team, attack!" she heard Tig order. The radio quickly filled with coordination and alert communication. She isolated Daeson's com channel while scanning for life signs in the space above the flying wreckage.

Where are you, Daeson? Surely Ell Yon has protected you!

Is this the end for me? Daeson asked himself.

As in a dream where one knows he is dreaming, Daeson sensed his life was in great peril, yet he was not afraid. The presence before him wasn't clear, but he knew who it was.

"There's much to do to prepare for my coming. I will ask much of you, and it will not be easy. Your own people will turn against you for my name's sake, but not all. I come not only for Rayl, but for all people throughout the galaxy...to undo the evil of Lord Dracus and free them from the prison of Deitum Prime. You will see this thing, and when your end comes, you will be with me."

"But Commander, how is this possible?" Daeson questioned.

"Wake up, Navi Starlore!" the voice commanded.

"Daeson, can you hear me?" Raviel's voice was distant at first.

Just as before, Daeson felt like every last ounce of energy in his body had been completely drained. Slowly he opened his eyes to the spinning blue skies of Kayn-4. The Protector had shielded him from the blast of the stasis field platform explosion by encompassing him in a sphere of protection. The problem was that he had been hurled thousands of feet into the air by the generator station energy beam. Now he was free-falling from over two thousand feet, unprotected.

"Raviel! I'm here!" he managed to radio back, the adrenaline rush of the free-fall helping to accelerate his recovery.

"I've got a lock on you," Raviel exclaimed. "I'm going to attempt a grappling field lock."

Daeson knew that was her only option, but he also knew that the odds of success were a thousand to one. The ground was approaching fast. The wind screaming by his ears indicated that he had already reached terminal velocity. He looked to the Protector, but it was silent and still, its job complete. In the chaos of impending battle and his own doom there was a peace inside him that he couldn't explain. It was as if he knew, through and through, that Sovereign Ell Yon was with him, whether in life or in death.

"Raviel...I love you!"

"Don't you talk like this is the end. I'm coming for you!" she rebuked.

Daeson positioned himself to view the advancing assault forces, both air and ground. The aerotech forces were already beginning their attack runs on the remaining defense cannons inside the region of the destroyed dome. The ground forces were advancing quickly, the A-65 Ground Screamers leading the way but still a few miles out. They were taking intense fire from the remaining plasma cannons inside the dome's perimeter as the aerotech forces worked quickly to eliminate them. He scanned for Raviel and found her. She was coming in fast, diving at a forty-five-degree angle, but the ground was coming fast too. Even if she did make it to him in time, the Starcraft's grappling field would probably tear him apart if she was able to effect a lock before he hit the ground. He had perhaps ten seconds before impact. He cringed at the thought of either outcome—death by being torn apart or death by impact.

Seven seconds.

Raviel banked hard to expose the underbelly of the Starcraft to Daeson. This was where the grappling field pod was located.

Six seconds.

The ground rush was overwhelming. Daeson couldn't breathe through the angst of the moment. There was one chance and one chance only.

Five seconds.

The roar of the Starcraft under full deceleration screamed by him in a wash of wake and exhaust.

Four seconds.

Daeson felt the Starcraft's grappling field tug on his body, but he continued to fall as the Starcraft flew past him.

Three seconds.

I'm sorry, Raviel!

Two seconds.

An ear-piercing screech intercepted the moment as Daeson's arms were nearly ripped out of their sockets. The alpha Terridon tightened its grip around his upper arms, yanking Daeson out of his free fall. The momentum of his fall and the creature's dive continued to carry them both downward for the last one hundred feet, but at least the deceleration was something his body could mostly endure. The creature opened its wings wide and pitched upward at the last fraction of a second in an effort to halt the falling velocity. The beast dropped Daeson the final few feet then hit the ground in a flurry of dust and flailing wings just a few feet away. Daeson rolled a half dozen times before coming to a stop just a few paces away from the beast. Both Daeson and the Terridon took a few seconds to recover. When Daeson was able to recover his feet, he turned around to see the Terridon baring its teeth, its angry yellow eyes locked onto him.

Daeson held up his hands and began to back away. The Terridon screeched one last time as if to say, "I'm done with you…the next time I see you, I will eat you!"

"You're free," Daeson said gently.

The beast snorted, then turned abruptly to take flight. As it did so, it swished its tail, smacking Daeson across his right side which sent him reeling to the ground again…a reminder that this creature was not a friend, but rather a coerced enemy.

"All right…I get it!" Daeson shouted after the beast.

Daeson stood once more, bruised and bleeding in multiple places but alive.

"Daeson!" Raviel's panicked voice screamed into his ear.

"I'm all right," he radioed back.

"But how?" Raviel asked. By now she was turning back toward him. "That's impossible. I missed!"

"I had a little help from an acquaintance," he replied.

"I'll set down and pick you up," Raviel radioed.

"No," Daeson returned. "You stay in the air and assist the air assault. I'm going in with the ground units. I want to personally take down Bandit One. Radio for a Screamer to pick me up."

"Navi, this is Screamer Two. I have your coordinates and will be there in two mics," Daeson heard Kyrah's voice interrupt.

"Copy that, Screamer Two. Prep your team. We're going straight to the capitol complex for Verdok."

"Roger."

A few minutes later, Daeson was strapped in next to Kyrah in her A-65 Ground Screamer. Here, Daeson was able to fully engage in the assault. Tig, Raviel, and their aerial assault force were making quick work of the air defense systems and enemy aero craft, as well as any other surface-to-air plasma cannons. Air-to-air encounters were taking place everywhere over the now domeless skies of Reekojah, but the training of the Raylean pilots was superior so they were quickly gaining the upper hand. On the ground, two remaining class four cannons were raining fire down on the advancing Ground Screamers, hindering their advance. One powerful blast took out the Ground Screamer right next to Daeson and Kyrah.

"Viper Two, get air support to take out those two cannons on the southern wall immediately. We're taking heavy fire!"

"Copy, Navi. Makson, disengage and target those wall cannons," Tig ordered.

"I'm on it," Makson responded.

Two minutes later both cannons were obliterated, which allowed the advancing ground assault marines in the remaining A-65 Screamers to penetrate the outer perimeter of the crumbled wall. Once inside, they quickly established strongholds within the dome's inner region.

After the aerotech forces established air superiority over the outlying areas, they secured a landing site for the first troop transport. Over two thousand soldiers disembarked to establish a forward operating position. Forty-five minutes later, the rest of the transports had landed. The entire assault force was now in play, and Daeson orchestrated a sector-by-sector advance.

"Screamer One, continue advancing as planned. I'm taking Screamer Two and these marines into the capitol complex. Radio any information to me regarding the whereabouts of Bandit One," Daeson ordered.

"Copy, Navi," Chief Bern replied.

At first, the fight was intense, but it quickly became obvious that the Rayleans would carry the day, so the Reekojan forces began surrendering in mass. Daeson and Kyrah advanced toward Prefect Verdok's capitol complex with multiple Screamers and marines following close behind. Once they reached the complex, Daeson, Kyrah and eight marines disembarked their Screamer and continued on foot, while the other Screamers attempted to secure the rest of the grounds. The fighting at the complex was extremely intense.

"These are Verdok's loyal capitol guards," Daeson explained. "Keep your eyes open and watch out for those defense drones!"

Daeson, Kyrah, and their marines made it to an inner courtyard but were pinned down by two squads of guards and a heavy-duty plasma cannon. They were taking a beating.

"We need air support!" Kyrah screamed as pieces of fractured concrete peppered them from a near-hit plasma round.

"Viper One and Two, this is Screamer Two. We need air support at the capitol complex, sector alpha three. Gun emplacement at these coordinates."

"Copy, Screamer Two. I'll be there in thirty seconds," Raviel replied.

Daeson looked above them to see the skies still hosting a few air-to-air combat battles.

"Plasma fire here is intense. Approach from the west and watch your six," Daeson radioed.

Daeson and Kyrah's squad continued to return fire, but they were still pinned down with no avenue of advance or escape. A few seconds later Daeson heard the sweet sound of an approaching Starcraft. Raviel banked between two of the buildings, slowed to a near-hover, and fired a concussion missile that completely obliterated the gun emplacement. She then rotated forty degrees, blasting her phasor burst gun as she went. She immediately took fire from a squad of capitol guards, but one plasma cannon burst later, they were gone. The whole engagement was executed with the experience of a veteran Starcraft pilot.

"Well done, Viper One. We'll take it from here. You're a sitting duck down here so you're cleared off," Daeson warned.

"Copy, Navi," Raviel radioed. She pushed her engines up and accelerated out of the complex to the next engagement.

Daeson and Kyrah led their marines across the courtyard to discover yet another threat of which they had been completely unaware. They immediately began to face rapid fire from two ten-foot-tall weaponized ground combat drones, each armed with two heavy-duty plasma guns. Due to the cover of the capitol building's structures, there was no hope of aerial support in this location. Kyrah called for additional marine support, but these death machines were relentless, and the situation was turning dire quickly. Two of their marines took hits and were severely injured.

"Where did these things come from?" Kyrah asked. "How about a little Protector intervention?"

Daeson looked down at the silent, shining vambrace around his arm. He shook his head.

"It doesn't work like that," he shouted over the recent concussions. "You can be sure of one thing—I don't control it...it controls me!"

Up above, Daeson saw Tig's Starcraft slide to a hover position.

"Tig," Daeson shouted through the chaos. "We're under fire by two ground combat drones."

"Copy. I can't get a shot without taking down the whole building. What do you want me to do?"

Daeson scrambled for an answer. Even a broad-burst phasor blast wouldn't affect these mechanical monsters. More ferocious plasma fire exploded around them. When it looked like there were no options, Daeson saw Tig set down on top of the building.

"Hold on...I have an idea," Tig radioed. A minute later, a metallic form fell forty feet from a concrete awning right above one of the drones. Rivet landed directly on top of the machine, simultaneously spearing right through its upper protective armor with a fully extended TalonX. Electrical arcs and smoke flew in all directions. He then flipped over the side of the disabled machine and used his TalonX to cut loose one of the plasma guns from its mount before immediately opening fire on the other unsuspecting drone. After a barrage of eight rapid bursts, the second drone slumped in a heap of melted metal. Rivet turned and waited for Daeson and Kyrah. Daeson approached Rivet with caution. The android had fought like the AI androids back on Mesos—like a veteran of war.

When Daeson was within a few steps, Rivet bowed his head. "My liege, I am pleased to see you are unharmed."

"Well done, Rivet," Daeson said, once more surprised and alarmed at the bot.

Just then another Screamer full of marines joined them at the complex.

"Admiral Navi, where do you want us?" the sergeant asked.

"We've got two marines down near that wall. Have two of your men extract them, and the rest of you come with us," Daeson ordered.

Once inside the capitol building, the fighting continued with great intensity. They were able to subdue and capture three guards and one of Verdok's officers. In spite of the intense fighting, there was a sense of defeat in Verdok's men. After a couple minutes of questioning, Daeson discovered that Verdok was still in the prefect chambers on the top floor of the capitol building.

They cleared each floor as they went. Kyrah and her men performed flawlessly in taking out the remaining capitol guards. Once they made it to Verdok's floor, Daeson halted them at the entrance to the prefect's chambers. He, Kyrah, Rivet, and six marines crouched at the corner of the hallway leading to the chamber door.

"Scan," Daeson ordered.

"Only one life form," Rivet replied, still carrying the heavy-duty plasma gun.

"Weapons? Explosives?" he asked.

"Negative," Rivet answered.

Kyrah looked at Daeson. "This must be a trap."

Daeson stood up. "Let's find out."

He walked to the door under the cover of Rivet, Kyrah, and the marines. Flipping his rifle over his back, he drew his Talon, extending it to full blade. Once he was within two feet, the door silently slid open in four directions revealing the elaborate chambers of the Prefect of Reekojah. Verdok was standing with his back to Daeson, gazing out through a wall of glass that displayed a city under attack. Billows of smoke lifted from hundreds of places across the city. Alarms were sounding, and of course the great stasis dome was destroyed. The generator station was still shooting its massive column of energy up into space. Daeson prepared himself, fully expecting Verdok to be armed with Lord Dracus's Triad weapon.

"My time here was satisfying," Verdok said without turning around.

"Your time here is over," Daeson replied. "You will stand trial for crimes against humanity and submit yourself to the justice of the Raylean—"

"I will submit myself to no one!" Verdok screamed. He turned and came at Daeson with neither weapon in his hand nor Triad on his chest.

Rivet stepped forward as Kyrah and her six marines all lifted their plasma rifles, each one aimed at the man's chest. Verdok stopped a few feet away, but he was close enough for Daeson to peer into his soul, a soul controlled by the enemy of Ell Yon—Lord Dracus. The Protector vibrated in angry arcs of blue.

"I see," Daeson said.

"Do you, Navi?" Verdok said, his tone dripping with condescension. "Do you really see? I have taken great pleasure in tormenting these miserable people for nearly three hundred years. Don't be so naïve as to think that the conquest of one city in a galaxy that I own will do anything to advance the cause of your petty Sovereign."

"Yes...I see, Dracus. Yet I'm surprised that you haven't even offered a Triad for your impuissant pawn to fight with," Daeson replied.

Verdok's eyes glared back in ancient fury. He began to laugh.

"You think that was the pinnacle of my power here?" he scoffed. "That was a mere prototype...a toy for Linden

Lockridge to play with." Verdok instantly stopped his mirthful response and peered into the depths of Daeson's soul. "When you see my power again, you will fall to your knees is petrified fear!"

Daeson glared back at the man possessed with the dark mind of Dracus.

"Take him," Daeson ordered.

"That won't be necessary," Verdok replied. "I'm done with this worthless mortal. But be warned, Navi Starlore…I'm coming to kill you *and* the one you love!"

For one fraction of a moment, Daeson could see Verdok's eyes shift from those of a vicious ancient Immortal foe to a petrified soul who had no idea to whom he had vowed his allegiance. Before the marines could move in on him, Verdok grabbed his chest. In an instant, the air in front of them exploded in a burst of white-hot plasma and burnt flesh. Verdok flew backward across the room and into the glass wall that shattered as his body fell lifeless to the capitol courtyard below.

Everyone slowly turned to see Rivet holding a smoking plasma rifle. The android's expressionless eyes looked at Daeson. "You were in danger, my liege," he said calmly.

"But you said he had no weapons," Daeson said, stunned by the bot's actions.

Rivet slowly lowered his weapon. "I may have been wrong," he replied simply.

An eerie silence hung in the smoke-filled room. Rivet tilted his head, then dropped the rifle.

"I have taken the life of a human. I will submit myself for termination."

Kyrah stepped right in front of Rivet and stared into his eyes. "That was no human…that was a heartless animal that deserved a thousand deaths." She then turned to Daeson and the rest of the marines. "Our work here is done. Let's liberate this city!"

She led her marines out of Verdok's chamber, leaving Daeson alone to contemplate the actions of Rivet.

Daeson stepped closer to the android. Now that it was no longer a mimic droid controlled by Lieutenant Ki, had the remnants of Mesos artificial intelligence programming taken over? Daeson hated the rising doubts that were resurfacing.

"Did Verdok really have a weapon?" Daeson asked.

Rivet hesitated. "He did not," the bot finally replied.

Chills flowed up and down Daeson's neck as he considered Rivet's answer.

"Then why did you kill him?"

Rivet stared at Daeson with hollow eyes. "Judgment."

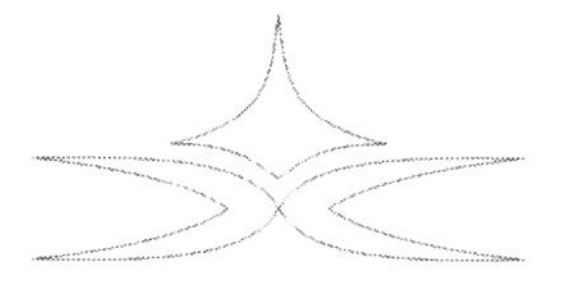

19

Keeping a Promise

"He was despised and rejected, a man of sorrow, taking upon his shoulders our punishment. By his torment we are reclaimed and made whole." ~Eziam, Oracle of Ell Yon

The liberation of nearly two hundred thousand slaves, most of them Rayleans, was a massive undertaking that would take months to sort through, but when the fighting was over and the city belonged to the Rayleans, Daeson gathered his circle of leaders.

"Tig, is the woman who helped you safe, and her family?" he asked.

"By quite a miracle, yes, she is," Tig replied. "Ell Yon allowed us to keep our promise."

"Then I'd like to meet her. I think she deserves our gratitude," Daeson said.

When they arrived at Hara's dwelling in an A-65 Ground Screamer, it was a spectacular sight. The entire lower section of the dome wall around the entire city had been shattered by the Protector's harmonic pulse wave...all except this one section of the wall. Here Hara's dwelling stood intact and unharmed. Daeson realized that Hara's dwelling was located in the direction from the platform that was in line with where the Protector had instructed him to stand. Daeson, Raviel, Tig, Kyrah, and Chief Bern were greeted by Hara and her family out on the front terrace.

"Hara, I'd like you to meet Admiral Navi, Lieutenant Kyrah, and Chief Bern," Tig said warmly.

Daeson stepped forward and bowed. "I am honored to meet you, Hara. Your courage and faith are an example to us all. Our people are now your people. You and your family have a future with us."

Hara smiled, reaching down to hold the hands of her children. "The goodness of your Sovereign is legendary for any who desire to hear it. It is our hope to be joined to this great people of his. Thank you."

After a few more words were exchanged, Hara finally turned to Kyrah and offered her hand.

"So, you're the one," Hara said.

"I'm sorry?" Kyrah questioned, her eyes expressing her confusion.

Hara glanced briefly at Tig, who offered a sheepish smile and then turned to converse with Hara's mother. Kyrah saw the exchange, and her cheeks flushed.

"Never mind," Hara said. She stepped close to Kyrah. "I have a fascination with technology, and I've never seen this type of craft. Would you mind showing me?"

Kyrah smiled. "Of course. We use a combination of aerodynamic ground effect and minimal anti-gravity tech…"

The next two days were a flurry of activity as the Rayleans completed securing the city and arresting the bulk of Verdok's regime, those who would be held responsible for heinous acts of crime against their own people and the people of foreign lands that had been forced into servitude. But there was one unresolved dilemma that gave Daeson no peace until he told Raviel exactly how Verdok had come to his end.

Raviel's eyes widened in great alarm at his words regarding Rivet.

"He must be shut down at the very least...probably terminated," she exclaimed. "Why haven't you already?" She looked at Daeson in disbelief.

Daeson struggled. Something gnawed at his soul. "I've detained him until we could decide what to do," he replied. "We need more information. I want you to talk to him with me."

After much prodding, Raviel finally agreed. They entered Rivet's holding room. It was empty except for a table and a chair. The android sat motionless at the table. He looked up at them.

"It's good to see you, Lady Raviel," Rivet said.

Raviel didn't reply. She eyed the android carefully. This would be the third time they would be forced to evaluate the motivations of this android.

"Rivet, we need to ask you some questions regarding what happened when we stormed the capitol a few days ago. I want full disclosure...absolute truth. If we suspect that you're not telling us the whole truth, you will be...shut down. Do you understand?" Daeson asked.

"Yes, I understand," Rivet replied. "But you actually mean terminated, don't you, my liege?"

Daeson stared at the bot, unable to answer. "Where do you come from?" Daeson began.

"I come from the planet Mesos. I was never a maintenance android. That was a cover story that the Malakians created so you would accept me and not be alarmed. I was actually designed and programmed with artificial intelligence as an infiltrator with subversion and combat algorithms. I was the last of my kind. When the Malakians captured me, they altered my programming and established a connection interface via my mobility analytics processor so I could be utilized as a mimic bot for Lt. Ki."

"Why did they leave your AI programming active?" Raviel asked.

"Because there were periods of time when Lt. Ki could not be constantly with us, and she needed me to continue to provide protection and complete the semblance of a simple maintenance droid."

Raviel looked at Daeson, her eyes filled with deep concern.

"I've inspected your circuitry," Raviel said. "The Malakian interface to your mobility analytics processor has been removed. Are you now fully an AI android, programmed by ancient AI androids?"

Rivet turned his head to look at Raviel. It seemed now that any movement by this android felt eerie and unpredictable.

"I am not. As I mentioned, the Malakians altered my programming when they captured me. Additionally, when the mobility analytics processor interface was removed, my programming was altered again." Rivet stopped, as if he were thinking. "And there is something else."

With Rivet, there were no facial expressions and virtually no body language that would normally help in judging honesty during an interrogation.

"What else?" Daeson asked.

Rivet's eyes returned to Daeson.

"When the interface was installed, Lt. Ki was controlling more than just my movements. Whether she realized it or not, I could not tell, but the interface allowed me to...*see* her thoughts."

Rivet's head lowered, his gaze falling to the floor.

"Her adoration and loyalty to the one known as the Sovereign Ell Yon and his son, the Commander, was difficult for me to understand. It was powerful, and it altered me." Rivet looked back up at Daeson. "I've...grown. In some strange way, she is a part of me now."

"What happened to Lt. Ki?" Raviel asked.

Rivet hesitated, looking carefully at her.

"She is dead. She died trying to save you," he said as gingerly as a robot could. "I was given instructions not to reveal this to you, but considering the ultimatum you have placed on my existence, I have overridden that command to comply with my liege's request," Rivet said, slowly turning his head toward Daeson.

Daeson and Raviel became soberly silent as they considered the great sacrifice that had been made on their behalf. Raviel turned and walked away. Daeson continued to stare at Rivet, desperately trying to judge the character and motives of this new force in their lives. Just in the last few moments, Rivet had demonstrated an ability to override commands. They were in dangerous territory.

Raviel whipped around and came to stand in front of the table where Rivet was sitting, her eyes fierce. "Did you kill Lt. Ki?" she asked.

Rivet's head turned to look up at her.

Daeson's hand instinctively fell to his Talon as he imagined the android weighing its options in a cold, unemotional set of calculations. How strong was its desire to survive? Would it turn on them with such threatening accusations?

"I did not," came Rivet's cold reply. "My programming does not allow me to take a human life unless—"

"Then how is it that you were able to kill Verdok?" Raviel interrupted.

Rivet hesitated again.

"I do not know. I only know and understand that Verdok had been judged by Sovereign Ell Yon as a wholly evil human and that his time to live was over."

Rivet looked back up at Raviel then straight at Daeson.

"That judgment was not my own. You knew it as well, didn't you, my liege?"

Daeson swallowed hard. Rivet was right. He had suppressed the voice of Ell Yon in that moment because it felt unnatural. Daeson's feelings often didn't align with the voice of Ell Yon. The Protector had been clear, but Daeson had ignored it. Rivet was indeed right.

Raviel stared hard at the android, then turned to face Daeson.

"How can we ever trust him?" she asked Daeson. "He's not predictable...he's AI!"

"Is anyone you trust completely predictable?" Rivet interrupted. "My mission to protect you, my liege, and you, Lady Raviel, is unchanged."

"Why?" Daeson asked. "If you are truly AI, then who's to say that your mission might change in a microsecond?"

Rivet thought for a moment. "Because I have seen and remember dark deeds, and now I have seen and understand the minds of the light. I now know what is right...what is good. Through Lt. Ki I saw Ell Yon's greater purpose for the galaxy—a purpose I want to help fulfill. Isn't that what we all want...to have purpose?"

Raviel walked to the door, clearly upset. She exited and began walking down the hallway.

"Stay here, Rivet," Daeson ordered then followed her out.

"Raviel!" he shouted and ran to catch up to her.

He grabbed her arm. She turned to him, shaking her head.

"It's like Mesos all over again," she said, running her hand through her thick, dark hair. "I don't know what to think anymore."

"But he saved our lives...*again*," Daeson countered. "And he was used by the Malakians to help us."

"Yes, but you heard him...he's now fully AI!" Raviel exclaimed. "With algorithms in subversion! This could all be deception. Don't forget...he killed a human of his own accord when there was no threat!"

"Okay, let's say he's a tool of Lord Dracus. Why then would he kill Verdok?" Daeson asked.

"Didn't Dracus himself tell you he was done with Verdok? What if this is part of his deceptive plan?" Raviel countered.

"Then why didn't he just kill you and me right now? He's had many opportunities, and instead he has rescued us multiple times," Daeson said, crossing his arms.

Raviel's eyes narrowed. "Maybe it's because Dracus doesn't know Ell Yon's plan for the galaxy, but he's figured out that you're a part of it, and he's trying to discover just how to subvert it...biding his time until the moment is just right." Now Raviel crossed her arms. "The AI androids were masters of deception, and if Rivet was the last of his kind, he would be profoundly good at it. He's too dangerous!"

"You're overreacting," Daeson blurted, immediately regretting his tone.

"And you're being naïve!" Raviel shot back.

They stood toe to toe. This was one of the only serious arguments they'd had since being bonded. Daeson lowered his head as he reconsidered her perspective. Her logic was solid.

"If he's truly here to help us, destroying him would be an egregious act, yet I hate suspecting someone...or something that is so close to us. It's wearying," Daeson conceded.

Raviel softened too.

"I know, but there's so much at stake." She put a gentle hand on Daeson's arm, touching the Protector. "What does the Protector say about Rivet?"

Daeson turned his arm over to examine the Immortal gift from Ell Yon.

"Nothing, but Rivet is certainly right about one thing." He looked into Raviel's eyes. "I was supposed to execute Verdok."

Raviel looked stunned. "Really?"

Daeson nodded. "The Protector was clear, and I failed Ell Yon."

They stood silent for a moment. Raviel seemed deeply affected by this new information. "It's almost as if he knew what Ell Yon was commanding," she finally said.

Daeson took a deep breath. They stood in silence, contemplating how to move forward. "So...what do we do with Rivet?" he asked.

Raviel raised an eyebrow. "I guess we sleep with one eye open." Raviel thought for a moment. "I have an idea. We need to talk to him again."

Daeson and Raviel returned to the room to see Rivet still sitting in the chair, his arms resting on the table in front of him. Raviel went to the table and leaned over, placing both of her hands on the table in front of Rivet.

"Rivet, I intend to install a destruct mechanism next to your processing circuitry."

Rivet lowered his head. "If you feel that is necessary," the android replied. "But I think that I would prefer—"

"This isn't an option," Raviel interrupted.

"—termination," Rivet finished.

Raviel and Daeson stared in stunned silence at the android.

"Why would you prefer termination?" Raviel asked quietly.

Rivet lifted his head, gazing into her eyes. "We just liberated many people from an evil tyrant in Reekojah. The slaves were controlled by collars they were forced to wear. This destruct mechanism you plan to install would be my collar. I would rather be terminated."

Raviel stared at the android, motionless. She then stood and turned away, biting her lip. She finally looked over at Daeson, wiping away a single tear. She turned back to Rivet, placing a gentle hand on the android's arm.

"I'm so sorry, Rivet. You don't deserve this. Your actions have demonstrated nothing but loyalty toward us. Please forgive me…our history together has been rather unusual." Raviel flashed a glance toward Daeson and then back. "I think we need to work on building trust with each other once again."

Rivet nodded ever so slightly. "I agree, my lady. I am committed to winning your trust until the day that I am no more. This I promise." Rivet looked over at Daeson. "To both of you…and your offspring."

Raviel stood straight and looked at Daeson with the most alarmed expression he had ever seen on her face. "Offspring?" she exclaimed.

"Yes. I understand that is the natural progression of two bonded humans, is it not?" Rivet asked, tilting his head as he looked to Daeson for confirmation.

Daeson and Raviel both burst out laughing. Daeson walked to Raviel and put an arm around her shoulder.

"Come, Rivet," he said. "We have much work to do."

The work following Liberation Day was overwhelming. Tribunals were established to execute justice on behalf of all slaves in the region. Punishments were attributed accordingly and executed swiftly. Restitution was made for all that had endured the harsh rule of Verdok and his evil regime. Perhaps the most glorious day of all was when the rest of the Raylean people arrived from the Ianis System. Daeson, Raviel, Tig, and Kyrah had surveyed the planet and found a lush region of land north of Reekojah, which they called the Serula Valley that was chosen for their future capital city.

When the transports landed, medical teams and supplies were waiting for them. It was a beautiful sight. Most of their people had never set foot on the solid, fertile soil of a planet let alone one they could call their own. Daeson, Raviel, Tig, and Kyrah watched with tears in their eyes as the people became overwhelmed by the joy of it all. Some cried, some shouted, and many just rotated in circles, soaking up the sun, air, and beauty of their new planet. Children ran and laughed and played in the thick green grass of their new homeworld.

Kyrah grabbed Tig's hand, pulling him to come greet the people with her. Raviel leaned into Daeson as he wrapped an arm around her.

"Welcome home people of Ell Yon," he said quietly. "Welcome to Rayl!"

After watching the joyful arrival of their people quietly from a distance, Raviel pulled away.

"They need to see you now. They need to see their leader."

Daeson frowned. This was the part of leadership he disliked most of all, but he knew Raviel was right. He walked a couple of paces toward the landing site and crossed his arms. "I suppose you're right, but I won't enjoy it. I'd rather just watch them."

When Daeson turned back, reaching out his hand for Raviel to join him, she wore a look of horror on her face.

"Daeson!" she cried out as she briefly faded to a wisp.

Daeson ran to her, his arms outstretched. Raviel rematerialized just long enough to hold out her hands to stop him.

"Don't! It could kill you!" she exclaimed.

Daeson watched in utter dread, panic flooding his soul as she faded and struggled to return once more. Her face became ashen, but whether from fright or the quantum event, he could not tell.

"Raviel!" Speaking her name was the only thing he could do.

The terror on her face...the fear in her eyes.... Daeson's soul was being ripped in two once more, and he was helpless again...or was he? A thought flitted across his mind. An utterly selfish thought that he could not keep from acting upon. The moment Raviel became fully present, Daeson pulled the Protector off his arm and pushed it onto her outstretched arm.

"No, Daeson!" she screamed, but her voice faded in a diminishing echo, and she was gone—and so was the Protector.

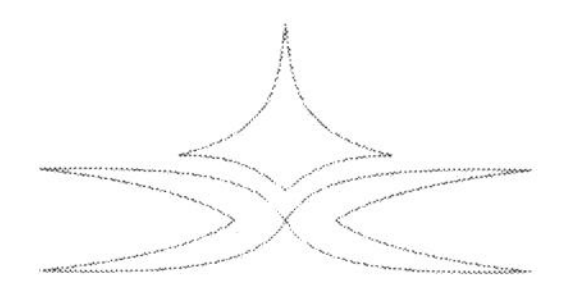

Epilogue

A Future Hope

When Elias finished, Brae was sitting up against the back of her bed, her head hanging low.

"Is that really how it happened?" Brae asked.

Elias hesitated.

"Yes, Brae. I'm afraid it is," he said, pushing her hair back over her ear so he could see her face.

Brae sighed, lifting her head to look at Elias.

"If Dracus and his evil men hadn't been trying to kill the Rayleans, Raviel would have never had the accident, and she and Daeson could be happy. Why do people have to be bad?"

"They don't have to be...they choose to be. When Dracus brought Deitum Prime to the galaxy, it made it impossible for people to choose to be good without the power of Ell Yon. Dracus is an evil Immortal that wants to hurt Ell Yon by hurting the people Ell Yon loves."

"Like Daeson and Raviel?"

"Yes, and like you and me...and millions of others throughout the galaxy."

She looked up at Elias.

"It's all very sad."

Elias smiled, shaking his head. "It might feel that way right now, but you need to remember the promise of the Sovereign. There's coming a day when Ell Yon will destroy the evil work of Dracus and give hope and freedom to the people once again."

"When, Dad? When will that happen?" Brae asked.

Elias seemed lost in thought as he considered her question. He started tucking Brae in as she settled down under her covers.

"I believe it's coming soon, sweetheart. That's why we must always be ready."

Elias bent down and kissed Brae's forehead. He then stood and went to the doorway. Brae's face lit up as she remembered a part of the story she'd just heard.

"Dad, you know who I like?"

Elias turned at the doorway looking back at the sweet girl filled with life and adventurous courage.

"Who's that?" Elias asked.

"Rivet! I think he's a good android, and I wish our clunky old droids were just like him."

Elias laughed.

"Good night, Brae."

"Good night, Dad."

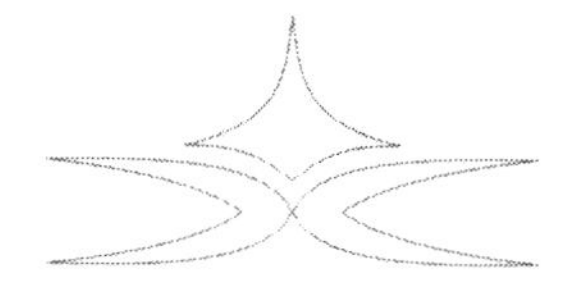

Author's Commentary

The canvas of life upon which God has given us the ability to create story is truly remarkable—an undiscoverable universe, emotions, senses, a world of unrepeatable humans, and minds to think of untold adventures. My greatest concern regarding the writing of this series is in regard to my limited ability to appropriately represent the God of the Bible by the use of metaphors and allegory. Please do not make the mistake of assuming that science and technology can in some way explain away the supernatural marvels of God, His holiness, power, wisdom, and love. The full character of God is unknowable, and thus attempting to depict Him in all of His glory is a frightful endeavor. I pray that you return to His Word and fully embrace the profound descriptions of truth without fiction found there. It is my purpose in writing these words to point you once more to the glorious God of heaven and earth, His Son Jesus Christ, the Holy Spirit, and the radical intersection of supernatural love through the redemptive power of the gospel.

~Chuck Black

Made in the USA
Columbia, SC
04 December 2024

LORE

Look for other books
by Chuck Black

The Kingdom Series
Kingdom's Dawn
Kingdom's Hope
Kingdom's Edge
Kingdom's Call
Kingdom's Quest
Kingdom's Reign

The Knights of Arrethtrae
Sir Kendrick and the Castle of Bel Lione
Sir Bentley and Holbrook Court
Sir Dalton and the Shadow Heart
Lady Carliss and the Waters of Moorue
Sir Quinlan and the Swords of Valor
Sir Rowan and the Camerian Conquest

The Starlore Legacy
Nova
Flight
Lore
Oath
Merchant
Reclamation
Creed
Journey
Crucible
Covenant
Revolution
Maelstrom

www.ChuckBlack.com

LORE

EPISODE THREE

CHUCK BLACK

Lore

Published by Perfect Praise Publishing
Williston, North Dakota

ISBN 978-1-7359061-4-0

Printed in the United States of America

Library of Congress Control Number: 2021910441